Dear Reader,

No matter how busy your day, there'll *always* be time for romance. TAKE 5 is a new way to indulge in love, passion and adventure. Each TAKE 5 volume offers five condensed stories by top Harlequin and Silhouette authors. Now you can have the enjoyment and satisfaction of a full-length novel, but in less time—perfect for those days when it's difficult to squeeze a longer read into your hectic schedule.

This volume of TAKE 5 features five sizzling love stories...five *hot* escapes! *New York Times* bestselling author Jayne Ann Krentz turns up the heat with two tales of seduction—*Call It Destiny* and *Velvet Touch*. The love is unexpected—and forbidden!—in Candace Schuler's *Soul Mates* and *Designing Woman*. And passions flare when lovers reunite in *Heartland* by Sherryl Woods.

Why not indulge in all four volumes of TAKE 5 available now—tender romance, sizzling passion, riveting adventure and heartwarming family love. No matter what _____ ___ __ ___ in, you'll have the perfect escape!

Happy reading,

Marsha Zinberg
Senior Editor a__

D1053999

Jayne Ann Krentz is one of today's best-loved authors of women's fiction. With multiple *New York Times* bestselling novels to her credit, she is a prolific and innovative writer—much to the delight of her legions of fans around the world. She has delved into psychic elements, intrigue, fantasy, historicals and even futuristic romances. Jayne lives in Seattle with her husband.

Sherryl Woods can't be far from the sea without getting downright claustrophobic. She's lived by the ocean on both coasts and now divides her time between Key Biscayne, Florida, and her childhood summer home in Colonial Beach, Virginia, where she has also opened a bookstore. When she isn't chatting with customers about her favorite topic, books, she is doing her other favorite thing—writing books about falling in love and living happily ever after. Sherryl has more than sixty romance and mystery novels to her credit.

Candace Schuler was raised in the San Francisco Bay area, but since marrying her husband, Joe, she has lived in almost every corner of the United States and traveled extensively abroad. When she isn't writing, she likes to relax by taking adult education classes— the more offbeat the better. Almost all the skills she learns—from being a private detective, driving a limousine, using a handgun and belly dancing, to performing witchcraft and designing landscape— eventually show up in her books!

TAKE5
Quick Reads. Great Escapes.

**NEW YORK TIMES
BESTSELLING AUTHOR**

Jayne Ann Krentz

Sherryl Woods

Candace Schuler

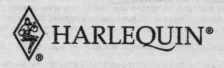

HARLEQUIN®

TORONTO • NEW YORK • LONDON
AMSTERDAM • PARIS • SYDNEY • HAMBURG
STOCKHOLM • ATHENS • TOKYO • MILAN • MADRID
PRAGUE • WARSAW • BUDAPEST • AUCKLAND

ISBN 0-373-83493-4

TAKE 5, VOLUME 2

Copyright © 2001 by Harlequin Books S.A.

The publisher acknowledges the copyright holders of the individual titles as follows:

CALL IT DESTINY
Copyright © 1984 by Jayne Ann Krentz

VELVET TOUCH
Copyright © 1982 by Jayne Ann Krentz

HEARTLAND
Copyright © 1989 by Sherryl Woods

SOUL MATES
Copyright © 1988 by Candace Schuler

DESIGNING WOMAN
Copyright © 1986 by Candace Schuler

Visit us at www.eHarlequin.com

Printed in U.S.A.

CONTENTS

CONTENTS

CALL IT DESTINY

Jayne Ann Krentz

"**I**'ve brought along a draft of the prenuptial agreement. Take your time looking it over." Heather Strand sipped her chardonnay and smiled at the man sitting opposite her.

Jake Cavender smiled back at her. Heather was getting accustomed to that smile with its faint twist of amused speculation. "Why have you come back to Tucson, Heather?"

"You know the answer to that," Heather replied. "My father is retiring and I'm prepared to step into his shoes."

"What can your father's hotel offer that can compete with what you had established in California?"

"A chance to be in total control. San Francisco and San Diego were excellent training grounds—"

"You could have learned everything you needed to know by working at your father's side."

"Not when I was younger." Heather's mouth curved ruefully. "We clashed on almost everything. Even now I doubt a partnership would work."

"You must know that your parents are delighted you've decided to return," Jake remarked casually. "They've been hoping for a long time that you'd come back to the Hacienda."

Heather smiled, her hazel eyes deliberately bland and unreadable. "I left Tucson under something resembling a cloud."

"I've heard the story," Jake said. "You were last seen heading west on the back of a black Yamaha motorcycle. I believe you had vowed to marry the guy before you reached California."

Heather felt a distasteful chill. Jake Cavender, it seemed, had indeed been adopted into the family circle. "Rick Monroe was every adolescent's fantasy of a reckless boyfriend. He was a loner. Much like me, I thought at the time."

"You were hardly a loner," Jake said. "You had the full protection and support of a loving family."

Heather blinked uneasily. Jake Cavender could be blunt at times. She assumed it was one of the reasons he had been so useful to her father and would continue to be useful to her. A good executive did not want to surround herself with yes-men. On the other hand, there was such a thing as tact.

"Whatever happened when I was eighteen really doesn't concern you, does it?"

"I beg your pardon," he said quietly. "Did I stray over the line?"

"Yes. Do you make a habit of doing it?"

Jake nodded his head once. "I'm afraid so. I'm not particularly good at handling people."

"You're in a strange line of work for someone who isn't good at dealing with people."

"Hotel work? It is a little off base, isn't it? But it's worked out very well for me. Your father always took the role of jovial host. I dealt with the financial facts and figures."

"I assume the same arrangement will work between us," Heather said bracingly.

"I'm sure it will," Jake retorted smoothly.

"So you have no objections to a prenuptial agreement?" Heather needed to pin him down.

"Did you have a contract with your...young punk?"

Heather's eyes chilled. "As it happens, Rick and I were never married. And if the actions of my youth offend you, I suggest you reconsider my offer of marriage."

"Your family would be crushed if I did that," he said with one of his quick unreadable smiles.

"Yes," she agreed. "You've practically become a member of the family, haven't you?"

"Practically, but not quite."

"Is that why you're marrying me, Jake?" Heather demanded. "To become a full member of the family?"

He lifted his intent gaze to meet hers. "It's part of the reason, yes. Does that worry you?"

It was Heather's turn to consider a question. "I don't see why it should. When you failed to panic at the idea of marrying me, my father probably thought finally he was living in the best of all possible worlds. His wayward daughter had returned to assume her preordained role as president of Hacienda Strand, Inc., and his handpicked son was willing to become her consort and faithful assistant. A nice neat package."

"You don't seem to have any objections to being part of that nice neat package," Jake observed mildly.

"I'm no longer eighteen and determined to rebel against all authority."

"You're twenty-nine and willing to submit?" Jake taunted.

Heather laughed. "Hardly. I'm back in Tucson to take over my father's hotel, Jake, but I'm back on my own terms."

She could sense he was adding up all the information he had about her and running it through the computer he called a brain.

Jake gave her an odd glance. "When your father told me he had suggested the idea of us getting married, I expected you'd go through the roof. Based on what I'd been told of your character I assumed a more or less arranged marriage would bring out all the old spirit of rebellion. I told Paul he'd made one hell of a mistake. That's when he informed me that you were a changed woman."

"You sound as if you don't believe in the change," she returned, mildly irritated by his skepticism. She'd seen traces of it during the two weeks she'd been back in Tucson and during her visits home the past year, but tonight it seemed more pronounced. "I assure you I'm not the wild child who left here all those years ago."

Jake stared at her for a moment and suddenly Heather wished that she could read his mind. That polite mask he wore gave few clues to what he was really feeling.

"How reassuring for both of us." His gray eyes went to her face. "Would you care for dessert?"

Heather shook her head, and Jake signaled for the check, then got to his feet.

She was vividly aware of his presence as they made their way out of the restaurant and into Jake's white Mercedes.

Jake broke the quiet. "Do you regret leaving home?"

With a sigh, she shook her head. "At the time there didn't seem to be much choice. My father and I fought constantly and if I'd stayed and gone to university here there would have been more problems. Dad was determined to direct my life and I was just as determined to do things my way. His fury over my relationship with Rick Monroe was the last straw for both of us."

"Who financed your education in California? The infamous Rick Monroe?"

Quashing the faint stirrings of her long-dormant temper, Heather tried to answer as if it didn't really matter. "I financed my own education. Rick didn't have a dime to his name, I'm afraid. Lots of rebel-without-a-cause charm but no money. We parted ways before we even reached California."

Jake's head came around sharply. "You did?"

"He and the bike made for a dramatic exit from Tucson, but when he started demanding that I phone home for money I told him to get lost. Unfortunately he took my bike." Heather forced a superficial laugh to cover the memories of fear and loneliness that had assailed her on that traumatic trip.

"Being on the road isn't particularly romantic, is it?" Jake guided the Mercedes toward the foothills outside Tucson where the Hacienda Strand was located.

"No."

"But your pride wouldn't let you come home?"

"I couldn't—not until I'd shown everyone I didn't need Dad's money to cushion the way," she explained starkly.

"So how did you finance your hotel course?"

"Got a job in a fast-food hamburger place. No benefits and

low salary but the road to the manager's job was wide open for anyone who wanted to work the bad hours. I became manager in three months," Heather said. "Now I can make forty hamburgers a minute or supervise a gourmet hotel kitchen."

"You did things the hard way," Jake growled. "All because you were too headstrong to appreciate what your family wanted to give you."

Something snapped briefly inside Heather. Her hazel eyes flared in the dimly lit interior of the car.

"Let's get something straight, Jake. I am not the wild and reckless girl I was when I left town. You'll see just how realistic and businesslike I am these days when you read that prenuptial agreement."

"I'll go over it tonight," he promised. The gleam was back in his gray eyes.

"You do that, Jake. I wouldn't want you getting involved in something you can't handle!"

SHE LOOKED GOOD sitting there on the terrace, Jake noted the next morning as he approached the private garden area where the Strands customarily took breakfast. However, there was more than a hint of assertiveness in the firm lines of her chin and jaw, and that hint, coupled with Heather's rather formidable self-confidence, was all the warning Jake needed.

Unconsciously Jake's fingers locked tightly around the contract in his hand.

Heather glanced up as he crossed the brick terrace with easy familiarity. Something in her bristled. She should have known by now that he often had coffee with Paul and Ruth, but this morning she instinctively resisted the idea of how much a part of the family he really was.

Then again, perhaps that was one reason she was willing to marry him. A part of her longed to regain every foothold she'd ever had with her family. Marrying a man of whom they approved was one more way of cementing the new relationship.

"Good morning, Jake," Ruth Strand said warmly.

"Good morning, Ruth. Paul." Jake nodded and then strode directly to Heather and leaned over with a casual possessiveness to kiss her.

The decidedly familiar caress came as a shock to Heather. Before she had time to assimilate the hard feel of his mouth on hers, he had withdrawn to take the empty chair at the round table. A crinkle of paper made her look down at her lap where he had left the contract he'd been carrying. When she glanced up questioningly, Jake gave her a strange half-amused smile.

"I only made one small change," Jake said, lifting the white napkin off the bread basket.

Heather's brows came together as she hastily began to flip through the contract. Ignoring her, Jake and her parents immediately fell to discussing the weather.

"We were safely tucked away, discussing the, uh, business of our marriage when last night's storm hit," Jake assured Paul. "Would you pass the jam, please, Ruth?"

"Of course, dear." Ruth handed him the tiny silver jam pot with a fond glance. "I was thinking of having the reception in the gardens. What do you think, Heather?"

Heather only half heard her mother's question. She had just flipped back the next-to-last page of the contract and found Jake's one "small" change.

"Heather? Did you hear me, dear?"

"Yes, Mother?" Heather's head came up finally.

"Really, dear, you shouldn't get involved with business until after your marriage. You know your father and Jake have tried to keep you away from the office until everything is settled. You need to take the next couple of weeks off and enjoy yourself. Think of all the fun you'll have planning your wedding."

"Fun?" Heather wrenched her eyes away from Jake who seemed patiently oblivious to the message in the hazel gaze. "Weddings aren't supposed to be fun, Mother."

It didn't take Paul Strand's uneasy disapproval to make Heather realize she'd made a mistake. But something about the quietly arrogant manner in which Jake had modified the prenuptial agreement had caught her on the raw.

Heather got to her feet and waved the contract at him. "If you'll excuse me, I think I'll go have a look at the kitchens. I promised myself a tour of them today."

"Heather, there will be plenty of time to get to know Hacienda Strand again after the honeymoon." Paul frowned at Jake. "Won't there?"

"All the time in the world," Jake agreed equably, polishing off his croissant. "On the other hand, perhaps a tour of the kitchens would keep her out of trouble."

Heather caught the flicker of anguish in her mother's eyes and instantly paused to drop a quick kiss on her cheek.

As Heather left the terrace on Jake's arm, she heard her father remark with satisfaction, "I told you they were going to make a terrific team, Ruth."

Beside her, Jake's mouth twisted in amusement. "I think he means a perfect management team," he murmured so that only Heather could hear. "What do you think?"

"That he might be right. So long as both members of the team remember which of them is ultimately in charge." Heather kept her words light but gave them a definite emphasis that could not go unnoticed.

As they walked through the lush grounds, she shook the contract in her hand. "Jake, about that clause you marked out. I think we should come to terms."

"What terms?" he asked flatly. "I agreed to every other clause in the contract, including the one that stipulates that if the marriage is dissolved both of us will leave with only our own property before the wedding. I can't see you have any cause to complain just because I crossed out one small clause."

"A rather important small clause!"

He glanced down at her. "Why do you need that clause about giving the marriage six months before deciding whether or not to take matters beyond the platonic level?" he asked.

"Jake, on the few occasions when I've been back to visit my parents, you and I have talked on only a very casual basis. If all goes according to schedule we'll be married at the end of the month. Four weeks is hardly long enough to build a relationship. We need time before we take this marriage beyond the business level."

His mouth tightened. "But I have no interest in contracting a purely business arrangement. I want a real marriage." Jake stopped and put his hands on her shoulders, turning her to face him. Something softened in his expression. "You're getting nervous, aren't you?"

"I am not nervous." She stood quite still and lifted her chin challengingly.

"Are you sure you're not starting to wonder just what you've gotten yourself into by coming back to Tucson?"

"I'm home, Jake, because this is where I want to be. This desert and those beautiful mountains are in my blood. Just as my family is a part of me and just as the Hacienda Strand is a part of me. I am a very different person than I was at eighteen. I had to leave or all these things would have smothered me."

Jake regarded her intently. "Heather, this battle over the clause I crossed out of the contract is not worth fighting."

"And if I happen to believe differently?"

"Then I shall have to decline your kind offer." He smiled rather wistfully. "You're not the only one who's come home, Heather. The Hacienda Strand is my home now, too. Your parents have made me feel like a part of the family. And unless you plan on running off again with some punk on a motorcycle, we're in this together for the duration. But if I'm going to link my life and my career with yours then I want a full, one hundred percent commitment. I don't want a ridiculous sham of a marriage."

Heather caught her breath, suddenly fiercely aware of the strength in his hands and the unyielding intensity of his eyes. There were many things she could have said, should have said. She ought to have pointed out that his career at the Hacienda could be terminated at any time by her. She could have argued that she hadn't actually ruled out intimacy in the marriage, merely postponed the decision. She might have stressed her refusal to be pushed beyond certain limits.

Instead she heard herself say crisply, "We'll talk about it later."

"We'll talk about it now, Heather. I want this settled."

His stubbornness threatened to trigger her carefully buried instinct to rebel. With an extreme effort of will, Heather reminded herself that she was in charge here. It was up to her how much territory she decided to yield.

"You're the one who's nervous, aren't you?" she challenged softly. "It's your future here at the Hacienda that's on the line, not mine."

"Let's just say I'm willing to work hard to get roots, a family and a place to call home. All the things you once threw away so casually and have come back to claim."

"I didn't realize marrying me was going to be such hard work!"

"I'm beginning to think it's going to be the hardest job I've ever undertaken." He sobered. "Heather, let things happen naturally without restrictions and contractual clauses. Is that too much to request?"

She stared up at him wonderingly, startled by the genuine honesty in his voice. He was so close, so quietly insistent that she didn't know how to handle the situation. She needed time.

"Jake—"

Heather got no further in her demand. Jake lowered his head, a smoky quality invading the gray depths of his eyes.

His kiss wasn't quite what she had expected. For one thing she certainly hadn't anticipated this degree of controlled hunger. His mouth moved on hers, exploring, in an incredibly intimate fashion. The flickering uncoiling sensation in the deepest places of her body warned Heather that Jake could make her want him.

Slowly, with infinite reluctance, Jake lifted his head. He held her against the length of his lean body, and the gray smoke of his gaze reflected the lingering, heavily restrained desire in him.

"What kind of wife will you make?"

She shrugged fatalistically. "Who knows? I've never had any experience. What are your qualifications as a husband?"

Jake moved his head in a slow negative, the brackets deep on either side of his mouth. "My experience is quite limited. I was married once, Heather. A long time ago. We were both very young, very immature and very broke. I think we thought marriage would somehow cure all that. It was a romantic fantasy that didn't last eighteen months. At the end of that time we were still young and broke but perhaps a little wiser."

Heather's eyes gentled. "What happened, Jake?"

"She found someone who could support her in the style to which she wanted to become accustomed." There was no bitterness in his words. "She got the security she needed and I had the freedom to spend every dime I could earn on an education. After I got my business degree I was too busy building a career to think about marriage. I don't know. I do know," he added with quiet emphasis, "that I am ready again for marriage, and this time I intend to make it work."

"You sound very certain of that."

"I've grown used to getting what I want out of life, Heather. Even if I have to get it the hard way."

Heather turned away with a small frown. Drive and determination were normally qualities she admired in others and had an abundance of herself. But in Jake Cavender those two attributes were loaded with an intensity that sent uneasy chills down her spine.

*

ONE WEEK BEFORE the wedding Jake stood beside Paul Strand on the Strands' private garden terrace and watched Heather circulate through the crowd of beautifully dressed people her mother had invited. The party was in honor of the engaged couple but somehow it seemed to have turned into Heather's party.

Jake sipped meditatively at his Scotch. In another week he would be married to the vivid creature across the room. He wanted her. He'd been wanting her for three weeks. It seemed like forever. He took another swallow of the Scotch and broodingly observed his future bride.

Paul grinned complacently at the younger man. "I always knew she had the brains and the willpower to make something of herself, and it used to drive me to distraction to see her rely on easy charm to get what she wanted."

"She seems to have developed both brains and willpower," Jake observed. "You don't get her kind of reputation on charm alone."

Paul chuckled. "I know. Actually, she's a great deal more lethal now than she was when she was a kid."

"Charm and intelligence can be a dangerous combination," Jake agreed.

"And you, Jake, are just the man to handle that combination. The two of you are going to make a perfect team."

And she's going to be my woman, Jake told himself, trying to squelch the reckless excitement that idea brought.

"Excuse me," Jake said a little grimly, "but I do appear to have lost track of my fiancée. I'd better go find her." With a nod to Paul, Jake strode determinedly into the crowd.

"Good evening, Cavender." Cecil Winthrop greeted him in a far more jovial manner than usual as Jake handed Heather the glass of Chenin Blanc he'd procured en route.

Jake nodded politely. He didn't fool himself. Winthrop's cordiality tonight was strictly because of Heather. "Hello, Cecil. I'm glad to see you're enjoying yourself."

Heather smiled brilliantly. "Cecil and I were just discussing the time I practiced riding my motorcycle on his land." She shook her head in rueful apology. "I'm not even sure where the Hacienda Strand's land ends and yours begins!"

"Jake knows, don't you, my boy?" Cecil asked. One bushy gray brow arched behind his wire-frame glasses.

"I admit I've studied the matter," Jake replied.

"Your husband-to-be has some plans for all that acreage I've got that borders the Hacienda Strand property," Cecil confided cheerfully to Heather.

Jake hid his irritation at having the subject brought up. "I had some thoughts of using that land to put in a private golf course for the Hacienda," he told her brusquely. Taking her arm very firmly, Jake nodded at Cecil Winthrop. "Sorry to drag her away, Cecil, but..."

Heather managed an unconcerned smile in return but as soon as they were out of earshot she disengaged her arm. "What in the world was that all about?"

Jake sighed. "Heather, you're supposed to be socializing, remember? Your family doesn't want you being concerned with business until after the honeymoon."

"I know," she said wryly. "Dad won't even talk about the details of turning over the reins to me. Every time I bring up the subject he just goes on and on about what a fine management team you and I will make."

Jake's expression was stony. "There will be plenty of time after the wedding, Heather."

It was another hour and a half before the first guests started to leave, two hours before everyone had departed. But eventually Jake was able to pry Heather away from an in-depth postmortem of the successful event with her mother. Firmly he guided her onto a garden path.

"You were the queen of the evening," he said after a moment of silence. "You charmed the socks off everyone."

Beside him Heather exhaled softly. "Everyone who showed up tonight did so to see how I'd turned out." Her tone was dry but not bitter. "I had to put on a good performance."

"I don't think it was all a performance. You're in your

element dealing with people, Heather. That's a talent I wish I had.''

"From the way my father talks about you, your talents in finance and business administration more than make up for any lack of social skills you feel you have.''

"Very diplomatic," he approved.

They walked the rest of the way to his place in a companionable silence. "I have some cognac," Jake began as he unlocked the front door and ushered her inside.

"That sounds delightful. I'm exhausted.''

As he poured the cognac and carried it across the Navajo rug, Heather curled into the love seat, drawing her stockinged feet up under the hem of her silk dress.

"To us," he said, gently tapping his glass against hers.

"And to the Hacienda," she returned.

Jake sat down beside her, casually allowing his thigh to come in contact with her curving knee.

"Do you think going away for a few days to Santa Fe is really necessary, Jake?"

He was silent for a moment. This wasn't the first hesitation she had voiced about their honeymoon. "Your family will expect us to go away for a while," he pointed out, seeking the most powerful argument he had at his disposal.

"I suppose so." She lifted one shoulder languidly beneath the beautifully hued silk. "Well, it might be a nice break for both of us before we get ready for the season.''

Jake's head came up. "It's supposed to be a honeymoon, not a 'nice break.'''

"Jake—"

"Why are you fighting it, Heather?"

She didn't pretend to misunderstand. "Because there's something in you that I don't quite understand. Something I don't know about you. I just know I need time.''

He leaned forward to brush his mouth lingeringly across hers. "I think if we are honest on this level," he said in a voice that was thickening slightly, "the rest will follow.''

Deliberately he lowered his mouth again, delighting in the small tremor that went through her when he crushed her lips beneath his own. Jake was certain he tasted the beginnings of passion as fierce desire stoked the fires that had been simmering in him all evening.

He began to explore the alluring curve where her throat and shoulder merged. There was an intriguing vulnerability about her there.

She wrapped her arms around his neck, a low moan parting her lips. His head spinning with anticipation and skyrocketing need, Jake buried his lips against her throat.

"Oh, Jake…" Her head arched back over his arm as he deliberately allowed the heat of his palm to blend with the heat of her body.

"You're going to drive me crazy. Feel what you're doing to me!" He moved his hips against her. "I want you, Heather. Very badly."

"Jake, I—" Her small tongue emerged to dampen her parted lips as she struggled for words. "We can't. Not yet. Too soon. Much too soon."

"How can it be too soon when we want each other this much?" He traced a small erotic pattern on the inside of her leg. She gasped and shifted beneath him.

"Jake, you promised you wouldn't rush me."

He felt her willpower reassert itself over her growing passion, and longed to overwhelm it. He could kiss the protests back into her throat, pull away the crumpled silk dress and take her. She would respond.

But he resisted the impulse, and instead lifted himself to a sitting position. The sweep of her sleek, bluntly cut hair swung forward to shield her expression for a few critical seconds.

"I'll walk you back to your cottage." Jake got to his feet, reaching the door ahead of her. He walked her through the gardens in silence and left her at her door just as she wished. He heard the click of the bolt.

If she had locked her door against him it might mean she would not be able to get him out of her mind tonight.

In another week he would make certain he was the last thing on her mind every night.

RUTH STRAND EYED her daughter approvingly the next morning on the terrace as they waited for Paul and Jake to join them for breakfast. "Santa Fe will make a lovely spot for a honeymoon. Whose idea was that?"

Heather shrugged. "Jake's, I think. I wasn't really planning on taking one."

"Well, at least you'll be having a more luxurious one than your father and I were able to afford," Ruth said, chuckling. "We couldn't afford to go any farther than that old cabin Paul had for hunting up in the hills."

"I haven't thought of that place in years."

Before Heather could continue the discussion, a cheerful greeting announced the arrival of her father. Beside him Jake looked dark and restrained, his teak-brown hair still damp from the shower.

Uncomfortably, Heather reached for the coffeepot, unwilling to betray the fact that last night had been on her mind all morning. "Your coffee," she quickly offered, and then chided herself for being even slightly nervous around Jake. She ought to have a bit more poise under the circumstances!

"I was telling Heather where you and I spent our honeymoon," Ruth said as her husband sat down.

Paul Strand laughed. "Did you tell her where we'll be spending our second one?"

"What's this all about?" Heather demanded.

"Ruth and I are going to take a three-month cruise while you two are settling down to married life and the business of running the Hacienda." He gave his wife an affectionate smile.

Ruth said laughing, "He's set a goal of playing on all the major golf courses of the world."

"And I plan on playing the new Hacienda Strand course, hmm?" Paul reached for the jam pot.

"If we can get Cecil Winthrop to sell us that land," Jake agreed, his eyes on Heather.

Heather said dismissively, "I'm not at all sure the Hacienda needs a course of its own."

"If we don't pick up the land fairly quickly he'll probably sell it to someone else," Jake said carefully.

"We'll discuss it some other time," Heather said, and a sudden tense silence descended over the small table.

ON THE EVE of her wedding, Heather stood quietly in the shadows of her parents' garden and watched the crowd that jammed the terrace. This last party her mother had insisted on giving was for the staff of the Hacienda.

Normally she would have been in the middle of the crowd. But about an hour ago she had suddenly begun to feel a little trapped, hemmed in by people. Bridal jitters, she reassured herself. Or too much champagne. One of the two.

Bridal jitters, indeed!

The real problem, Heather decided abruptly, was that she was getting restless. Her family and Jake just hadn't understood that by keeping her away from the hotel offices they hadn't made things easier for her. When she was back at work she would feel normal.

On a sudden impulse Heather started down a deserted path toward the main lodge. No one called after her or demanded to know where she was going. For the moment she was free.

A few moments later she stepped inside the plush offices that belonged to her father until tomorrow morning. This would be her domain, Heather thought, as she trailed a finger along the mahogany desktop. The deep leather chair looked inviting. With a smile of distinct pleasure Heather sank down in it. How many times had she wandered into this office as a child and clambered into this chair?

Absently she began opening desk drawers. Strange. Jake

had taken over much of the day-to-day accounting work during the past two years. Heather wondered why a great deal of the financial information hadn't been transferred to his office. From what she had been able to tell, Jake appeared to work out of his cottage.

Perhaps her father hadn't been good at delegating authority. When she took over she would see that Jake took charge of these records. After all, he was supposed to be the financial wizard.

Her eye paused on some recent entries, noting the handwriting. Frowning, she reached for some of the official records of the corporation.

Five minutes later she sat staring at the copy of a recent corporate resolution. The document clearly stated the owner of the Hacienda Strand, and it was not Paul Strand.

Heather read the name again and again. Jack Cavender owned the Hacienda Strand, and had owned it for the past six months.

It had been about four months ago that her father had first approached her about returning to Tucson. Three or four months ago that her parents had begun to hint very seriously just how beneficial a marriage between herself and Jake would be.

A perfect team, her father had said. A perfect management team. No one had bothered to tell her that she was not going to be the ranking member of that team.

Fury, intense and passionate beyond anything she had ever known, began to uncoil in her. No wonder Jake hadn't seriously objected to signing the prenuptial agreement. He was the one who would retain possession of the Hacienda in the event the marriage was dissolved.

Calling herself a fool and an idiot in a hundred different ways, Heather managed to let herself out of the office.

The music drifted through the balmy night air. Jake would be standing there, knowing he owned all he surveyed. And tomorrow morning at ten he was scheduled to acquire the last item on his shopping list.

"Hello, Heather. I've been looking for you."

Her head snapped around. For a second, it seemed as if her enraged imagination had conjured him up out of the darkness. Then an icy calm settled on her.

His face hardened as she began to step past him. "You've never left one of these parties early. Bridal jitters?"

"Umm, yes. I expect so."

"That's not like you, either, is it?"

"Jake, as I keep pointing out to you, you don't really know me that well, do you?" She sighed.

"I'm learning." It sounded like a threat.

"Don't worry, I'll be fine by tomorrow."

"Good. Because it's much too late to change your plans."

"Don't worry, Jake, I'll show up at the wedding. After all, it's my first one and I'm bound to be curious." She slipped free of his grasp.

AT NINE-FIFTEEN the next morning Heather turned to her closet and pulled out black designer jeans, a black cotton-knit pullover and sleek riding boots.

When she glanced into the mirror there was no trace of a glowing bride. A proud, coldly angry woman stared back at her.

A short time later she found the busboys hanging around the back of the hotel kitchens. When she offered Jim fifty dollars for temporary use of his new motorcycle he stared at her.

"I don't know about this," the teenager said worriedly. "Maybe you should borrow the bike another time?"

"Now is exactly the right time." The massive black motorcycle accepted her unprotestingly. She slid it into gear and rode off.

The narrow path that wound picturesquely up to the little chapel was almost empty. The threatening roar of the cycle made everyone turn. Her parents and Jake were standing together on the front steps of the chapel.

With one booted foot bracing herself and the machine, Heather flexed her fingers on the handlebars and focused on the man who waited for her. Of all the people gathered there only he seemed to realize exactly what was happening.

"I understand there's a wedding here today," Heather remarked so that all could hear. "I just wanted to come by and congratulate the groom. I understand he's the new owner of the Hacienda Strand. The news came as something of a shock to the bride, I'm afraid, so if I were you I wouldn't stand around waiting for her. She's a bit indisposed at the moment. Feeling like a manipulated idiot will do that to a woman. Especially on her wedding day!"

She twisted the accelerator and the bike growled down the path toward the main entrance to the lodge and then she was free, heading down the road toward Tucson.

Behind her, Jake strode down the steps and the crowd at the bottom parted for him in the same way they had parted for the woman on the motorcycle.

Perhaps they sensed a similar potential for raw violence in man and machine.

*

SLOWLY HEATHER began to cruise toward the airport, seeking one of the new motels that had been built near it. Some time later a frankly suspicious desk clerk handed her the key to Room 235.

In the anonymous room she picked up the telephone. Jim Connors was going to be frantic about his beloved bike. After saying where he could pick it up, she added, "I'll leave another fifty in an envelope along with the keys. Goodbye, Jim, and thanks." Heather replaced the phone before the teenager could argue.

The hours stretched out ahead of her—hours in which depression replaced the savage high Heather had found herself riding. How long she lay—overcome by guilt and seething anger—Heather didn't know…

There was no knock on her door. It simply swung open without any warning as a key was slipped into the outside lock. The remote mask Jake had always worn in her presence had disintegrated.

"Bastard," she breathed tightly.

"Is that a question or a comment? Whichever it is, it happens to be true." Jake's gray eyes never wavered. "My father wasn't in the picture long."

"I'm not in the mood for a sob story, Jake."

"This was supposed to be our wedding night," he reminded her silkily.

"An interesting thought. When would you have bothered to tell me that you owned the hotel? Before you seduced me? The next morning over breakfast? What a lovely wedding gift."

He exhaled slowly. "Paul and I knew that you would never come home or give any relationship between you and me a chance if you thought I owned the Hacienda."

"Go to hell!" She hadn't allowed herself to feel such fierce emotion in so many years and the result was dizzying. "You manipulated me as though I was a rival!"

"You were. I couldn't risk telling you everything until you were committed to me, as well as to the Hacienda Strand."

"Such arrogance."

"Was I any more arrogant than you were to think you could descend on the Hacienda after all these years and pick up where you left off? I'm the one who poured money and time and everything I had to give into that hotel during the past two years. I'm the one Paul Strand came to when the place was in trouble and I'm the one who put it back on its feet. It's going to be my home and it can be yours, as well. Do you really want to run off to California again?"

She reacted violently, leaping to her feet and shoving at his lean, hard body with both hands. In a flurry of arms and legs Jake tumbled her onto the bed, pinning her by her wrists and using the weight of his body to hold hers quiet.

"I can't let you go, Heather," he groaned heavily as he lowered his head. "You're a part of it. I need you to make it all work. Don't you understand?"

"No, no, I don't, and I don't want to," she heard herself say on a note of panic. The last thing she could risk was giving herself to Jake Cavender. Not now when everything had gone so terribly wrong.

"If you can walk away in the morning, after we've been together tonight, I swear I won't stop you. But I want tonight, Heather. You owe me a wedding night."

His mouth came down on hers with a rough intensity. Frantically Heather tried to find the words she needed to free herself. She managed to pull her mouth from his. "Would you want me so much if I had nothing to do with the Hacienda? If I offered you one night instead of marriage?"

"What the hell are you talking about?"

"If you make love to me tonight it will be on my terms," she vowed. The emotions in her were an uncontrollable flood. Pain and passion and rebellion and rage seethed in her veins. "No promises, Jake. No guarantees. No neat tidy package consisting of me, my approving family and a home at the Hacienda Strand."

"Another contract, Heather?"

"You won't sign this one. There's nothing in it for you."

"You said yourself that you don't know me very well," Jake muttered as his mouth closed once more over hers.

No, HEATHER REALIZED she didn't know him very well. If she did, she would have understood that the depths of his emotions were even more raw and powerful than her own.

She learned that shattering fact the moment he began to consume her with his passion. The spectrum of his blazing emotions was suddenly savagely revealed to her. In him there was pain and passion just as she had known. There was anger, too. And a purely masculine desire to find the key to her surrender. But above all there was a hunger unlike anything she had ever known.

Heather found herself responding fiercely to that undisguised hunger, and she heard his growl of pleasure. It was the most satisfying sound in the world. He came to her in a rush of strength and need that dazzled. In a fever she opened herself to him, parting her legs at his touch, lifting herself in silent pleading invitation.

Heather gasped as he probed the entrance to her throbbing feminine core. For an instant fear rose up through her.

"Heather, don't fight me." Suddenly he was overwhelming her body's instinctive protest, sheathing himself deeply inside and drinking the cry of excitement and fear from her lips.

Heather clung to him. She had no other choice. It was as if, finally, after all these years, this was the answer she had been seeking. The world narrowed down to a single brilliant focal point. Tonight Jake Cavender was the only thing in her life that truly mattered.

He swept her into the powerful rhythm of his lovemaking, tuning her body's response to his. Her pulse leaped and the desire in her shimmered in reaction.

"Jake! Oh, Jake!"

"Let it happen, honey," he rasped. "Just let go and take me with you."

He sank his fingers deeply into her flesh and Heather cried aloud. She heard Jake's answering shout of release and exultation and then they were locked together in a world of shattering intimacy.

Hours later, Heather woke to find herself curled closely around Jake's warm body. Her wedding night, she thought bleakly. No, her night of surrender. She'd come back to Tucson on her own terms, she'd said. But it was devastatingly clear to her that the only way she could stay would be on

Jake's. And the upshot was she had fallen in love with Jake
Cavender.

A frisson of genuine fear tingled through her veins. Somehow she had never imagined that being in love would leave
her in such an emotional tangle.

"Heather?" Jake moved his face into her tousled hair.

"Jake, you've turned my whole world upside down."

"We're even, then."

"No. Your world is humming along exactly as you planned.
I want some time to reorganize my own world. Some time by
myself."

"How much time?" he asked harshly.

"I don't know. A few days. Maybe longer."

"Heather, you belong to me now. You know that."

"Do I?" she challenged huskily, unwilling to give him that
final verbal victory.

He hesitated then asked softly, "Where will you go?"

"My father's old hunting cabin up in the canyon. I have to
go," she told him flatly.

Jake watched her shadowed face and knew that he would
have to let her go for the moment. He'd taken her world apart
and he told himself she had a right to figure out whether or
not she wanted the new one he was offering.

"In the morning, Heather. I'll let you go in the morning,"
he said roughly. "Grant me what's left of my wedding night!"
He pulled her into his arms.

HEATHER TURNED THE KEY in the Mercedes, watching through
the side window as Jake fired up the motorcycle. He gave her
a sidelong glance. "A few days, Heather," he reminded her
over the muted roar. "That's all."

She nodded and drove off. Making only a brief stop for
groceries and camping supplies, she soon resumed her journey.

Heather shook her head wryly as she guided the Mercedes
along the highway that led into the hills. Jake had done more
than compel her physical and emotional surrender last night.

He had succeeded in reviving the passionate outlook on life that she had subdued so successfully for the past few years. Marrying for convenience or for business reasons, no matter how satisfactory to all parties concerned, was simply no longer good enough.

When she turned off the road to take the much narrower, less-used canyon trail, the desert terrain gave way to shrubs and trees.

When she arrived at the cabin, she remembered that it didn't have electricity, but there was running water. No hot water, of course, but she could live without it for a couple of days.

A couple of days. Jake had let her go this morning with hardly any argument. Not like him at all.

Visions of Jake coming after her danced through Heather's head. The romantic side of her longed for such an event. The realistic side warned her that nothing would be changed by such an occurrence.

Tears burned for a few seconds in her eyes. Hastily she brushed them away with the back of her hand. Then she set about taking her mind off her problems by concentrating on starting a fire in the old cookstove. She heated some water and started cleaning up the cabin.

As she worked all afternoon, huge billowing masses of unstable air whirled in the sky. She hoped the cabin roof didn't have too many holes.

The distant sounds of thunder hid the noise of the car until it was already in the driveway. Heather leaped to her feet. Jake had come after her. She felt a fierce gladness as she threw open the cabin door.

Heather stared in shock, her attention riveted on the weapon. She jerked her eyes up to meet the menacing, dark eyes of...Rick Monroe, last seen when she and Rick had parted ways en route to California so long ago. Now, he had a gun in his hands.

"Small world, isn't it? How have you been, Heather?"

"Oh, my God." When he showed every sign of pushing

past her, Heather stepped back into the cabin. "Why the gun, Rick?" Thunder cracked overhead as the sky continued to darken. "Why are you here?"

"Me?" He sat down on an overstuffed arm of the old sofa. "Well, Heather, I'm afraid I'm here on business." He grinned unpleasantly. "I guess you could say this place is my corporate headquarters." He eyed his surroundings derisively. "Remember when you and I used to come up here all those years ago."

"Rick, you're not making any sense." Determinedly Heather walked to the door. She was in shock but her instincts were warning her to put as much distance as possible between herself and Rick Monroe.

Her hand was on the old glass doorknob when he spoke. "I'm afraid I can't let you waltz out of here, sweetheart. I've got an important meeting of the board this evening and I'd kinda like you to attend."

"I don't want any part of your schemes," she hissed.

He rose and moved toward her. "You might like finding out what you missed when you told me to get lost eleven years ago."

Heather was trying to think of a way to handle his threat when the heavens chose that moment to send down the first sheets of water. A scowl appeared on Rick's heavy features and he glanced at his watch.

"What happens now, Rick?"

"We wait."

"For what?"

"The arrival of Joe. My partner."

This evening's storm was bound to make driving all but impossible. He shrugged, his fingers idly toying with the handle of the gun. It was a small gesture of tension and it made Heather more nervous.

"What happens after?"

"You mean what happens to you? Funny you should bring up the subject. I've been thinking about that little matter myself. I'm going south after this deal goes down tonight... Mexico, or maybe Panama. Somewhere I can enjoy myself and my money without having a lot of people asking nosy questions. Maybe, if you're real nice to me, I might think about taking you along. Least for a while."

Heather panicked at the leer in his tone. "And if I don't want to go with you?"

"Well, babe, I'm sure you can understand that I'm not in a position to tolerate witnesses."

Heather's eyes squeezed shut for a fraction of a second. "I think my decision is rather simple."

His gaze cruelly mocked her. "Just like old times, huh?" Rick strolled toward her, surveying her as though examining new property. "I always wondered how you'd be in bed. But I never got the chance. This time everything's going to be on my terms."

My terms. The words rang in Heather's ears. How many times had she said that to Jake? I'm coming back to Tucson on my terms. The marriage was to have been on her terms. The Hacienda Strand was to have been run on her terms. As she listened to Rick Monroe make a similar declaration she realized how appallingly arrogant she must have sounded to Jake.

The storm was raging more violently than ever outside. The sound of the nearby swollen stream was a dull roar.

"I'll remember you're in charge, Rick." Desperately she sought to inject suitable meekness into her tone.

"Good. Let's see what you can rustle up for dinner. I'm going to the Jeep."

Leaving the door open so that he could keep an eye on Heather, he dashed out to the Jeep and grabbed a battery-powered lamp. A moment later he was back.

As the minutes ticked past she became increasingly frightened. Rick was concentrating on watching the road to the cabin. He seemed more tense than ever.

If she was going to do anything it had better be before the

man named Joe arrived. Heather eyed the pan of bubbling soup she'd made for their dinner. Such an impossible long shot.

Heather was standing very still, the rag-wrapped handle of the soup pan in one hand when she saw shadowy movement outside the side window. She barely stifled her gasp of alarm. Perhaps Rick's friend Joe had some plans of his own this evening. He's clearly into something sinister, Heather thought. Drugs seemed likely. Deals such as the one Rick apparently had going tonight all too often left the bodies of witnesses and former "partners" in their wake.

Heather cried out as the dark form of a man came hurtling through the side window. Both men fell to the wooden floor with a jolting thud.

Whatever chance she was going to have was here and now. Whirling she dashed for the door.

Outside the rain was coming down as violently as the fight behind her was raging. The storm had turned into a nightmare of roaring water. She was standing on the porch, trying to find the Mercedes keys in her pocket when the two men, locked in savage combat, burst through the doorway.

Heather's startled scream was broken off abruptly as the two figures tumbled past her. She recognized the low-cut desert boot even as it nearly tripped her. "Jake!"

The man on top briefly straddled the one on the ground, then raised an arm for a final blow. It landed an instant later with a sickening sound, and then the man slowly struggled to his feet.

"Jake?" she whispered tremulously.

"I swear, Heather, if you intend to give me this kind of trouble for the next fifty years..."

"Oh, Jake!" She hurled herself against his mud-splattered figure.

Jake stroked her back. "Heather, what's going on? Who is that guy I punched out?"

"It's Rick Monroe, who I left town with all those years

ago. He's using the cabin as some kind of hangout. And his partner, Joe, will be showing up soon. They have a deal going. Drugs, I think.''

''Oh, hell. That's just wonderful,'' Jake growled in disgust. He glanced skyward as another roll of thunder crashed above them. Then a beam of light flashed around the curve of the road. ''That really tears it. Come on, Heather. If we stay here we're going to be sitting ducks in the beam of those head-lights.''

Jake tugged her after him, forcing her to run blindly in the pelting rain. She realized that they were circling the cabin, putting the structure between themselves and whoever was in the approaching vehicle.

''Jake, we can't go much farther in this direction. The can-yon walls—we'll never be able to climb them in this rain.''

Jake swore. ''We'll have to ford that stream.''

''That stream is a river by now. We'll never make it.''

A shot rang out in the darkness, then another. A beam of light arced through the night, slicing over their heads. Jake froze, holding Heather absolutely still.

''Keep your head down. We're going to have to get across that stream.''

Heather knew how treacherous the canyon streams could become in this kind of storm. But she had no better plan to offer.

The powerful beam of the light flashed, barely missing them. And then she heard Rick's voice.

''Heather, come back here. I told you I'd take you to Mex-ico. You can't get out of this canyon.''

''I knew I should have hit him again,'' Jake gritted. ''They're focusing the searchlight on this side of the canyon,'' Jake muttered, watching the sweep of light. ''They obviously don't expect us to try the stream.''

''Rick'll assume we'll have more sense.''

''Then we haven't got much choice.'' He circled her wrist

in a grip of iron and plunged into the raging stream. Heather nearly lost her breath as the impact of the water struck her.

"Jake!" A stronger surge of water crashed into them and under the force of it Jake was shoved sideways. His grip on Heather's wrist slackened momentarily. Heather clenched her teeth and fought for the next step.

Another few feet and they would be on the far side. But the roar of water cascading down the canyon was deafening.

She felt Jake come to a halt. Her body crashed into his, and his hands were suddenly under her, lifting her toward the boulders that promised safety.

Desperately Heather grasped the wet slippery surface. She was free of the pull of the water because she'd had someone to lift her. There was no one behind Jake.

"I'm going to pull you out, Jake!" she shouted.

"You can't. You're not strong enough. Let go!"

Heather wriggled along the rock until she was over a small ridge in the boulder, and tugged with every ounce of her being, feeling as though her arm was about to be torn from the socket. As long as she could hold on…

Abruptly Heather jerked her head up, aware that something had given way. Either Jake had found a way to free himself and was being carried helplessly downstream or…

And then she was in his arms, clinging madly. In the wet darkness she could barely distinguish the gleaming depths of his eyes. Then he turned, catching her wrist one more time. "Come on, honey. We can't stay here." Together they forged an awkward path through the rain-soaked night.

"There used to be a couple of old deserted cabins on this side of the stream," Heather said hesitantly, trying to pick out familiar landmarks in the shadows.

The only source of comfort was Jake's firm grip on her hand. "I was contemplating throwing soup at Rick when you came charging through the window. How did you know something was wrong?"

He turned with an expression of amazement. "I find you

with another man within twenty-four hours of having been in
my bed, and you wonder how I knew something was wrong?''

Despite the increasing chill of the night air on her damp
body, Heather warmed. ''But how did you know the situation
was dangerous?''

''I drove up here to try to talk some sense into you. Then
I saw Monroe go out to his Jeep and realized he had a gun.''

He gave her hand a squeeze. ''Where did you learn to hang
on in a situation where you should have let go? I owe my life
to you.''

''We're even. I owe you mine.''

The cabin proved to be on high ground, well above the
threat of flowing water. And when Jake pushed open the unlocked door the single room appeared relatively dry.

''You're shaking,'' Jake muttered, pulling her close.

''Oh, Jake, I was so scared.'' She wrapped her arms around
his waist.

She'd never felt so safe in all her life.

*

THE HEAT OF HIS BODY was more satisfying than the fire he'd
built. The strength of his grasp chased away the last of the
night's terrors.

''I should have known better than to let you head for that
cabin this morning. By the time I got back to the Hacienda I
realized I'd been a fool. Never let a headstrong female go
chasing off on her own to think things over. That's my new
motto.'' Jake sounded complacent and satisfied. ''Hold me,
honey. Wrap yourself around me and let me know you're safe
in my arms.''

The feel of his hardening body made her senses sing. ''I
won't let go,'' she heard herself murmur into his chest.
''Ever.''

He heard the promise on her lips and reveled in the way
she drew him even closer, her nails biting deeply into his back

as her legs clung to his hips. Every nuance of her response
fed his own desire. When she tightened beneath him, arching
her head back over his arm, he thought he would never know
such satisfaction as he did in that moment. Jake lost himself
in the woman he was holding and it was a moment or two
before he realized exactly what she was saying over and over
again.

"I love you, Jake. I love you, I love you, I love you."

The litany caught at him. "Oh, Heather, Heather, go on
saying it. Just go on saying it forever."

After a time Heather stirred languidly in his arms. Her eyes
reflected her happiness. "I love you, Jake."

He stared at her for a long searching moment and then without a word, leaned over to kiss her softened mouth. She responded happily, her face glowing as he raised his head again.

"This—" she informed him, leaning down to nip his shoulder teasingly "—is the point where you're supposed to tell
me that you love me. Honestly, Jake. For a supposedly brilliant
businessman, you're a little slow on the uptake sometimes."

"I've had a rough time of it lately," he murmured by way
of apology. He was toying with the curve of her breast where
it lay pillowed against his chest.

"Jake, you do still want to marry me, don't you?"

"Oh, yes, honey. I still want to marry you. I'll give you
everything I can."

"All I want right now is for you to be honest with me. Do
you love me?" She sucked in her breath when he remained
silent. "You don't love me."

Jake's expression darkened. "You're talking to the man you
left standing on the chapel steps with a couple hundred wedding guests and your parents to face alone. Remember?"

"Jake, I didn't mean…I mean I was furious. I felt betrayed." She stared at him uncomprehendingly. "I didn't
know I was in love with you then! I didn't realize it until—"

"After I'd taken you to bed and dragged a surrender out of
you. After I'd shown you how good we are together."

"That had nothing to do with it," she cried, and shook her head in horrified understanding. "You don't believe in love, do you?"

"Dealing with you is like dealing with a keg of dynamite." Jake sat up and reached for his clothes. "Aren't you about to withdraw your declaration of undying love?" he challenged, voice hardening for the first time.

"No."

That brought his head up sharply, gray eyes coolly narrowed. "No?"

She watched him from proud unflinching eyes. "No. I love you, Jake...and nothing will change that. I agree that we have a lot in common businesswise and we both seem to want a home. I agree, in fact, with all the intellectual and realistic reasons why we belong together. I'm even willing to acknowledge that we might just possibly be able to work together, even if you do own the hotel."

Relief flashed into the gray eyes. "Then what is this all about?"

"Simple. The other side of me, the side you say is dramatic, passionate and given to scenes, won't be satisfied with a marriage based purely on lots of nice rational reasons. I won't marry for anything less than love."

Jake's eyes closed in dismay. His scowl turned into a full-fledged glare. "Growing up in foster homes was an excellent example of just how unreliable love can be," he shot back savagely. "Do you have any idea how often someone has told me she loves me? My mother. All those women who ran the homes. So did the woman I married. Whatever emotion they were experiencing sure didn't last long."

"You liked hearing the words from me. You said so!"

"Of course I like hearing them," he stormed. "But no one but a fool would trust them. I put my trust in other kinds of bonds. Those bonds form the real basis on which a marriage between us can work."

"We can have a terrific working relationship based on those

bonds. We can even have an affair based on them. But I will not allow them to be the basis of marriage between you and me."

He stared at her in bewilderment. "You think I'm going to wake up one morning and realize I'm deeply in love?"

"Why not? That's the way it happened to me."

He ignored that. "And in the meantime you're prepared to have an affair?"

"People in love tend to be generous," she assured him kindly.

"The hell you are," he growled softly. "You're willing to make the offer because you know I can't accept. I told your father that when I brought you back, everything would be under control."

"That was very foolish of you, Jake. No one has ever succeeded in managing me. I live my life on my own terms."

Jake reacted to the challenge with cold assessment. "So you keep saying. But in me you've met your match. We're not going to have an affair, Heather Strand. You're going to marry me. On my terms."

THERE HAD BEEN NO SIGN of life on the opposite side of the canyon the next morning when Jake and Heather had hiked out. The driver of a pickup stopped willingly enough, regaling them with stories of storm-caused damages he'd seen that morning. Heather climbed gratefully onto the worn seat and sat between the driver and Jake.

"Not too smart to go into these canyons when a thunderstorm's brewin'," the rancher advised.

"Actually, I'm a runaway bride," she said chattily. "I left Jake standing at the altar and he came after me."

The rancher cast a questioning look at Jake.

Jake sighed, sinking more deeply in the seat. "I had visions of spending my honeymoon in Santa Fe, not that blasted canyon."

"It wasn't a honeymoon because we never did get married," Heather pointed out. "We may never get married. Jake has decided he doesn't love me."

"Shut up, Heather."

"He's very bossy at times," Heather went on cheerfully. "You hear that warning tone in his voice? He sounds that way just before he lays down the law."

"If you don't close your mouth I will do it for you."

Heather smiled devastatingly and said nothing for the remainder of the trip.

By mid-afternoon they'd found their way back to civilization. Before returning to the hotel, they stopped at the police station and notified the authorities about the activities of Monroe and his pal, Joe. A short time later Jake parked the rental car in the private parking area of the hotel, much of Heather's earlier breezy assurance faded.

"Oh, Jake. What am I going to say to them?" she groaned.

"Just tell your parents to reschedule the wedding for two weeks from today. The day before they leave on their cruise," Jake pointed out heartlessly. "That's what I'm going to tell them."

"You'd better not unless you want to find yourself standing alone at the altar again!"

He turned to look at her, the cool gray eyes level and utterly unyielding. "You'll be there this time, Heather. Believe me."

BY THE TIME JAKE had told the Strands the whole story, Ruth and Paul were vastly relieved.

"I wouldn't have believed she had such stubborn strength in her," Jake said at one point, his gaze roving over Heather. "I told her to let go, and there wasn't anything I could do except climb out of that stream. It was obvious she wasn't going to give up."

"You should have seen Jake in the brawl," Heather put in quickly, uncomfortable under the cool admiration in his eyes. "They don't teach that sort of thing in accounting classes."

"Just as long as the two of you are okay, that's all that matters," Ruth assured them in heartfelt tones.

It was Paul who broke in with the one remaining question. "Well? What are you two going to do now?"

"Go to work," Heather said.

"We work very well together," Jake agreed coolly. "So well that we're going to reschedule the wedding. I thought two weeks from today would do nicely." He watched Heather over the rim of his coffee cup, daring her to contradict him.

THAT NIGHT HEATHER had dinner with Jake and her parents. She helped her mother prepare the tacos and enchiladas, working in a companionable manner that was very soothing to Heather's heightened state of tension.

"I was astounded that those two would mislead you that way. I knew Paul intended to sell the Hacienda eventually but I thought he and Jake would strike a deal after the two of you were married." Ruth shook her head as she arranged the enchiladas. "Men. They always think they know what's best. Paul told me that he thought everything was all right because—" She cast a sidelong glance at her daughter. "Are you going to marry Jake in two weeks?"

"I love him. But I don't know if we'll be married."

"Are you trying to punish him for what he did?"

Heather firmly denied that with a shake of her head. "No. I'm trying to make him understand exactly how he feels about me."

As if she sensed her daughter was uncomfortable revealing anything more about her relationship with Jake, Ruth lifted the tray of enchiladas and said, "I'll let you off the hot seat if you'll slip these in that hot oven, okay?"

"Okay, mother," Heather said, laughing.

AFTER DINNER JAKE took Heather's arm as they started back through the hotel gardens.

"You had everyone so grateful that I was alive that they

forgot to be angry at me for having caused that scene at the chapel. I owe you one, Jake.''

He smiled. ''Good. Maybe if I get you deep enough in debt you won't cause me any trouble when it's time to drag you to the altar.''

Her mouth curved upward as she lifted her face in the moonlight. ''I love you, Jake.''

He groaned and pulled her close, crushing her mouth hungrily beneath his own. ''Then don't fight me.''

''I won't fight you tonight. Shall I come back to your cottage with you?'' She traced a pattern against the nape of his neck.

''A week ago, I'd have stumbled over my own feet accepting the offer.''

''Tired of me already?''

''You know very well that's not the case. The way I feel I could make love right here on the grass.''

''I'm not fighting you, Jake. You're fighting me.''

''Do you think that if you seduce me often enough I'll give you what you want?'' he asked bitterly. ''It won't work, Heather. Stop playing your dramatic little games.''

Heather tried to hide the hurt she knew must be reflected in her eyes. ''Good night, Jake. I'll see you in the morning.''

He'd hurt her with that last crack about playing games, he realized. It was odd to have the power to hurt someone. He didn't think he'd ever possessed that kind of power before and it made him uncomfortable.

He was made considerably more uncomfortable by the stark loneliness of his bed. He muttered savagely to himself as he lay staring at the ceiling. Jake had never felt so utterly determined in his life as he did in that moment. He would put a halt to Heather's dramatic little fantasy of love and force her to accept the situation between them for what it was. After all, there was still that practical businesslike side of her nature to tap. He'd use it to resolve the conflict between them.

The decision made, Jake climbed out of bed and opened the

drawer. He pulled out a copy of the prenuptial agreement he'd signed and began to study it in detail. Then he reached for another sheet of paper and a pen.

HEATHER FELT unaccountably suspicious of the dinner invitation from the moment she accepted it the following afternoon.

Jake drove them to an elegant restaurant in the hills overlooking the city, saying little en route. After he had guided her firmly indoors she realized that he was in a dangerous mood. There was a hard relentless determination in the depths of those gray eyes.

"I think it's time we got down to business. You don't want to be my wife—"

"I never said that," she protested urgently.

"Let me rephrase that. You insist marriage be on your terms. Terms I find unacceptable."

Heather's mouth went dry.

"You are willing to work for the Hacienda and be my mistress. I have drawn up a contract that covers your chosen job duties."

Heather's fingers closed tightly around the stem of her wineglass as Jake withdrew a folded document from inside his jacket.

A horrible sense of déjà vu struck her. "You've been busy," she tried to say offhandedly.

"I'll want your signature by the first of next week, Heather."

"I see."

"I'll be glad to outline the main points."

No, she wanted to scream.

He leaned forward, holding the glass of Scotch in one hand. "Basically you will be my personal assistant. In addition you will perform the duties of hostess for the Hacienda. You're good at that and I need those skills. Above all you will carry out my wishes."

"Will you be standing over me with whips and chains?" she challenged.

"I don't think there will be any need for that. The second half relates to your duties as my mistress."

"Your lover," she corrected distantly.

"For purposes of the contract, the word is mistress. As owner of the Hacienda I feel obliged to maintain a certain image."

"You mean you think it might be a bit tacky to be sleeping openly with the daughter of the former owner?" Heather asked bitterly.

"Very tacky. Because being my mistress is just another job, I am willing to pay a separate salary."

Heather went white. Watching her from across the table Jake faltered. "It doesn't have to be like this, Heather."

"Doesn't it?" She stared at him, wounded.

"Marry me. You'll share ownership of the Hacienda and you'll share my life."

"It's not enough," she told him evenly.

Jake's face tightened. "Why do it the hard way?"

"Asking you to love me as I love you is the hard way?"

"Heather, I know you want—" Jake broke off abruptly, his eyes lifting. "Oh, hell, Cecil and Connie Winthrop."

"How lovely," Heather breathed bitterly. "Invite them over and you can make another pitch to buy their land for your precious golf-course project."

Jake's gaze flicked to her tense face. "Why not? I'll let you handle the whole thing." He rose to his feet as he signaled to the Winthrops.

Before she could protest, they were upon them, beaming with avid curiosity. The Winthrops had been among the two hundred or so guests at the chapel a few mornings earlier.

"How are you, Cecil?" Jake extended his hand politely.

"Fine, just fine. I might ask the same question of you, young man. It sounds to me as if our Heather has been giving you a hard time lately."

"Cecil!" his wife admonished hurriedly.

"I think I'll survive," Jake murmured, his gaze on Heather's face. "We're getting it all ironed out, aren't we, honey?"

"Steamrollered, not ironed out," Heather responded with a shred of her natural spirit. She turned to Connie Winthrop with her most brilliant smile. Jake said he wanted that land. Very well, she would get it for him.

*

THREE DAYS LATER, Jake stood in the doorway of Heather's office and watched as she pored over a new menu. Ever since the night he had taken her out to dinner she had totally involved herself in work, spending up to sixteen hours a day in the office.

Warily he had tried a few business conversations with her but Heather had merely listened politely, nodding agreement to everything he said.

As Heather became aware of his presence, he tried a smile. "Does the menu look feasible?"

"It's going to cost us...you, a fortune."

He heard the way she tripped over the word us, and swore inwardly. "I just had a call from Cecil Winthrop."

Heather nodded, saying nothing.

"You're the reason he and Connie finally agreed to sell," Jake went on doggedly.

"You can show your appreciation by throwing in a Christmas bonus."

"Heather!"

That brought her head up. "I'm sorry, Jake. I forgot myself. I'm a little tired this morning."

He surveyed the coffee cup beside her desk and the half-empty pot. "You're drinking too much coffee."

Heather glanced at him, about to make a crack about paying for the coffee, but something stopped her. Surely he wasn't actually worried about her. And then, quite suddenly, she knew he was.

Jake straightened and moved toward her desk purposefully. "How much longer, Heather?" he asked softly.

"Until I sign the contract? You gave me until Monday, remember?"

"You know it's not what you want."

"I know." Her smile was sad and a little whimsical. "Excuse me, Jake. I've got to get back to work."

Jake's mouth firmed. Without a word he removed himself from her office.

As soon as she heard the door close behind him Heather's body went limp. They were tearing each other apart. If she signed the contract she would be committing both herself and Jake to an endless siege. If she gave in and tore it up, agreed to marry Jake, she would tie herself to a man who might never learn to love.

"Heather?"

She turned awkwardly at the sound of Paul Strand's voice.

Paul gave her a searching glance. "I just passed Jake in the lobby. He looks as though he's engaged in a war."

Heather stared at her father and knew she could never explain that the man he had chosen and groomed for her didn't love her.

Paul looked at her with a trace of pity. "Heather, I know better than anyone how stubborn and strong you are. But I've also learned a lot about Jake Cavender. If you didn't love him you might have a chance of winning a pitched battle. But loving him..." Paul shrugged unhappily. "I just wish to God I had realized what I was starting two years ago when I hired the man. On the other hand—" Paul kissed his daughter "—the guy's not exactly stupid."

Not exactly stupid. Heather repeated the words to herself. It was true Jake wasn't an idiot, but she wasn't so sure about herself.

ON SATURDAY, Heather spent the evening alone. She carefully unfolded the contract. Jake didn't want a mistress. He wanted a wife. Jake wanted a partner; she wanted a passionate lifelong love affair. Jake could go on playing manipulative games indefinitely. She couldn't. She could not go on battling the man she loved.

Slipping open the door, Heather headed for the garden path that led to Jake's cottage. It was starting to rain.

A moment later Jake opened the door and stood staring down at her. The gray eyes narrowed and he seemed to tense as if for battle. "What are you doing here?"

"I thought we should discuss this contract." She held up the folded document. Never had he seemed more remote or, in some indefinable way, more dangerous.

She stepped through the door just as rain started to come down in torrents. "I haven't signed it."

The relief that flashed into his eyes disappeared almost immediately but Heather had seen it. Very deliberately she smiled and tore the contract. Then she stepped toward him and dropped the document at his feet.

"I love you, Jake. I couldn't possibly sign that silly contract." Her arms went around his neck and she pulled his head down toward hers.

"Heather!"

Her name was a rasping cry against her mouth. She heard untrammeled relief.

Jake pulled her into the strength of his body, his broad hands flattening along the length of her back and down to her hips as he sought to force every inch of her against him. "Heather, Heather! You'll marry me?"

"Yes."

He buried his lips in her hair, inhaling the scent. "I was so afraid you'd fight me until there was nothing left."

"I know, Jake," she soothed, translating the gentling tone of her voice to the tips of her fingers as she massaged the hard curve of his shoulders. "I know, darling. It's all right now.

Everything is all right. Don't say anything else. Just let me make love to you.''

"I've been aching for you." With a husky groan he scooped her up and settled her onto the love seat. "I need you so badly."

The feverish desire flared between them, cutting off further conversation. Heather shimmered under the overwhelming assault of Jake's body. When the white-hot intensity of their shared need consumed them both, Heather no longer cared whether Jake viewed her love in terms of surrender. She gave herself completely and in the process received everything she could ever need or want.

IT WAS A LONG TIME before Jake stirred lazily against the sweetly limp form entwined with his. He smiled to himself, enjoying the feel of her leg as it lay trapped between his muscular thighs. What had he ever done to deserve his present contentment?

The answer to that question slammed into his head with uncomfortable certainty, forcing him up to a sitting position. Heather murmured a catlike protest, opening her eyes.

"Getting ready to kick me out so soon, Jake?" She teased him with her eyes. "Don't worry, I understand completely. Can't have the entire staff gossiping about us, can we?"

Very seriously he looked down at Heather. "What made you come here tonight?"

"You know the answer to that. I love you. And I want a home with you. I'd marry you regardless of whether or not the Hacienda came with the package."

He tried to find the words to communicate the unsettled driving message in his mind. "Honey, I've got to talk to you."

"So talk." She dropped a delicate kiss on his cheek.

"I should be taking you home." He didn't know how to tell her what he was feeling.

"If you're determined to take me back to the cottage, I suppose I'd better put some clothes on. If one of the security people saw me dashing naked through the rain, your reputation would be in tatters!''

When she swung a quick amused glance at him he caught his breath at the love shining out of her hazel eyes. ''Heather,'' he started in desperation, ''I didn't want it to be like this. I didn't want surrender....''

''I know,'' she responded simply. Then she was on her feet, tugging on her panties and jeans. ''Better get dressed, darling, unless you want to be the one who walks naked back through the gardens.''

He obeyed slowly, aware of the tension in himself. ''Honey, I'm trying to explain—''

''Oh, look, it's stopped raining. We won't get soaked preserving your image.'' She had the door open.

He caught up with Heather just as she stepped out into the night. Urgently he grasped her arm, aware that he had to say the rest of the words now, tonight. He had realized he didn't want victory the moment he'd seen her standing at his door this evening.

She'd surrendered so sweetly, he thought in shock as they walked silently through the grounds. And he'd taken everything she had to give. A woman as passionate and headstrong as Heather should be railing at him, screaming her anger and frustration, trying to punish him for lacerating her pride. If the situation had been reversed he'd have...

No, there was no way the situation could have been reversed. He would never have been able to find the courage to surrender.

He didn't like the taste of victory, Jake discovered.

''Heather, listen to me, I want to explain something. Something very important....''

The quickly moving storm clouds fled through the night sky, slipping past the moon. The pale light caught the length of the gun barrel just as the man crouched in the shadows beside Heather's front door raised the weapon and fired.

HEATHER WAS PLUNGING headfirst into the carefully tended shrubbery on her left. The propulsion power came from the hand with which Jake had been guiding her and it was followed by the full force of his body.

"Jake!"

"Shut up," he hissed, his hand clamping over her mouth. She nodded and then he released her, rolling free. She saw him digging into his belt and an instant later a small handgun appeared in his fist.

Jake scanned the bushes, telling himself to ignore the lack of feeling in his right arm. From the direction of the main lodge he thought he heard a shout. That would be security.

A flash of light shot through the shadows followed instantly by another crack of sound. The bullet went wild. Willing himself to concentrate completely on the least trace of movement, Jake waited.

The man broke cover a split second later and ran, crouching, for the small private-parking area. Jake leaped to his feet, aiming not at the running man but at the steady unmoving target presented by the Jeep. He fired once, twice, three times.

The engine squealed protestingly to life but the Jeep raced forward for only a few yards before another of Jake's shots caught it. This time one of the tires seemed to explode. The vehicle slowed to a stop just as the three security guards converged on it.

"You, in the Jeep. Out!" The man in charge of the three guards barked an order.

Rick Monroe tossed down his gun and stood scowling furiously in the pale gleam of the overhead parking-lot light. The security guards surrounded him instantly. Heather ignored the scene, struggling to her feet and reaching for Jake.

"Jake, are you all right?"

Jake lowered the gun in his hand, aware of the chill that climbed his arm and radiated into his shoulder. His head began a slow steady spin that annoyed him enormously. There was something he had to do.

"You've been hit!" Heather's expression went from concern to horror. "Your arm. You're bleeding!"

"Heather, I want to tell you…"

"Hush, darling. Can you make it to the steps?"

He ignored that. "No, this is more important. Listen to me, damn it!" Her pale face was swimming in and out of the fog that was starting to cloud his vision. So much to say. What if he never came out of the fog? And the pain was starting. Oh, God, the pain.

"One of the guards is calling an ambulance."

"Heather, shut up and listen to me." Her hand was clamped around his arm. He could see his blood welling up between her fingers.

"I'm listening, Jake," she said gently.

"Heather, I love you."

There, it had been said. Jake let himself slip into the soothing darkness.

HEATHER WAS SITTING by his bedside the next time Jake opened his eyes. She felt his hand tighten convulsively around hers and then his lashes lifted uncertainly. Jake stared at her as though he wasn't quite sure she was real. Then he scanned his surroundings.

"Hospital?" he got out a little hoarsely.

"I'm afraid so. Cheer up, though, you had the good taste to collapse away from the guests." She looked at him with love, concealing the tremendous relief she felt.

"Mustn't disturb the guests," he agreed slowly. "What time is it?" He searched her face.

"It's morning, Jake."

He frowned intently. "Last night. You came to me."

"Yes." Her mouth curved gently.

"And tore up the contract. You're going to marry me."

"Mother's going to spend the day rescheduling the wedding for the end of next week," she assured him.

"You'll be there this time, won't you?"

"Yes."

"Because you love me."

"Oh, yes, Jake. I love you."

"I knew for sure last night." He closed his eyes again and Heather worried that he might go back to sleep. But a moment later he opened them. "I should have been certain that first time. You're too strong, too proud to surrender for any other reason."

"So are you," she said quietly.

"I wanted to, Heather. God knows I wanted to. I just didn't know how. Until you showed me last night. Did I tell you I love you?"

"Just before you passed out."

"Good. I meant it, Heather."

"I know. If I'd been thinking straight I wouldn't have needed to hear the words. But I was running blind myself until the very last."

The half smile quirked his lips. "A heck of a team."

"I think things will function very well from now on."

"Just keep telling me you love me," he insisted.

"Forever," she vowed.

He was silent for a moment.

"Jake, does your arm hurt very badly?" Heather frowned in concern at the tight lines around his mouth.

"They get Monroe okay?"

"The guard rounded him up after you'd stopped him. Since when did you start carrying a gun?"

"Since we got back from the canyon."

"You suspected Rick might come back for me?"

Jake muttered something explicit. "You were really the only person he had to worry about. You knew he was involved in something illegal."

Heather shuddered. "I didn't even see Rick until he ran for the Jeep. That bullet you took was meant for me."

"Any word on his pal?" He ignored her last comment.

"One of the cops who came to the hospital earlier said they

picked up a Joseph Kincaid trying to cross the border last night. He's wanted on several counts of drug dealing, I gather.''

"So Ruth is replanning the wedding, hmm?" He looked content for a moment.

"She certainly is. She's going to have the chef prepare the entire reception menu again. I still feel terrible about what must have happened to all the goodies he fixed the first time!"

"Don't worry, he'll be delighted," Jake said dryly.

Heather smiled. "I think it's time you got some more sleep. You look a little peaked, to put it mildly.''

"I shouldn't be feeling this drowsy," he complained. "What have they got me on, anyway?"

"Something to keep you off your feet for a while. Don't worry about it, Jake. Just go back to sleep.''

"And where are you going?"

"Nowhere.''

His hand tightened on hers in thanks. "I love you, Heather.''

"You're getting very good at saying that.''

"And I'll get even better. It gets easier with repetition. I'll be practicing a lot.''

He was asleep when the young nurse came into the room fifteen minutes later. "How's our patient?" she asked Heather cheerfully.

"He woke up for a few minutes.''

"I assume he sounded reasonably rational?" The nurse checked the bandages on Jake's arm.

"Never more so.''

"Good. Maybe you should go catch a nap yourself, Miss Strand. You've been awake all night.''

"I told him I'd stay here." Heather didn't move.

The young woman grinned. "Like that, is it?"

Heather nodded. "We're partners, you see. A team.''

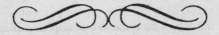

VELVET TOUCH

Jayne Ann Krentz
writing as Stephanie James

"**Y**ou're crazy!"

The words echoed in Lacey Seldon's ears as she guided the snappy red Fiat off the Washington State Ferry. She'd been hearing those words ever since she'd exploded the bomb of her decision. The shock waves were probably still ricocheting around the small, Midwestern university town where she had lived every one of her twenty-nine years.

"You're crazy!"

Everyone had told her that. The head librarian had said it when she had handed in her resignation.

Her parents had said it, her mother in tears, when she gave them the news.

Her father had taken the rational approach. "Leave a good job just when you're in line for another promotion? Don't be an idiot, Lacey!"

"Take the money from the sale of your house and live on that? But that should be set aside for the future!"

Her mother's arguments, predictably enough, were more emotional. She, at least, was saying the things everyone else was thinking.

"But you can't move away! This is where you belong. Why won't you be sensible and marry that nice professor of psychology? You'd make a wonderful mother for his children.

"Why are you doing this? You were always such a source of pride to your father and me." And then, more thoughtfully, "Except for the divorce, of course. But that was over two years ago. You've had plenty of time to get over it. You don't belong out there on the West Coast. You've always been such a *nice* girl!"

The yard sale had been the largest in the town's history. Everyone came, mostly out of curiosity. But it made for a very profitable sale. Aunt Selma, the one who had never married, took a look at the avidly interested crowd pawing through Lacey's things and winked at her niece. She had been the only one to show some understanding of Lacey's decision.

"I'll take your mother home," Selma had announced firmly. "She'll never make it through this day if I don't!"

Lacey's mother, however, had survived, just as Lacey had known she would. The descendants of the women who had made the Midwest into the heartland of America were made of stern stuff. When Lacey finally found herself standing beside the packed Fiat, her family grouped on the sidewalk in front of the home where she had been born, Lacey had kissed them all. And for the first time since she had made the decision, Lacey herself had cried.

So many years, she thought now as she followed a narrow road which encircled the island. The years when she should have been seeing the world, taking risks, and perhaps finding out what real romance and passion could be. All that time gone with nothing to show for it but a broken marriage, a job which had become incredibly routine, and no prospects of ever finding the exciting side of life.

But this summer, she, Lacey Seldon, would change all that. Finally, before it was too late, she was going to *live!*

The winding road slipped beneath the wheels of the Fiat, towering pines on one side, sweeping views of Puget Sound on the other. Eventually the small sign announcing the turnoff came into view and Lacey swung the little car around the corner, following an even narrower road as it curved along the edge of a quiet bay.

There, nestled cozily on the shore, was the Randolph Inn. Lacey smiled. It looked exactly as it had in the brochure. In front of the lodge a wide lawn stretched to the shore. Behind the main building she could see tiny cottages snugly fitted into the pine and fir trees. One of those was hers.

Lacey parked the car, pulled off the scarf which had kept her shoulder-length hair in place in the open car and shook the fiery tresses free. As she stepped from the Fiat, the yellow, crinkled gauze cloud of a dress swirled about her. She walked toward the main entrance.

The lobby was empty, no one waiting behind the antique front desk. Tentatively she rang the bell. When no one appeared, she shrugged and walked over to gaze out the window. She had the rest of her life ahead of her.

That thought was shaping her lips into a secret smile when a deep, grave voice spoke from behind her. "I'm sorry, miss, but I'm afraid the inn is full. Unless you have a reservation?" The tone said clearly that he didn't think she did.

"I do," Lacey hastened to assure him, swinging around to confront the man leaning against the doorjamb. The smile which had been edging her lips widened as she bent her head to dig about in her shoulder bag. "I've got the confirmation somewhere in here. I'm renting one of the cottages for the summer, not a room in the inn itself."

"But all the cottage tenants have arrived, except for..." He broke off, a strange expression flickering in his silvery hazel eyes. "You're not L. Seldon, the librarian from Iowa?"

Lacey gave him a serene, confident glance. "I'm afraid so. Don't fret, you don't look much like a desk clerk, either!" She handed him the reservation confirmation.

When he bent his head to scan it briefly, Lacey took the opportunity to study the man in more detail. He must have been around thirty-seven or thirty-eight. Tawny brown hair was combed carelessly back, nearly brushing the collar of his blue work shirt. Strong thighs were sheathed in close-fitting jeans which Lacey's mother would have severely frowned upon. When he came to stand behind the desk, she saw a look of lean, hard strength clearly stamped on his face. The impression it gave of quiet power was surprisingly attractive.

He glanced up and saw her watching him and his eyes flashed. He *enjoyed* her scrutiny!

"Welcome, Miss Seldon. We've been expecting you. And so, apparently, have a number of other people!" He ducked down behind the desk. When he straightened he was holding a stack of mail.

"We did as instructed in your letter, Miss Seldon," he informed her politely. "We held all mail for your arrival. You intend to spend the summer corresponding?" he remarked dryly.

"I intend to spend the summer job hunting." She chuckled, flipping happily through the envelopes. "I've been sending out resumes for the past couple of months. I used the inn for the return address. With any luck, you'll be getting mail for me all summer long!"

"You've come all the way out here just to job hunt?" He looked genuinely bewildered.

"I've come to do a great deal more than that," she assured him. "Now, shouldn't I sign in somewhere?"

Without a word he slid a form and a pen across the polished countertop. When she finished he handed her the key and started out from behind the desk. "I'll help you unload the car."

"You're the chief bellhop as well as desk clerk?"

"I'm afraid so. At least for today. My assistant, George, isn't feeling well," he explained easily. "My name's Randolph, by the way. Holt Randolph. I...own this place."

"Do you?" Lacey remarked, a little surprised. "How long have you had it?"

He flicked a speculative glance at her as he paced beside her across the lawn. "I inherited it," he said slowly, "from my grandparents."

"Oh." Lacey nodded. "I understand. I didn't realize you people out here did things like that, though."

"Have grandparents?"

"No." She laughed. "I thought everyone out here went off on his own to find himself."

"Sometimes," he admitted, halting beside the little car. "And sometimes we find out it isn't necessary."

Lacey glanced at him sharply. She could well believe he was the sort of man who had always known what he wanted. The only surprising thing, to her way of thinking, was that he wanted to run an old-fashioned inn tucked away on the edge of a tiny island.

"Well, to each his own," she returned breezily.

"Is that an old Midwestern philosophy?"

"Are you kidding? One of the reasons I'm here is to be among people who really *do* practice that philosophy! Now, which cabin is mine?"

"The one at the top of that rise. I'll meet you there," he added. "You obviously don't have room to give me a lift!"

Lacey laughed happily, her hand sweeping out in a gentle arc to indicate the boxes piled high even in the passenger seat. "I feel like those people on the old wagon trains must have felt when they packed what they could and sold off everything else!"

Holt stared at her for a second and she could see the mingled astonishment and curiosity mirrored in those eyes. Lacey could have given a shout of sheer satisfaction. Back in Iowa no one had been consumed with curiosity about her. Everyone knew her life history. But Holt merely nodded and started up the path to her cabin.

She reached the cottage ahead of him and hurried to unlock the front door. Yes, it was exactly as promised. Heavy cedar logs framed a cozy parlor, complete with stone hearth. Wide windows provided the view of the main lodge and Puget Sound.

"Will it do?" her host asked, walking up behind her.

"It's perfect," she told him enthusiastically.

"Some of the furniture's a little ancient," he said somewhat apologetically, his eyes on the quaint, overstuffed sofa and lounger chair. "But the bed is new and the bath was redone during the winter."

"I'm sure it will be fine," she said.

"Good, I'm glad you like it," Holt said. "Where are you planning on moving after your summer vacation?"

"Haven't the foggiest," Lacey said lightly.

He stood for a moment, watching her. "You know, I hate

to say this, but frankly, you just don't look like the small-town librarian we were expecting.''

"Good. And you," she went on crisply, "don't look like the sort of person I imagined would be running this place. So much for stereotypes, I suppose!" Lacey tilted her head to one side, studying him.

"Actually," drawled a new voice behind her, "Randolph's a born innkeeper!''

Lacey whirled to find a lanky young man with warm brown eyes.

"And you must be the librarian he promised! Hi. I'm your neighbor for the summer, Jeremy Todd."

"Good afternoon, Todd," Holt said. "I see you're not wasting any time."

Lacey blinked, disconcerted by the element of masculine hostility which seemed to have entered the atmosphere.

Jeremy grinned, a charming, boyish grin. "Are all the librarians in Iowa like you?"

"No," Lacey retorted. "Some are blond."

Holt chuckled approvingly. "Come on, Todd. If you're going to hang around Lacey's front door, you might as well make yourself useful."

With both men assisting her, it wasn't long before Lacey had her belongings neatly piled. "That," she observed, "is everything I own in the world."

"You must have left an awful lot behind in Iowa."

"I left twenty-nine years behind in Iowa," she replied with a hint of grimness.

"Going back for them someday?" Holt asked.

For an instant they met each other's gaze across the room. *"Never."*

Holt nodded slowly and Lacey felt herself grow vaguely uneasy. She turned brightly to Jeremy.

"Which cottage is yours?"

"The one right across the way," he said quickly. "And if you're not doing anything else this evening, there's a brandy hour and dancing in the lounge," Jeremy explained. "You can watch Randolph mingle with the guests. Want to come along?''

"Thanks, I'd like that," she said with a smile.

"I'll see you both later this evening, then," Holt said in a slightly formal tone as he made for the door. Lacey watched him disappear down the path to the lodge.

"Need any help putting all this stuff away?" Jeremy inquired.

"No, thanks. I'll want to think about how to organize it. Will people dress up for this evening?" she asked.

"No, we keep things pretty casual around here. A pair of jeans and a swimsuit will see you through the summer," he said with a grin.

"Those I've got! Are you here all summer, too?"

"Yes." He gave her a somewhat sheepish glance. "I'm going to try and write a book."

"That's great! What kind?" Lacey was an old hand at encouraging such projects.

"It's one of those men's adventure novels. You know, lots of intrigue, a bit of sex."

"Your first?" she hazarded.

"Yeah. I'm trying to get out of insurance."

Lacey smiled. "It would appear we're both going to spend the summer looking for new careers!"

Jeremy's eyes warmed happily. "You, too?"

"Uh-huh. New career and a new life."

Jeremy smiled broadly. "Something tells me we're going to find a lot in common, Lacey."

Lacey smiled back. A lot more in common than she would ever find with a man who had probably never wanted anything else except to run this inn.

"THE INN is the most popular night spot on the island during the summer," Jeremy told Lacey as they walked into the lobby. "Ah! We've been spotted."

Holt was making his way toward them, every inch the

charming host. In one hand he carried a bottle of brandy and two small glasses.

Tonight was the first chance she'd had to wear the new, exotically patterned silk dress from India. She saw the flash of pleasure in Holt's expression and wondered why it pleased her.

"I'm glad you could make it," he said suavely, handing her and Jeremy a glass. "Jeremy, I'll leave you on your own while I introduce Lacey."

Lacey found herself whisked away. "One of the few privileges of being in charge," Holt murmured, one hand locked firmly under her arm. "The boy's too young for you, anyway," he added outrageously.

Lacey retorted coolly, "At my age a woman starts appreciating younger men!" Never would she have made a remark like that in Iowa, she thought happily.

He cocked one tawny brow. "Surely even Midwestern women have learned the value of the...vintage stuff over the brashness of younger material!"

Lacey drew a breath. "I came West to find variety, Mr. Randolph, not to prove the wisdom of old adages."

He brought her to a halt in front of the fireplace. "You're determined to leave all the old ways behind?"

"All of them."

"Does that include a man?"

"I don't think that's really any of your business," Lacey said, growing uneasily aware of the intensity of that silvery gaze.

"I only wanted to be prepared in case some irate male shows up and accuses me of harboring a runaway wife," Holt assured her.

"You're quite safe. There's no husband to come running after me. He left me willingly."

"Sure you're not just on the rebound?"

"Do you always get this personal with your guests?"

"Only the ones who interest me," he said smoothly.

She hesitated, debating about whether or not to answer the

compelling look in his eyes. Then, with a tiny shrug she decided to outline things for him.

"You needn't fret. I'm not on the rebound. It was over two years ago. Right after I'd finished paying off his medical-school bills. He married another doctor," she explained briefly. "And I don't think you need worry about Harold, either."

"I hate myself for asking, but who's Harold?"

"A professor of psychology," she told him breezily. She couldn't possibly have joked about poor Harold back in Iowa. Everyone knew him. "He asked me to marry him. Thought I fit the profile," she explained dramatically.

"This is like sinking into quicksand. What profile?"

"The earth-mother type." Lacey chuckled, remembering Harold's little inkblots. "But his two kids brought out aggressive tendencies in me. The day I told him they needed a wallop instead of an encounter session he withdrew his offer of marriage."

She saw the smile lurking in Holt's eyes and sighed ruefully. "Another shot at marriage down the tubes. Time's running out, you know," she told him wisely. "After thirty a woman's chances go down rapidly."

"You're here to hunt for a husband along with a new job?"

Lacey's voice lost its bantering quality and rang with conviction. "The next time I become involved with a man, it will be strictly romance and passion. No strings and no hidden bargains!"

The flash of surprise in the metallic eyes was barely concealed. "What you're looking for shouldn't be hard to find," he gritted with deceptive gentleness. "Is Jeremy Todd slated to experience the all-new you?"

Lacey hadn't come all this way to find more of the disapproval and advice she could have gotten back home! "I haven't decided yet," she said in liquid accents.

Holt said in a cold drawl, "You can always scratch an unsuccessful experiment and start over if things go wrong!"

"You misunderstand, Holt," Lacey told him with a seething

calm. "I've given this a great deal of thought. I'm looking for an interesting, reasonably long-lasting relationship which, when the excitement fades, can be terminated without the bitterness of divorce."

"So you're going to indulge yourself in a series of affairs?" he asked derisively.

"Why not? I found out what the traditional marriage has to offer. I spent twenty-nine years putting up with the values of small-town life. Now I'm going to make up for what I missed!"

"Oh, my God," he breathed, looking appalled. "You're going to go through a midlife crisis at my inn!"

Lacey didn't like that appalled look on him. It reminded her of the expressions she had left behind. "Why not? I took one look at the brochure you sent me and decided this island looked like the ideal place to go through such a crisis." Turning on her heel she smiled to herself and walked off.

THE SMILE was still mirrored in her eyes an hour later when Lacey slipped into Jeremy's arms on the dance floor. He pulled her closer as the music flowed around them and Lacey didn't resist. He was nice, she told herself. And they understood each other very well. She listened attentively as he talked about his novel.

"And if it doesn't sell right away?"

"Then it's back to insurance in the fall." He groaned.

On the way to their small table in the dimly lit lounge, Jeremy introduced her to some of the guests.

"I didn't notice Randolph making good on his claim that he was going to handle introductions." He chuckled wryly as they moved away. "What was that conversation in front of the fireplace all about, anyway? You sure left him with a frustrated expression on his face!"

"We were discussing my future plans," Lacey said dryly. "He doesn't entirely approve."

Her escort laughed, seating her. "He had such a firm image of you and you're not fitting it at all!"

Lacey lifted one brow interrogatively. "What?"

"He explained he had a sweet little librarian coming in from the Midwest. I think he wanted to let me know he wasn't going to provide any free summer entertainment of that nature."

"He does seem a little on the...uh...conservative side," Lacey observed vaguely. "I mean, considering the fact that he's single...."

"According to the Millers—" he named the couple to whom he had just introduced Lacey "—that status may not last. They've been coming to the inn for years and remember his ex-fiancée. She apparently ran off to marry another man and has since divorced. Edith says that the mystery woman from Randolph's past has made reservations here sometime during the summer."

Lacey's eyes lit up. "Fascinating! Maybe he was scorned once by a free-thinking woman in the past and has been hostile toward the species ever since!"

Jeremy shrugged, clearly losing interest.

Lacey took the hint and changed the subject. They were deep in conversation when Holt once again appeared out of the large crowd.

Lacey, for one, wasn't altogether surprised. She'd caught sight of him dancing with several guests.

"I'm making my social rounds." Holt reached down to encircle Lacey's wrist with a grip that felt like a manacle. The gleam in his eyes dared her to refuse.

"There's really no need to include me on your list of duty dances, Holt," she began firmly.

"But I insist," he countered, forcing her to her feet. "I take my responsibilities very seriously."

Lacey found herself being led in the direction of the dance floor. He drew her into his arms.

"Do you dance with all the women who stay here?"

"At least once."

Lacey thought about the imminent arrival of his ex-fiancée

and knew she had enough feminine curiosity to want to see him dance with the woman from his past.

"Do you mind some of the social obligations of your job?" she heard herself ask with genuine interest.

He shrugged, somehow managing to maneuver her a few inches closer in the process. "It's not the dancing I find unpleasant," he countered. "In fact, you feel quite good in my arms. All silky and light..." He paused. "What I'm not expecting to enjoy is your reaction when I give you the standard lecture on Jeremy Todd."

She groaned. "Shall we just skip the whole thing?"

"Sorry, my conscience would bother me for weeks. The plain truth is, Todd fancies himself as something of a playboy. He stayed here for a few weeks last summer and I had the unenviable privilege of watching him in action."

"Don't you think I'm old enough to take care of myself? As I recall, you were telling me he's too young for me, anyway." Lacey lifted one eyebrow.

"I think," he said very distinctly, "that you're more vulnerable than some women your age might be, Lacey. Divorce doesn't give you any special immunity to men who use women."

Lacey couldn't resist. "Perhaps I'm not entirely opposed to being used!"

"I don't think you understand just what you're saying. Jeremy Todd is looking strictly for a summer affair."

"Perhaps being swept off my feet is one of my plans," Lacey retorted. "You know, you'd be right at home in Iowa. My family would love you!"

"Which recommendation is enough to damn me, right?"

"Let's just say that the members of my family haven't proved to be excellent judges of character."

"They loved the doctor and the psych professor?"

"I'm afraid so."

"What makes you think I'm in the same category?"

"A certain intrinsic, pompous authority," she claimed with relish.

"Pompous!" A slow grin suddenly revealed very white teeth. Lacey felt a flicker of uncertainty in her assessment. If there was one thing neither her ex-husband nor Harold had been able to do, it was laugh at themselves.

"Wouldn't you think the same of me if I attempted to warn you off another woman within hours of having met you?" she pointed out reasonably.

He sighed, his hand sliding to the curve of her waist. "I might take it as a sign of interest...."

"Are you interested in me, Holt?" Lacey challenged.

"You're not quite what I'd expected," he hedged.

"Is that the reason you're so concerned?"

"No," he finally admitted reluctantly. He drew a breath as if about to plunge into a cold stream. "You remind me of someone I used to know."

"I should have guessed," she said dryly, thinking of the ex-fiancée.

"How could you?" he countered. "You didn't meet me when I had my own lifestyle crisis. You're not the first to arrive at the earthshaking conclusion that you're missing something critical in life, Lacey Seldon," he told her quietly, his eyes serious. "Want to hear what I learned?"

"No!" The single negative almost exploded from her. "Because I *am* going to change my world, Holt. And I don't particularly want lectures from someone who didn't. One needs successful role models!"

"Not failures?" he concluded for her.

Lacey felt the red wash into her cheeks. She would never have been so openly rude under normal circumstances. Deliberately she took a grip on her temper. "We have to make our own choices, Holt. You made yours. And I'm sure you can understand that I don't want you or anyone else making mine."

"Lacey, listen to me...."

"If you'll excuse me, I should be getting back to Jeremy." She gave him her most brilliant smile. "You can rest assured you've done your duty!"

*

SHE WAS sitting cross-legged on a mat, palms curved upward, facing the rising sun the next morning when Holt Randolph again intruded.

"Meditation? Perhaps you do belong out here, Lacey. I can imagine that sort of thing was rather frowned upon back home." His voice was dry but there was an underlying humor which found a response in her.

She flicked open her long auburn lashes and absorbed the running shoes, shorts, and bronzed torso. "Anyone who goes jogging at this hour of the morning has no right to remark about my personal habits."

"I run, Miss Seldon—I do not jog." He crouched beside her and grinned wryly. "Give me a chance to apologize?"

"Apologize!" She stared at him.

"I realized after you left last night that I had been behaving in a totally uncalled-for manner," he told her with sudden seriousness.

In spite of herself she recalled the feel of his arms around her on the dance floor.

He grimaced. "All I can say is, I'm sorry for coming on like…like…"

"Like any one of a number of other people I left behind in Iowa?" she suggested helpfully.

He shot her a quick, probing glance and then smiled crookedly. "I can see where you might be a little sick of other people always knowing what's best for you."

Lacey bit her lip and then grinned spontaneously. "I didn't really mind listening to your lectures." He looked genuinely astonished. "You see, back home I had to listen to that sort of thing and conform, or risk scandal. It was rather exhilarating being able to tell you off last night. Sort of symbolic, if you know what I mean."

Holt ran a hand through his hair and shook his head. "I don't like the idea of playing that particular role."

"But you do it so well!" she protested.

"As I said, there were extenuating circumstances."

"I know," she said, voice softening. "You told me. You felt obligated to protect a poor, sheltered creature from Jeremy. On top of that, I appeared to be making the same struggle to escape that you once made."

"That, Lacey, is only part of it," he stated meaningfully. She blinked. "What's the rest?"

"Sheer resentment of another man's swift maneuvering!"

"Oh!"

"You're a rather intriguing woman, Lacey Seldon. Will you let me apologize for my behavior last night?"

"How?"

"Have breakfast with me on my boat this morning. We can leave in about an hour."

She nodded as he straightened, watching as he set off in an easy, loping run. Then Lacey got to her feet and headed for the cottage. Life was looking up nicely. Two different men in as many days. Who would have believed it?

AFTER anchoring the white cabin cruiser in a sheltered cove on the tip of the island, they consumed the delicacies in the basket with civilized greed. Holt made coffee in the tiny galley of the boat. The conversation flowed freely between them, each careful not to bring up the one topic which threatened discord.

"That's the best breakfast I've ever had! Or maybe it's just that everything is going to taste better out here than it did back in Iowa!"

Holt put out his hand and tipped her chin, his face intent and serious.

"Let's find out, shall we?" he murmured, leaning forward before kissing her in a bold, exploratory manner. With a swift movement of easy strength, he lifted her onto his lap.

"Holt!" she tried vainly, her voice a broken thread of sound as her breathing quickened. "I don't think we should…"

He stopped her faltering words, burying his mouth in the curve of her throat and sliding his hand along her denim-covered hip, up under the flowing peasant blouse to the counter of her stomach. Lacey shivered at the touch and a small sigh escaped her.

She lifted her fingertips to the thickness of his hair. "Oh, Holt…"

Her words seemed to release another bond in both of them. The warm hand on her stomach flattened possessively against her skin and began gliding upward to her unconfined breasts. She twisted in his lap, intending to slide off his lap.

"Lacey, don't fight me. I only want to sample some of your sweetness. I wanted to kiss you the moment I saw you yesterday…"

"I don't want a meaningless encounter with a man I barely know."

"Give it a chance, Lacey," he half ordered, half pleaded. "Nothing this strong could be without meaning! Damn it! You can't go this far and then call a halt."

"I can do anything I damn well please," she flung back, letting a mounting anger supply the necessary motivation to stop him.

Lacey knew she had won the battle of wills as she watched Holt's mouth tighten and his eyes harden. Without a word, he heaved himself to his feet, turned away with a low, savage exclamation, and threw himself out of the cabin.

A wave of guilt and a grim acknowledgment of her own responsibility for what had happened made her gather her courage and head for the outer deck.

"Holt, I'm sorry. You have every right to be angry. I should never have allowed that to happen. I take full responsibility. I should have made my position clear to you from the beginning."

"Have you forgotten," he asked very gravely, "that I'm the one who initiated that kiss which got so out of hand?"

"Of course not! I told you I was interested in an affair and it's not your fault I didn't explain that I meant something a little more enduring than a one-night, or rather, a one-morning stand!"

He regarded her with a slow grin. "I prefer the notion that I might possibly have been doing a good job of seducing you!"

Her own sense of humor bubbled forth at the teasing light in his eyes. "Shall we toss a coin to see who gets to shoulder the blame?"

Holt laughed. "Whatever else happens this summer, I think I can predict life won't be dull with you around, Lacey Seldon!"

DURING the next few days, Lacey could see the desire in Holt's eyes whenever he was around her. He stopped to talk to her before his morning run, and at night, his dancing took on increasingly intimate overtones.

One week after their boat outing, Holt invited Lacey out to dinner in town.

Over their salmon dinner, Holt questioned her plans for the future. "What will you do if there are no positions that interest you?"

"Worried that you're still going to have me hanging around all winter? Don't worry. I've got a couple of ideas tucked away." She told him about her dream jobs.

"You're really searching, aren't you? I went searching once...."

"You promised we wouldn't discuss that topic," Lacey interrupted softly.

"I was merely going to tell you a little about myself. I practically grew up at the inn. My grandparents often took me to the island when my father had to travel because of his job. Everyone assumed one day I'd take over the inn."

"How did you feel about it?"

"I loved the place. After college, I took over running the inn full-time, but my grandfather had no plans of retiring, and having two stubborn Randolphs running the place just didn't work. So I told him I was going to find something else to do with my life and walked out. I think I'll tell you Chapter Two of my life story some other time."

Once Lacey gave up the futile attempt to coax Holt into giving her the rest of the story, the conversation moved easily again between them and they returned to the inn.

"Going to invite me inside?" he demanded softly as he walked her up the path to her cottage.

"Will you tell me the second half of your story?"

"Not a chance. I'm going to keep you dangling." Holt unlocked the door and was nonchalantly building a fire before she realized she hadn't invited him.

With a wry smile, Lacey went into the kitchen and made a pot of tea. Holt appeared to be staying awhile. When she emerged, Holt had put some music on. The full skirt of her soft summer dress spread across the sofa cushion as Lacey sat down next to Holt.

"Would you laugh in my face if I told you that what you're looking for isn't going to be what you really want? That when you find it, you're going to be disappointed?" Holt asked quietly.

"Yes, I'd laugh."

"I don't think I want to listen to any more of your laughter tonight," he whispered huskily, pulling her into his arms. Lacey didn't resist.

Her senses began to swirl around her as they did that morning on the boat, tuning out the rest of the world and concentrating only on the man who had stirred them to life.

She twisted beneath him as he swept his hand down her side, his thumb gliding briefly, thrillingly across the nipple of one breast before going on to shape her hip. Lacey moaned and heard his answering murmur of desire.

"I love the feel of you," he whispered gratingly, stringing kisses down her throat and across the swell of her small breasts. "You bring out more than desire in me, honey. You make me want to possess you completely, body and soul!"

She shivered at the determination in his words but she was past caring about anything but the present. Without protest, she arched her hips against him, coiling her arms more tightly around his body. Her head fell back in an agony of exquisite need and she heard his indrawn breath at the obvious surrender.

And then, with no warning, Holt was breaking the powerful contact, pulling away reluctantly but firmly as if he'd reached a preordained stopping point.

"I'm practicing a little of that restraint you were admiring earlier," he explained quietly. "We're in agreement on one thing at least, Lacey. Neither of us wants a one-night stand."

She stiffened at the cold words. "What do you want, Holt? Surely you're not going to claim you wanted anything more from me?"

"I don't intend to be the first in a long line of short-lived, experimental relationships."

"If you really understood what I'm trying to do with my life you wouldn't be implying such terrible things about me!"

"All I'm trying to say, Lacey," he ground out deliberately, "is that if we start an affair, it's not going to be the easy, uncomplicated arrangement you seem to think you want."

Holt left, much to Lacey's surprise. After a brief dip in the indoor pool with Jeremy, who was disappointed to learn the woman he'd been interested in was married, Holt broke up the fun by ordering them both of out the pool, since it was after the posted hours.

"We'll do things your way. You wanted an affair, Lacey Sheldon, very well, you'll have an affair. With me. And it's going to begin tonight!" Holt scooped her up into his arms and strode toward the Victorian-style summer home attached to the main lodge.

"I don't want a one-night stand. You know that."

"It won't be a one-night affair. We have the summer, remember?"

Her nails sank slightly into his skin as she felt the bathing suit stripped slowly, sensually down her body. The touch of his hands and the feel of his body were rapidly reviving all the restless need she had known earlier that evening.

She felt his hands gliding up to cup her breasts and moaned softly, far back in her throat. Her head fell onto his shoulder

in a small gesture of surrender and need. Slowly he worked
his way down her body while she twisted beneath him. When
at last he moved higher, finding her breasts with his lips, Lacey
gave in to the urgency driving her. With a desperate little
effort, she reversed their positions.

And then she was covering him with damp, lingering ca-
resses, her hair strewn across his chest. With delicate, passionate greed she enveloped Holt in a cocoon of soft feminin-
ity, pouring kisses across his shoulders, his chest, and his
thighs.

"We must have been fated to meet like this," he ground
out passionately.

"Yes," she agreed wonderingly, lost in the world of pure
sensation. "Yes, this is what I wanted...."

His leg moved heavily, insistently against her, parting her
thighs and making a warm, heated nest for himself against her
body. She cried out as he moved on her, heard his answering
groan and then they were both caught up in the deep, demanding rhythms of passion and desire.

The surging, spiraling pattern carried them higher and
higher, tossing them into the ultimate ending with a sudden-
ness that brought a sob of wonder and exquisite satisfaction
from Lacey. As if he had only been waiting for her to find
the threshold, Holt gasped hoarsely, his face buried in the
curve of her shoulder, his hands holding her to him with incredible strength.

For long moments they lay together in the damp, tangled
warmth. Lacey's fingers trailed lightly, wonderingly, over
Holt's sinewy back, delighting in the heaviness of him. At
long last he stirred reluctantly, lifting his head to meet her
love-softened eyes.

In silence they regarded each other and then Holt said simply, meaningfully, "Was it what you were looking for?"

"I've never known anything like it. I only dreamed that
someday I would find something approaching this...."

A gleam of pure masculine satisfaction lit the silvery gaze.
"The feeling was mutual. I spent several years searching the

world for it, and all the time I was fated to find it here at home.''

She grinned mischievously. "I spent years searching for it at home and finally had to come looking!"

"Maybe that's because Iowa wasn't meant to be your home. Perhaps this island was to be the place where you would find home."

She slanted him a teasing gaze. "You're no longer in a hurry to pack me off to Iowa?"

"I never was in a hurry to send you back there. I just wanted to make sure you stopped here!" He grinned wickedly.

"I have the rest of the summer to find…" She broke off as she felt him go suddenly, savagely tense. "What's wrong, Holt?"

"I said I didn't want to be part of an experiment on your part, Lacey. I don't want a relationship with a preordained ending which suits your game plan."

A slow kind of anger began to build in her as she absorbed the implications of his words. "Are you saying you tricked me? That you seduced me tonight, hoping I would forget about my plans for the future?"

"What happened tonight was totally unplanned until I caught you in the pool with Todd. Now that it's done, you're not going to have everything your own way!"

"Neither are you! You couldn't talk me into seeing the light and doing things your way so you tried to seduce me into it!"

"Neither of us can walk away from the other now. Don't you understand? What we have is something special. Surely you can't believe yourself capable of enjoying yourself like this for the summer and then blithely leaving for Hawaii or Los Angeles!"

"What makes you think you can change my whole life by simply taking me to bed? I told you I was only looking for a summer affair. Everyone I've ever known has assumed he or she could talk me into doing things their way. Well, I changed that. I make my own decisions now. I will not let someone else decide what's proper for me. Nor will I allow you to coerce me into doing what you want!''

"If you're not willing to give yourself up to an honest relationship without an arbitrary ending established by you, then I'm not willing to let myself be used in an experiment!''

"You said you didn't want something that only lasted a night!''

"I said I didn't want it, not that I couldn't handle it,'' he growled pointedly. "I can cope with it better than I can cope with the trauma of an affair which is doomed to end in a couple of months. You're not going to use me like that. Get dressed, Lacey. I'm taking you back to the cottage.'' He surged to his feet, moving toward his closet with a determined stride, pausing to gently toss her clothes at her in a soft wad.

"You have to expect a certain percentage of your affairs to wind up like this. That's part and parcel of your new lifestyle, honey. Comes with the territory.''

*

EVEN NOW in the full light of morning she didn't want to think about it. How could she have been such a fool? How could she have let Holt take her into bed? In her tiny kitchen she morosely went about the business of making coffee. It was ridiculous, insane, some strange figment of her imagination, she decided as she sat at the little table by the window. But even during her marriage she hadn't experienced such a sensation of being fundamentally bound to a man.

It probably had something to do with the strength of the passion she had experienced, she told herself. But that didn't really explain things. Passion might make you crave a man but it wouldn't make you feel bound to him.

The dazzling future she'd planned for herself danced in front of her eyes. Lacey gritted her teeth. She hadn't come all this way to tie herself to one man. For heaven's sake, she thought grimly, living on this island for any extended period of time would have all the elements of small-town life in Iowa!

She would be trapped again. Could she even face the rest of the summer here? She needed to get away and think.

Lacey hurried down the path to the main building and was relieved to find only George, Holt's assistant, behind the desk.

"Good morning, George. I came to check the ferry schedule."

He smiled cheerfully. "Going for a little tour?"

"Yes. I see there's one due in about thirty minutes."

She made the ferry docks with a few minutes to spare. Lacey stood in line at the concession stand for coffee before heading out on deck. The hot coffee tasted good and the fresh air was invigorating. Leaning against the rail, she gazed reflectively at the multitude of green islands, which dotted the inland sea.

"Running away, Lacey?"

She whirled, slopping the coffee. "You followed me!"

Holt shrugged, slanting her a straight glance as he rested his arms on the railing. "George told me you were asking about ferry schedules, and I decided I'd tag along and point out a few facts of life. You're running away," he concluded in a flat tone.

"No." She shook her head. "I decided to spend some time hopping islands on the ferries."

"While you go over your options?"

"Something like that."

"And running away is one of your options?" he persisted, making Lacey grit her teeth in frustration.

"Doesn't it occur to you that my leaving might be sensible? The easiest thing for both of us?"

"It wouldn't be." He sighed. "Leaving isn't going to change what we have. You'll still be thinking about last night six months from now, just as I will. Last night was special. Very special. I had to make sure you knew that."

"You practically threw me out last night." She bit the words out scathingly.

"I was madder than hell last night. How do you think I felt

when you made it clear you saw me as just the start of your adventures?''

She flinched. ''How do you think I felt having you dictating my future just like everyone else in my life has tried to dictate it? You want things your way. It's your ego which can't stand the thought of me calling a halt to the affair, isn't it?''

He stared at her, his expression hard and remote. ''Do you really believe that?''

She closed her eyes. ''I don't know,'' she said finally. ''I just don't know.''

His face softened and he lifted his hand to her cheek. ''Poor Lacey,'' he murmured. ''Things aren't going quite the way you planned, are they?'' He bent his head and kissed her. When he raised his head again he was smiling ruefully. ''There's nothing out there that will compare with what we've got between us.''

''But I won't know until I've found out for myself, will I?'' she breathed, studying his face.

''Give us a chance, honey.'' She could feel him trying to compel her with every fiber of his will. ''You want me as much as I want you, Lacey. All I'm asking for is a compromise. Promise me you won't spend every waking minute planning a future that doesn't include me and I'll—'' He broke off suddenly.

''You'll what, Holt? What do you have to offer in exchange for my postponing the future?''

''A present that's better than the future will ever be,'' he said simply.

''I'll only have your word for that.''

He shook his head firmly. ''No. There will come a time when you'll know for certain that what you've found is what you were really looking for all along.''

She eyed him with sudden intuition. ''Is that how it was for you?''

He smiled. ''Since we seem to be committed to *several* ferry rides, why don't you come inside out of this wind and I'll give you the second half of my life story?''

Lacey struggled mentally for a long moment, telling herself she needed to come to her own conclusions. But it seemed ridiculous to deliberately avoid him on the small ferry. And she did want to hear the story.

They sat across from each other on padded seats near the massive ferry windows. He settled back against the seat cushion. "I think I was in Acapulco when I got word my grandfather was dying. I came back to say goodbye." He paused and Lacey watched the memories flit through his eyes.

"My grandfather had very neatly tightened the knot by willing the whole business to me. I either had to run it or sell it. I went over to the island to estimate how much it might bring."

"You intended to sell?"

He nodded. "When I arrived on the island I was shocked at the condition of the place. I hadn't seen it for several years and Granddad had let it run down terribly. I couldn't believe it. I kept walking around remembering how it had been in its heyday."

"So you got hooked and decided to stay?"

"Not exactly. I told myself I could double the price if I put in a few improvements. Well, one thing led to another and finally one day it dawned on me that I never intended to sell."

"So you accepted the chains," Lacey murmured.

"Nothing that dramatic," he retorted with a cool glance. "I'd found what I wanted to do in life."

"What, exactly, is the moral of this little story?"

"I got lucky, Lacey. Circumstances brought me back for another look at what I'd turned down a few years earlier. And I had the sense to recognize I'd found what I wanted. But life doesn't always provide neat opportunities like that. If you walk out on what we've got without giving it an honest chance, you won't get a second one!"

"I feel duly warned," she retorted. But it was becoming increasingly difficult to maintain the flippant defiance and Holt must have seen it because his response was a knowing smile.

"Now, which island are we heading for next?"

She blinked at the change of topic. "I don't know. I…uh…was going to check the map near the main lounge."

Holt was determined to restore the balance between them, Lacey acknowledged as the day wore on. He was every inch the cheerful, attentive escort as they hopped on and off ferries until late in the afternoon. He took her to the myriad arts-and-crafts boutiques sprinkled about the island villages and entertained her over a delicious lunch of steamed crab.

She gave herself up to the pleasant day, feeling genuine regret when it came to an end.

SHE WAS totally unprepared for the shock that awaited her that night as she slipped familiarly into the cheerful crowd sharing brandy and gossip. The raven-haired beauty clinging so elegantly to Holt's arm could be none other than his ex-fiancée.

"She's a knockout, isn't she?" Jeremy Todd noted with a grin. "The famous fiancée."

"Ex-fiancée, I believe you said," Lacey murmured, sipping at the glass of brandy Jeremy handed to her. Joanna Davis was, indeed, a knockout by most standards. "A tad overdressed for this crowd, don't you think?" She immediately winced at the catty words.

Jeremy lifted one eyebrow. "So that's the way it is, hmmm? I'm not surprised," he added cheerfully. "It's no secret that you weren't hustled directly back to your cottage last night. The only thing that puzzles me is I don't quite see you and Holt as a couple."

"Holt and I have had a couple of dates and that's the extent of matters," Lacey said firmly, lying through her teeth.

"You may be right, now that Joanna is back."

Lacey found herself flicking another glance toward the aloofly smiling woman on Holt's arm. At that moment, Holt glanced up and saw her. She had an instant's impression of a glacial cold in his silvery hazel eyes and then it was gone. He was disentangling himself from Joanna's embrace and heading toward her and Lacey wasn't quite sure how to handle the situation. She was saved from having to worry about an immediate response when one of the night clerks came through the door behind her.

"Oh, there you are, Miss Seldon," the young man said hastily. "Telephone call for you."

"Thanks." She hurried into the quiet lobby with a sense of relief. It was with shock that she realized it was her ex-husband Roger Wesley on the other end of the line.

"What in the world do you want?" There was a distinct silence as Roger assimilated her unencouraging response.

"Darling, you know your family is worried about you," he began, the bedside manner reflecting a doctor's sureness.

"And they've asked you to talk me into going home?" she interpreted astutely.

"I've been thinking a lot about you lately and I..."

"Roger, unless you want to get a bill from me itemizing all those medical-school fees I paid, you'd better forget about pestering me!" Without waiting for a reply, she slammed down the receiver.

"This seems to be our night for hearing voices from the past," Holt drawled from the doorway.

"You appear to have a bit more than a disembodied voice from *your* past."

"You're not jealous by any chance?"

She was saved from whatever inane remark she might have made next as the door behind Holt opened to reveal Joanna Davis.

"Darling, the dancing has started, and it's been so long since we've danced together."

Then Jeremy was cheerfully barging through the door. "Come on, Lacey." He started forward and grasped her wrist. "Randolph's booked a new band for tonight!"

Joanna had the last word. "Now you won't have to worry about your little guest being entertained."

Jeremy let the door swing shut behind them, mopping his brow theatrically. "Wow! She's pure poison."

During the evening she danced frequently with Jeremy and

every time, Holt was there with his ex-fiancée. They made a handsome couple.

It was nearly eleven o'clock when Lacey glanced up to see Holt and Joanna approaching the table she shared with Jeremy.

"Here comes trouble," Jeremy said. "What do you bet I'm about to have the privilege of dancing with sweet Joanna?"

He had guessed accurately, and the next thing Lacey knew she herself was in Holt's arms on the dance floor.

"What did Roger have to say?" he began.

"He's been appointed to try and talk some sense into me," Lacey retorted lightly.

"Will he succeed?" he asked crisply.

"Will Miss Davis succeed in talking sense into you? Has she realized she made a mistake when she broke off your engagement?"

"Pointed questions from someone who doesn't care what happens to me after September!"

"I just wondered if you were setting yourself up for another fall!" Lacey snapped.

"Kind of you to be concerned," he drawled, his hands tightening on her back. "You and Jeremy seem to be getting on well. Doesn't it bother him knowing you didn't return immediately to your cottage last night?"

Lacey flushed. "He doesn't know—"

"Honey, by now most of the people in this room know about last night," Holt informed her with a certain satisfaction.

"My God! This is as bad as Iowa!"

"You have to learn to handle this kind of situation."

"Just as I have to learn to handle one-night stands? How dare you, Holt Randolph! Go back to your ex-fiancée! Just don't come whining to me when she's through playing with you for the summer!"

Lacey strode across the floor toward the door, ignoring interested glances. She was almost there when Jeremy appeared magically at her side. "This kind of exit always looks better with a partner. Besides, you're not the only one escaping."

"She got to you, is that it?"

"She was furious at being foisted off on me. The lady has the manners of a she-cat!" Jeremy growled in the cool night air. "A word of warning, pal, she's aware of your role in Holt's life."

"I don't have a particular role, damn it!"

"Whatever you say, Lacey," he soothed as they reached her cottage doorstep.

"I'm sorry, Jeremy, I don't know why I'm acting like this! Thank you for trying to rescue me this evening!"

She stood watching as he set off for his own cottage. He was really a very nice man.

THE KNOCKING caught her unawares later that evening. As if mesmerized by an inescapable doom, she trailed across the living room and opened the door.

"Don't tell me you weren't expecting me." Holt lounged in her doorway, a bottle of cognac in one hand. He stepped past her into the room and threw himself down on the sofa. "Got a couple of glasses?"

She eyed him, trying to judge his mood and then went to fetch two glasses from the kitchen.

Wordlessly they sipped the cognac for a few moments, and then Lacey heard herself say, "How close did you come to marrying her?"

"Too close. Fortunately she realized I had no intention of being dragged off this island. She had visions of getting me back into the hotel business, I think. Saw herself living a jet-set lifestyle."

"Like me?" she couldn't help saying.

"Not quite. She wanted a man to pay her way."

"Were you...badly hurt?"

"My main emotion at the time was one of relief."

Lacey nodded understandingly. "That's how I felt after Roger finally told me he wanted a divorce."

"Speaking of Roger..."

Holt's words were cut off by the ringing of the telephone.

"Yes, speaking of Roger," she muttered, letting the phone ring again.

"Want me to answer it?"

A slow smile curved her mouth as she considered that. "You're wicked to tempt me like this."

Without waiting for a definite affirmative, Holt reached across and lifted the receiver from the cradle, his eyes still on Lacey's. "No, you don't have the wrong number."

There was a pause and a rather menacing mischief lit the silvery gaze. "Lacey's busy at the moment. Who am I? I'm the one who's keeping her busy, naturally. No, I'm not going to let you speak to her," Holt said calmly into the phone. "I never let strange men speak to my fiancée. Especially at this hour of the night!" Very gently he replaced the telephone.

She stared, not knowing whether to be shocked or amused. Then she grinned. "I would have given a fortune to see his face!"

"You're not angry?"

"I'll have to do some explaining in the morning, I suppose. He'll be on the phone to my parents as soon as it's light back there."

"You seem very calm about having to explain your 'fiancée,' " Holt murmured, staring down into his glass.

"There's not much to explain."

"Since the idea doesn't seem to bother you," he began slowly, "I wonder if you would mind returning the favor..." He looked up, his hazel eyes suddenly very serious. "Help me get rid of Joanna."

She stared at him, her thoughts chaos. "You don't need me to help you to do that."

"No, but it would sure as hell simplify things."

She couldn't deny the sheer, feminine pleasure it would give her to spike the other woman's guns. Holt had done her a favor in getting Roger off her back tonight. Why shouldn't she return it?

"If it will make life easier for you, go ahead and tell her you and I are going to be married."

His clenched fingers relaxed. "You don't mind?"

"If anyone else gets wind of it, we'll just say there's been a misunderstanding," Lacey said with an indifference she was far from feeling.

He stepped close and threw a possessive arm around her shoulders. "Come on, fiancée, let's go for a walk." He grabbed the shawl she had thrown across the back of the sofa earlier and settled it around her shoulders.

In the moonlight her eyes sparkled, at once wary and provoking. He drew her to a halt on the shadowy lawn.

"Sweetheart, I've been aching for you all day. And then, tonight, I had to listen to you talking to your ex-husband, watch you dancing with Todd. It's been a rough day!"

Lacey looking up at him, blue-green eyes shadowed as she acknowledged the extent of her own longing.

He bent to push aside the sweep of auburn hair and drop a warm, lingering kiss just below her ear. "I want you so much. Why don't we both forget about the future tonight and pretend we really are engaged?"

"Another one-night stand?" she asked sadly.

"No," he rasped huskily, finding the line of her throat with his lips. "After the second night I think we can classify it as an affair."

"And will there be a third night?"

"Yes."

Wordlessly he took her hands and started toward his Victorian home at the far end of the lodge.

UNDER THE impact of his touch, Lacey gave herself up to him completely, making no secret of her need, just as he made no secret of his. He seemed to delight in the increasing fervor of her demands as if his greatest pleasure lay in first invoking them and then satisfying them.

She grew impatient, pulling him to her with compelling fingers. "Please, Holt. Please love me!"

"You're mine, Lacey," he rasped as he took erotic command of her body.

In that moment she was his. She wanted to belong totally to this man and make him belong just as totally to her. It was all that mattered.

Holt's driving, graceful power swept them both into the irresistible tide of desire. Desperately she clung, and they found release together, holding each other in an unshakable clasp as it rocked them both.

The blinding realization came upon Lacey even before the final tremors had washed through her system. She shut her eyes against the knowledge, but when she opened them to stare blankly at the ceiling, the truth of what had happened was still there, taunting her, frightening her. She was in love with Holt.

She turned her head slightly to look at him. He lay beside her, his legs still twined with hers, the picture of satiated masculinity.

He regarded her with lazy satisfaction. "I'm not about to make the mistake I did last night!" He pulled her head against his perspiration-dampened chest, idly stroking her tangled hair. "I couldn't let you go again."

Lacey shut her eyes to keep back the hint of moisture. What was she going to do? Lacey knew one thing very clearly. She wanted Holt's love. But the knowledge didn't pacify her, it alternately infuriated her and depressed her! This wasn't what she'd planned on!

She hadn't expected to be able to even doze given the turmoil of her mind, but the next thing she knew, sunlight was illuminating the magnificent body of the man sprawled out beside her.

With a strange nervousness, Lacey edged carefully out of bed, heading for the bath. She was a bundle of agitation, she realized dimly as she stepped beneath the hot water in the shower.

In the light of day she should be able to put aside the illusions of the night. They had been the product of desire, she told herself again and again. Not love. Passion, excitement, anticipation, and adventure. That was what had been missing back in Iowa. Wasn't it?

With a groan she wondered if what had really been missing in Iowa was love.

Every iota of rational sense told her to fight the sensation. But how did you fight this abiding emotion for another human being? With one breath she told herself she couldn't possibly be in love with Holt. And with the next she knew it so firmly there didn't seem to be any defense against the knowledge. It was like trying to hide from herself.

Scrubbing vigorously with a washcloth, she hurried through her washing, anxious to escape the close confines of the shower.

*

BUT BREAKFAST was worse. To her horror she burned the toast, spilled the orange juice, made lousy coffee, and generally came apart at the seams.

"Funny," Holt said teasingly when she almost flung the overcooked eggs in front of him, "I thought any woman who came from Iowa could cook."

"I *can* cook!" she retorted vehemently, throwing herself into the seat across from him. "I'm just not used to your kitchen!"

"I understand," he soothed in that tone of voice men always use when they're trying to placate women.

Lacey tried to get through the meal, letting Holt do most of the talking, as she fought desperately to figure out what she was going to do.

She nearly dropped a cup when they started to clear the table. Holt looked up in mild concern as she caught the descending piece shortly before it struck the floor. "Good catch."

Lacey nearly hurled the offending cup at him. Holt didn't seem to be aware of his close call. He finished carrying his stack of dishes into the old-fashioned country kitchen, calling out to her casually as he disappeared, "I'm going to spend the morning in the office, if you need me. What are you going to do today?''

Lacey looked at the cup in her hand. ''Go through an entire midlife crisis in one day,'' she muttered.

''What?'' he called.

''I don't know yet!'' she shouted.

He reappeared in the kitchen doorway, smiling placidly. ''How about meeting me for lunch in the main dining room?'' He glanced at his watch. ''That will give you plenty of time for a nice swim before lunch and maybe a little meditation, too.''

''Yes, yes, that will be fine,'' she agreed hurriedly.

''Excellent.'' He nodded, looking totally satisfied.

He waved goodbye to her a short time later, striding to work with such good-natured enthusiasm that Lacey could have screamed.

THE PHONE was ringing authoritatively as she walked into her cottage. Lacey glared at it, intuition and logic dictating who was on the other end. She wasn't in the mood to talk to anyone, least of all family. She had a dilemma on her hands. Couldn't anyone comprehend that?

Lacey lifted the receiver in disgust. ''Hello, Mother,'' she said without waiting for the caller to identify herself.

''Roger says there was a man answering your phone last night at a very late hour. A man claiming to be engaged to you!''

''Roger has good ears,'' Lacey observed dryly.

''Well?''

''Well, what?'' She knew she was being deliberately obtuse and couldn't help it.

''Lacey! I want to know what's happening out there!''

''Don't worry, Mom, you're going to love him.''

Lacey hung up the phone and grabbed up her swimsuit before her mother had a chance to redial.

As she walked past George in the lobby on her way to the indoor pool she waved airily. ''Good morning, George. For the record, I'm not taking any more telephone calls from Iowa this morning.''

The pool room was empty at this early hour. Lacey changed quickly into the maillot and began doing what she seldom did in a pool. Laps. A lot of them.

But the activity only seemed to bring the facts into even harsher perspective. No matter what kind of logic she used, the only thing which really mattered any more was Holt Randolph.

Tossing her head angrily to shake off water as she emerged from the pool, Lacey reached for a towel and marched to the changing rooms.

Trailing dismally out of the pool room, she set out on a brisk walk along the tree-lined shore. Her thoughts continued to chase each other relentlessly. She was the one who was now desperate enough to take him on just about any basis. She tried to remind herself of how much the excitement of an unknown, adventuresome future had drawn her. And all she could think about was the excitement and passion she had found in Holt's arms.

Lacey swung around at the end of the shoreline path and headed back toward the cottage. Still her mind whirled.

At the cottage, Lacey stalked around the living room, trying to marshal her thoughts. It wouldn't be long before she was due to meet Holt for lunch. What would she say?

With the air of one choosing a last resort, Lacey walked out to the grassy area behind the cottage. Deliberately she settled into her meditation position. For long moments she didn't try to think at all. Then gradually, steadily, she began to seek a focus for her thoughts.

Slowly the tension eased out of her, leaving her calm and clearheaded at last. The sense of being totally unnerved faded to be replaced by a certainty which people out West labeled Midwestern stubbornness. She knew what she wanted now. It only remained to be seen if Holt wanted the same thing.

Lacey was unaware of time passing. Eyes closed, she let her senses drift, inhaling the scent of the woods and grass.

Lacey slowly opened her eyes. Holt was crouched in front of her, an incredibly gentle smile in his eyes. Beside him rested a small basket.

"Crisis over?" he asked softly.

She stared at him. "I love you, Holt."

"I know that," he murmured, settling into a cross-legged sitting position. "Hungry? When you didn't show up for lunch I decided to come looking...."

"What do you mean, you know it?" She gasped, ignoring the offer of food.

He looked up from his investigation of the contents of the basket, a whimsical twist to his lips. "Women intent on not getting totally involved with a man don't surrender in bed like that."

"You're an expert on the subject?"

"I know that what we have really counts," he said simply.

"Where I come from, barring complications, that means marriage," she said starkly.

He appeared to consider this carefully, his hands resting on the neck of the wine bottle. He went to work on the cork. "Then there aren't any complications, are there? Just ask your mother if you don't believe me," he added with a sudden hint of amusement.

"My mother!"

"Umm. Somebody had to talk to her this morning. Poor George was going crazy trying to explain that you weren't taking any calls from Iowa!"

"Oh, my God!" Lacey stared up at him.

"Don't worry, she's so damn grateful to me for saving you from heaven knows what that I'm practically a member of the family in her eyes." The humor going out of his voice, he gripped her tightly. "You're sure this is what you want, Lacey?"

"I'm sure," she whispered, her eyes serene and confident. "When you no longer demanded total commitment, it left my words ringing in my ears. Words about not wanting to tie myself down."

"You had to realize that permanency was what you wanted, too," he said quietly.

"Did you deliberately dangle Joanna in front of me?" she demanded accusingly.

"Perhaps, a little," he admitted. "I was willing to try just about anything...."

Her eyes narrowed.

"I wasn't in love with Joanna. I am most definitely in love with you!" He grinned, brushing a possessive kiss across Lacey's lips. "I'm permanently spoken for by a stubborn little Midwesterner who came a couple of thousand miles to claim me!"

Lacey sighed blissfully.

"You'll never know how terrified I was when I discovered you were intent on finding the fast life. But I realized as soon as I awoke this morning that things were going along nicely—"

"Nicely!" Lacey flared. "That's a fine way of describing it! I was a nervous wreck all morning!"

"Don't you think I knew that? It gave me great hope," Holt told her with patent satisfaction.

"I went through a severe emotional crisis this morning, Holt Randolph. I don't think it's very nice of you to tease me about it!"

"You're right. It's just that I'm so damned relieved!"

"What would you have done if I hadn't come to all my brilliant conclusions this morning?" she charged.

"I figured I had the rest of the summer. I would have let the affair continue under your terms until you finally realized what you really wanted," he told her sedately. And then a spark of vulnerability crept into his words. "I had no choice." He shook his head, the expression in his eyes naked.

"You're the only man I want, Holt. I do love you so much!"

"That," he murmured, "calls for a little celebration. I suggest we open that wine and drink to our future. If we don't,

I'm liable to start making love to you right here. Think what the guests would say!''

Holt finished opening the wine, poured it into two long-stemmed glasses. Silently they met each other's eyes and drank their toast to the future.

He became more serious for a moment. ''I almost forgot. George gave me this to bring to you.''

He held the long white envelope out to her. The return address was clearly marked, ''Hawaii.'' He watched her take it, his expression anxious.

Lacey glanced at the envelope and then slowly tore it in two. ''About my future career,'' she began softly.

''What about it, honey?'' he whispered, some of the raw vulnerability back in his voice.

''Remember that boutique I talked about opening? Well, it strikes me this island could use that sort of shop. All these tourists hanging about and nothing to spend their money on.''

The lines at the edge of his mouth relaxed and he took the wineglass out of her hand. Slowly he pulled her back into his arms. ''Welcome home, Lacey my love,'' he said with infinite gentleness.

She lifted her face for his kiss, perfectly satisfied with the shape of the future.

HEARTLAND

Sherryl Woods

Three Years Ago

From the top of the knoll, Lara's gaze swept over the barren winter landscape. Gnarled oaks stood stark but proud against the leaden sky. Flat, snow-covered fields stretched as far as the eye could see. For some it would be a scene of incomparable desolation. To her the view held beauty and simplicity and grace. Yet, undeniably, there was also heartache.

This land had killed her father, its demanding temperament too great a match for his ailing heart. It bore its share of blame for her mother's death as well, robbing her of the strength that might have made her fight against pneumonia a fair one.

"Please, Lara, keep the family together," her mother had begged. "Keep the farm. It's your legacy." Feverish eyes had burned into her soul.

For four years now she had done her best to keep her pledge. She had left college to do it. She had seen her brothers grow from skinny, awkward boys into strong young men ready to begin lives of their own. With them she had worked the fields from dawn to dusk in spring and summer, hired help when she could afford it and hauled her crops to market in Toledo. Her hands, which she'd once hoped would have the healing touch of a doctor, were raw and rough now, and her brothers—Tommy and Greg—would have the chances she had lost.

"We did it, Mama," she said, the words torn away by the wind. "We made it."

Against the odds, she had eked out a living. The bank had been lenient, granting extensions on the loans her father had taken out time and again to survive.

Through the struggle she had gained an appreciation of this farm and what it had meant to her father. She had understood at last why he had fought so hard to hold on to it, keeping the developers who would have bought him out at bay. She had come to love the farm's daily demands. She had come to respect the mighty quirks of nature that could destroy all that it had taken months to attain. Slowly, the farm had done what she'd thought impossible: it had claimed her heart.

She turned and gathered her things for the trip into town that would determine whether, after all she'd endured to keep it, the farm would remain hers.

At the bank Lara took a deep breath before entering Mr. Hogan's intimidating, mahogany-paneled office. The visit had been an annual one for four years now, but it had never gotten any easier. Her pride, that staunch Danvers's pride her father had instilled in her, had taken a beating each time she had been forced to admit that she needed yet another extension on the loans.

As she stepped through the doorway, her gaze was immediately drawn to the impressively built man seated across from the bank president. Brown hair, a week or two beyond the need for a cut, skimmed the collar of a beige shirt. Thick, curling hair that was all too familiar. Her heart thundered wildly in recognition.

Steven Drake.

Lara shivered as she had on the knoll. Eight years ago Steven Drake had taken the innocent world of an eighteen-year-old girl and turned it upside down. He had taught her about the incomparable beauty of love, then ruined it with a lesson in betrayal.

It took less than a minute for the bank president to confirm that this meeting had taken place by design, not chance.

"Lara, my dear," he began. "The payment on your loan is due today. Can you make it?"

She lifted her chin defiantly. Ignoring Steven, she told Mr. Hogan, "I have most of it." She handed him a sizable check, more than she'd ever been able to pay before.

He glanced at it. "What about the rest?"

She found herself pleading for continued patience. "If you can give me a few more weeks I'll have it. I've taken a job for the winter, and my brothers are working while they're at college. Tommy will graduate at the end of the semester and get a full-time job, in addition to helping out at the farm. Greg's already selling some of his paintings.''

''Art is hardly a reliable income,'' he pointed out. ''And Tommy has his own family to consider now. Besides, I thought he was studying business, not agriculture.''

''He is, but he and Megan have agreed to stay on at the farm until it's on its feet. There's plenty of room for them and the baby. We can do it, Mr. Hogan. This will be the last year I'll have to ask for an extension.''

The two men exchanged a look.

''Perhaps I have a solution,'' Steven offered.

Lara felt her heart begin to pound. Facing Mr. Hogan and never once allowing her eyes to stray to the man seated next to her, she asked the question that had been uppermost in her mind since she'd entered the room: ''Why is he here? This is between you and me, Mr. Hogan. It's bank business. We don't need an outsider to settle it.''

''Yes, my dear. I think we do.''

''I want to buy some of your land,'' Steven said.

She faced him at last, eyes blazing. ''How dare you! My father turned you down eight years ago. Wasn't it bad enough that you used me to try to get the land?'' She glared at him. ''I'd rather declare bankruptcy than sell you one square inch of Danvers land.''

A tiny muscle worked in his jaw. ''Then you'd lose the whole farm,'' he said. ''With my way, you'll keep some of it. You could go back to school yourself, Lara. All those dreams you had, they could still come true.''

''The farm is my life now. Those were just the foolish dreams of a girl.'' The dreams and her faith had been turned to ashes the night he abandoned her without a word. She'd been left with nothing but silence and regret.

''Listen to him, Lara,'' Mr. Hogan pleaded now. ''It's a sensible solution for all of you.''

Steven's solution was, indeed, sensible. His payment for the hundred acres of woods down along the stream would clear the family of debt and keep the farm afloat for several years. Best of all, he pointed out, it would not take any of the farm-land.

No, Lara thought, it would just take the most picturesque portion of the property, the section where they had made love under a midnight sky, an act that obviously held no meaning for him, while it had changed her life.

"What would you do with the land?" she asked, her voice laced with years of pent-up scorn. "Put in some housing project?"

"Only my own home."

"For now."

"For all time."

In the end the deal was made, because there was no choice. Mr. Hogan had made that quite clear. Too many small family farms were failing. The bank was being forced to foreclose.

And Steven was true to his word. A house of wood and stone on a slope of velvet green lawn surrounded by acres of towering trees was built on the property. It was the house they'd envisioned time and again eight years earlier as they had sat by the stream dreaming of the future.

The Present

THE HOUSE—Steven's house—had been empty for weeks now, and Lara had finally began to relax. She had no idea where he'd gone this time, but she was grateful for the reprieve. There had been no unexpected, disturbing glimpses of him fishing in the creek, faded cutoff jeans riding low on his hips, his bare shoulders burnished by the sun. Nor had there been any awkward chance encounters in town, those heart-stopping moments when their gazes would clash and all the passion and anguish would flare to life like tinder touched by a dangerous spark.

For a while she'd deluded herself that anger was responsible for the intensity of her responses, but on days she was being honest she admitted it was something very different. Fate had seemingly decreed that Steven would be the unforgettable passion of her life.

Considering her odd mood of late, it was good that Tommy had left the children with her for the summer, while he and Megan resettled in Kansas City. Jennifer and Kelly were a handful, giving her little time to dwell on other things. They filled the empty spaces in her life in a way that all the hard work and success with the farm had been able to do.

"I thought you didn't like us to go to the river," Jennifer said.

"I don't usually, but this is a special occasion."

The girls were dressed in their swimsuits, and the three of them were walking through the woods. Sunlight shimmered through the leaves, creating a patchwork of shades of green.

"What's this?" two-year-old Kelly asked, yanking a flower up by its roots.

"A buttercup."

"Everybody knows that," three-year-old Jennifer said with all the smugness of her advanced years.

"I want to swim," Kelly said, clearly tired of her sister's display of learning. "Want to swim now!"

Jennifer squealed with delight and ran to the stream's edge, putting one foot cautiously in to test the temperature before plunging ahead. Kelly toddled right in behind her on plump, sturdy legs, happily splashing in the shallow water.

As the girls played, Lara spread out the blanket and set out the things for lunch. She read for a while, then took off the T-shirt she'd worn over her bathing suit and walked down to join them at the water's edge.

"This is fun, Aunt Lara. Nobody's here. I don't see why we can't come all the time," Jennifer said, splashing water on her.

"Yes. Why not?" a deceptively soft and very masculine voice inquired. Lara's head snapped around.

"You—" she began in confusion, her heart pounding. "I thought you were away."

"I'm sure you did," Steven said, a wry note in his voice. "Otherwise, you wouldn't be here."

She was helpless to stop the rush of her blood, the hammering of her heart. His eyes were the same shade of vivid blue she'd remembered, his smile every bit as devastating.

"We'll leave," she said, determinedly gathering the picnic things she had just spread out.

Steven took the loaded hamper from her shaking hands and put it back down. "Lara, don't you think you're carrying this feud too far?" he said with a touch of impatience. "Let the girls enjoy themselves."

"Who are you?" Jennifer suddenly inquired. Dripping wet, she and Kelly were standing right beside Steven.

He stooped down to their height and introduced himself. "I'm Steven Drake. Who are you?"

"I'm Jennifer Danvers, and this is my sister, Kelly. That's my Aunt Lara. Do you know her?"

He cast a meaningful sideways glance at Lara. "I've known her for a very long time."

"Too long," Lara muttered.

Deliberately focusing his attention on her nieces, he said, "I see a fishing rod, but I don't see any fish around here. Didn't you catch any?"

"Fishing's yucky," Jennifer declared.

"Yucky," Kelly echoed.

"Then you must not be doing it right," he said.

He picked up Lara's fishing rod and, before she could protest, walked a little way upstream with it. Without so much as a glance for permission, the girls followed him as if he were some sort of pied piper.

Their laughter carried back to her on the still air. Lara suffered a sharp pang of something she could only label jealousy. It reminded her all too clearly of other times right here, times when they'd talked of having a family of their own.

Lara sighed and gave in to the inevitable. She distributed the peanut butter and jelly sandwiches and lemonade when they returned. Her sandwich seemed to lodge in her throat.

Suddenly warm fingers brushed hers as Steven took the sandwich from her hand. "If you're not going to finish that, I will," he said.

"Steven," she began impatiently, then got lost in the expression in his eyes. How many times had he stolen the last bite of her sandwich, the last cookie, the last swallow of her drink? It had been a running joke that she'd have to learn to eat faster or starve to death around him.

"We have to go," she said, hurriedly cleaning up the debris after lunch. The girls were half-asleep.

"Don't you think we could be friends again, if we tried?"

Friends? It was such a pale word for the way she'd once thought of him. Soul mate was closer. Lover even more accurate. But it had started with friendship.

He sighed. He reached out a hand to touch her, but she jerked away. "Oh, Lara, did I hurt you so badly? I'm sorry. I never meant to do that."

Blinded by sudden tears and determined that he wouldn't see them, she got to her feet. "It's far too late for being sorry, Steven. Just go on with your life, and let me go on with mine."

"I don't think I can do that, sweetheart. Not anymore." There was an apologetic note in his voice, but the gleam of determination glowed in his eyes. She knew that look all too well, and it made her quake inside.

Lara could take no more. "Jennifer! Kelly! Wake up, girls. It's time to go home."

As she led the girls off toward the path through the woods, she could feel his gaze on her, and she shivered, only barely resisting the impulse to run.

THE white frame house was bathed in moonlight. It had been years since he'd done this, years since he'd waited outside like a lovesick teenager hoping for a glimpse of a girl who'd caught his fancy. Even though he'd been twenty-seven back then, that's the way he'd felt from the moment he'd laid eyes on Lara Danvers down at the stream.

It had been a hot, dry summer day. A Thursday, he recalled, because his weekly meeting with his accountant to go over the books had been cancelled at the last minute. He'd decided to take advantage of the unexpected free time and explore the area. He'd even planned to take a swim to cool off, if he could find a deserted spot along the stream that edged much of the farmland he was interested in buying.

When he'd come upon the stream, dappled by sunlight, it had been irresistible. Seeing no one around, he'd stripped off his clothes and waded in, the cool water a welcome shock to his heated flesh.

That's when he'd seen her.

She was emerging from the woods maybe a hundred yards downstream. Her blond hair hung down her back in a shimmering wave. Her face was that of a Viking maiden, its structure and her coloring more than adequate hints of her Scandinavian ancestry. She was tall and moved with an easy, unselfconscious grace.

She had bent down to remove her shoes, then curled her toes into the cool grass. Still clothed, she had waded into the water, laughing like a child.

Perhaps if she hadn't been moving directly toward him, he would have kept his silence and carried the memory away like a rare and special dream. But she kept getting closer. He'd finally spoken, his voice a husky whisper, lacking its usual self-confidence.

"Hello."

Startled, she'd stared at him, and he'd seen that her eyes were an amazing shade of gray-blue.

She'd glanced along the shore then and had seen his hastily discarded clothes. Instead of embarrassment, a teasing smile had flashed across her face.

"I don't suppose you want to come ashore so we can have a proper introduction," she said.

He'd frowned with feigned severity. "You know perfectly well if I come ashore right now, there would be nothing proper about it."

She'd laughed at that, a sparkling sound. "Don't scold me. You're the one skinny-dipping in my stream."

That's how it had begun, amid taunts and laughter and smoldering sensuality. He'd tried to stay away from her, especially after he'd learned she was only eighteen. But even at that age, Lara was a lady not easily ignored. She'd lured him onto what he'd thought was no more than a merry-go-round of mild flirtation, only to discover it was as wild as any roller-coaster ride he'd ever taken. Never knowing what to expect, he'd awakened each day with a glorious sense of anticipation.

In time, though, it had had to end, but the leaving had been painful, worse than any he'd ever experienced before. Now here he was back again, risking the same emotional maelstrom.

With a last wry glance in the direction of the house, he set off for home.

*

LARA walked to the house two days later, thinking about this year's crop. With a good harvest, she'd be able to add to her special account meant to buy back Steven's property. A bad year could be devastating. She brought herself up short. She wasn't going to think about that today, not with a big holiday celebration waiting in town.

Dressed in red-and-white-striped shirts and blue shorts, Jennifer and Kelly made a patriotic pair. The downtown streets were crowded when they arrived. Main Street was already lined with families.

"Me can't see," Kelly protested, trying to wiggle between adult legs.

"Me, either, Aunt Lara."

Suddenly Steven was blocking their path. "Well, we'll just have to fix that, won't we?" Steven lifted Kelly and perched her on his shoulders, then took Jennifer's hand. "Excuse me, folks. Would you mind if the little one here gets up front so she can see?"

The family in front responded automatically to his smile and parted to create a space for Jennifer.

Kelly was wide-eyed as the first band came marching past. She waved her flag so enthusiastically it almost caught Steven in the eye. Lara reached out to take it away from her, but Steven intervened, his hand catching hers in mid-reach. "No damage done."

Instead of dropping her hand, he held it in the familiar way of lovers. His flesh was warm, his fingers gentle in their command over her senses. Just when Lara's blood was heating, he released her. She felt instantly bereft.

The last band marched past, and the crowd began to break up, most of the people heading for the square where a barbecue was being held.

When he'd retrieved Jennifer from her spot along the curb, Steven touched a hand to the small of Lara's back. "Come on. We'll be chaperoned by the whole town. How dangerous can it be?"

Lara's heart skipped a beat. She was unable to restrain herself from saying, "I seem to recall that eleven years ago the whole town wasn't enough to keep us from getting into trouble."

Their glances caught. He gave a quick look at the two wide-eyed children and held up a hand, silencing her.

"Hey, Nellie, my love," he called to the gray-haired woman who normally worked behind the old-fashioned soda fountain at Beaumont's. Lara noticed that a blush crept up her cheeks at the affectionate greeting he'd been giving her since he and Lara had gone into the drugstore for milk shakes eleven years ago. "Would you mind doing me a favor?"

"Steven Drake, I'd walk across hot coals for you," she told him, sharing a conspiratorial grin with Lara.

"How about taking Jennifer and Kelly to the barbecue for me so I can have a few minutes alone with Lara?"

"Steven," Lara protested.

"I don't mind a bit," Nellie said cheerfully. "With my

grandkids away, it's a real treat to have some little ones along on a day like this.''

As soon as the children and Nellie were out of earshot, Lara whirled on Steven. "How dare you use those children! I won't have it, do you hear me? I won't have you acting all sweet and attentive with my nieces just to get to me. They're little kids. They won't understand when you stop showing up.'' She turned away.

"Any more than you did?'' His voice was quiet.

She halted in midstep and turned slowly back to face him. His expression was unreadable, but his message had been crystal clear.

"Who says I'm playing up to those kids to get to you? I happen to like children. They always say exactly what's on their mind, unlike some adults I could mention.'' He stared at her pointedly.

"I think we've said quite enough for one day.''

He rolled his eyes. "Obviously reasoning with you is the wrong tactic.'' He grabbed her hand and started down the street. Lara had to run to keep up with him. He headed straight for a hundred-year-old oak tree in the park, its massive trunk the perfect backrest.

"Sit.''

She scowled at him, then sat, staying as far away as his firm handclasp would allow.

"Correct me if I get any of this wrong. You're still upset because of what happened eleven years ago. You're convinced that I betrayed you.''

"You did.''

"I didn't.'' When she started to protest, he held up his hand. "I did what I thought was best.''

"Oh, for heaven's sake, Steven,'' she said impatiently. "How could it have been for the best to walk out on me without a word? I was in love with you. We were planning a future together.''

He sucked in a deep breath. "I wanted to be with you more than I'd ever wanted anything in my life.''

Tears sprang to her eyes. "Then why didn't you stay?"

He sighed heavily. "There were so many reasons, starting with the fact that I wasn't much of a prize back then."

"I thought you were."

"You saw what I wanted you to see. Did you know, for instance, how much I hated my father? It was the only thing that drove me. I wanted to prove I wasn't like him." He gave a rueful laugh. "Instead, I found myself doing exactly the things he'd always done. I put my career above everything else. It was just beginning to go places when we met. I had to travel a lot."

"I knew all that. It didn't matter."

"It did to me. You were only eighteen. Too young to be making a commitment for a lifetime. I was nearly ten years older, and I'd already had one marriage fail because of my own inability to handle the responsibility of an honest, full-time relationship. I wasn't about to do the same thing to you. Besides, until I showed up, you'd been dreaming about going to college and being a doctor. I wanted you so much, I kept forgetting about that. Then your parents reminded me."

She shook her head. "I can't believe my parents would interfere."

"They just warned me to think very seriously about what I was doing. They were afraid that I'd never settle down entirely, that you'd wake up one day and realize I'd made you miss out on the only thing that had ever mattered to you." His gaze lifted and lingered on her face. "Remember that last night at the stream?"

"As if it were yesterday," she admitted in a choked voice. "You held me and made love to me and you...you cried." There was a note of surprise in her voice at the end. She had forgotten that, forgotten the shock of seeing tears in the eyes of the man she'd thought stronger than anything. "You knew what you meant to do then, didn't you?"

"I knew," he admitted. "And it hurt." There were tears in his eyes. "Do you remember what we talked about? You were so excited. Your grades had come in. Straight A's. You were absolutely certain you'd be able to get through undergraduate school in less than four years. There was no question you'd be accepted to medical school.''

Lara watched him with a puzzled frown.

''I'd been planning to ask you that night to leave town with me, but when I saw how bright your future was, how much you wanted that dream, I couldn't ask you to go. I had to let you have your chance.''

Lara swallowed hard. ''And that's why you didn't say anything? Couldn't you have given me a choice?''

A faint smile pulled at his lips. ''I knew you too well, love. You'd have gone with me.''

''Of course, I would have.''

''And it would have been wrong.''

''No, dammit,'' she protested, even as she realized the depth of his sacrifice. ''At least I would have had you. Instead, you left, then Papa died. Not so long afterward, Mama died, too. I had to give up any thought of medical school. So, you see, it was all for nothing.''

''It wasn't until I came back three years ago that I discovered it hadn't come true after all. By then your hatred of me ran so deep I didn't think there was any way to change it.''

''Why did you come back?''

''I couldn't stay away any longer. If you'd been happy, if you'd been married, I told myself I wouldn't stay, but you weren't. Even if you wouldn't let me back into your life, I felt I had to be here to watch out for you.''

''But you never said anything before now. Why?''

''Fear, I suppose. I could see how you'd reacted to my being back, especially since I'd practically forced you to sell me that land. I didn't know how to approach you to change that. Then I was gone a lot. I had a lot of business interests in other states. And in those years I'd been away, I'd had a lot of experience with engineering. I'd been in Mexico during the earthquake. I'd helped with the rescue operation. When similar disasters took place in other countries, I was asked to come and help. I always went. It was easier than staying here and seeing the look of betrayal in your eyes.''

Lara drew her knees up to her chest and wrapped her arms around them. She looked at Steven, saw the haunted expression in his eyes.

He got to his feet. ''You were the most important thing in my life. You still are. All I'm asking for is a chance to prove that to you.''

Before she could guess his intention, he leaned down and pressed his lips to hers, a touch of silk and fire that caressed her body and set it aflame. As he started to draw away, her fingers threaded through the hair at the nape of his neck. Their eyes met, questioned and knew. Their breath mingled during that instant of separation, and then she drew him to her again, as incapable of denying herself this moment as he had been. The unexpected, gently inquisitive kiss confirmed what she'd already guessed: the passion had never died, it had merely hidden in wait for his return.

''I'll give you your chance, Steven,'' she murmured finally. ''But I'll be one formidable enemy if you betray me again.''

The rest of the day passed in a haze. She rejoined the others. She ate, though she couldn't have said what. She played games with the girls, unaware of who won. She even danced just once with Steven, her body turning to liquid fire in his arms. The sensation both awed and frightened her, and after that dance she ran from it.

''JENNIFER Susan Danvers, you get back over here right this instant,'' Lara called out as Jennifer and Kelly ran ahead of her into the woods a few days after the town celebration. ''And bring your sister with you.''

She had no doubt at all they were headed for the stream.

''Jennifer, Kelly, I'm warning you,'' she shouted, starting after them. ''Get back here right this minute, or you'll spend the rest of the day in your room.''

Just then Jennifer burst through the stand of trees at the top of the knoll.

"Aunt Lara, Aunt Lara, come quick! S-s-something happened to K-K-Kelly." The words came out in a pitiful, scared tone.

Oh, dear God! Lara's heart slammed against her ribs. She set off at a run. "What happened?"

Jennifer sobbed. "She went in the ground, in a hole."

A terrible dawning apprehension swept through Lara. She picked up Jennifer and ran, stumbling, her arms aching under the child's weight.

When they reached the old well, there was no sign of Kelly. They could hear only faint cries from a long way down.

There was no time for hesitation. She had to have help. Taking a deep breath, she took hold of Jennifer's arms and said softly, "I want you to run to Mr. Drake's house as fast as you can. Ask him to come quickly. He'll know what to do."

As soon as Jennifer had gone, Lara lay facedown flat on the ground and called down to Kelly, talking to her, crooning songs, listening for any sound that would tell her that she was okay.

She was like that when Steven arrived. She took one look at him and the tears she'd been holding back began to fall. She flew into his arms seeking the comfort she knew she would find there.

"How's she doing?" he asked in a level, quiet voice, wiping away the tears on her cheeks.

"She's crying." Lara's voice was filled with dismay.

"That's a good sign," he reassured her. "It tells us she's still okay. I left Jennifer with my housekeeper, and I've called for some help. As soon as we get some equipment, we'll go in after her."

The afternoon turned into an eternity. When the men from town arrived, she was drawn away from the edge of the well by the volunteer fire chief's wife. A cup of coffee was placed in her hands.

"Drink this," Terry Simmons said in her naturally gruff voice, her manner brisk but somehow comforting.

A measuring device was lowered carefully into the well. It seemed to take forever before Steven finally came to her. She searched his face for some sign of hope, but his expression was grim.

"She's down a lot farther than I'd hoped. The well's not wide enough for any of us to go down after her. I've called for some drilling equipment."

She closed her eyes, then faced him with a quiet question. "It's time I called Tommy now, isn't it?"

Steven took her hand and squeezed hard, refusing to lie to her. "I think so."

Lara turned and found herself held in the ample arms of Terry Simmons.

"Come on, gal. Steven will take care of things from here on out."

Lara found herself leaning on Terry Simmons. In her quiet, brusque way Terry kept her sane, kept her focused on what had to be done rather than what might happen. She was desperately appreciative of the older woman's company as she placed the call to Kansas City and told Tommy, in a voice that shook but didn't break, exactly what was happening with Kelly.

"Tommy."

"Yes?"

"I'm so sorry." This time her voice did break, and she choked back a sob.

"Don't start crying, Sis," he begged, his own voice suddenly thick with unshed tears. "You've got to be strong until we get there. Tell our baby we love her."

"I'll tell her," she promised with forced bravery.

Once she was off the phone, she and Terry went back to the well. She was racked by a terrible sense of guilt.

If only she'd been paying better attention, she told herself, this would never have happened. She'd become too complacent, thinking of the farm as a safe haven for herself and her nieces. She'd forgotten all about the old wells scattered around the property. Most had been topped off for years, but as kids she and her brothers had been attracted to them. Only dire threats of punishment had kept them from trying to pry loose the tops themselves. Obviously some other children had found them an irresistible challenge, unaware that they were leaving a deadly temptation behind.

"Lara." Steven's voice lured her back to the present. It was nearly dark now, the air cooling rapidly. Huge spotlights were focused on the well.

"We've dug a shaft alongside her," he explained. "I'm going to try going down to see how close we are and see what we'll have to do to tunnel across."

With bated breath she watched as the men began to lower Steven into the newly dug shaft, watched as he disappeared from view, linked to the surface only by ropes and frantic hands.

Then she watched as the faces of the men fell. Her heart sank to its lowest point yet as Steven reemerged alone.

His expression was discouraged, the lines in his face etched deep. "We ran up against a problem. The ground is rocky down there. It'll take us a while to cut our way through."

Hour after hour the tension grew. The night dragged on interminably. Kelly's cheerful chatter diminished to tired whimpers and then nothing at all. Lara feared they had lost her.

"Lara, come with me and get something to eat," Terry insisted.

"I can't leave," she protested wearily.

"You don't have to leave. The ladies from town have set up a food tent."

Lara glanced around in amazement at the makeshift kitchen that had sprung up less than fifty yards away.

She went over to the women, grateful beyond words for their support.

"Thank you," she began, and then couldn't go on.

Terry interceded. "Go on and sit down. I'll bring the food right over."

Lara found an empty chair from which she could still see

the rescue operation and sank down on it. Her eyes burned from the strain of watching and waiting and from holding back scalding tears.

"Here you go," Terry said, putting a plate down in front of her.

Lara stared at the food. "Why did they come?" she asked, genuinely bewildered by their generosity. "I don't even know most of them. I mean I know their names, but I've never really gotten to know them."

"Even though Toledo's sprawling closer all the time, this is still country. Times like this, neighbors rally around. We'd have been here for you when your mama died, too, but you made it pretty plain you wanted to be left on your own."

Lara shook her head ruefully, recalling how her pride had kept her from accepting even a kind word back then.

"I was so angry back then," she admitted. "I was so afraid of relying on anyone. It wasn't just my parents dying, but..." Her voice trailed off when she realized what she'd been about to confess.

"Steven?" Terry prompted. At Lara's look of astonishment, the older woman smiled. "We all knew you'd fallen for him like a ton of bricks. We all wondered about it when he left so suddenly. You poked that chin of yours up in the air and looked so proud, we were all sure you'd given him the boot, but that wasn't the way it was, was it?"

Lara sighed and shook her head. "He left me."

"And now? From the way that man looks at you, my guess is he's still in love with you, assuming he ever stopped."

"So he says."

"Give it time, girl. Trust isn't something you have to give or withhold overnight. It's earned." Lara glanced toward the well where Steven's yellow hard hat was visible in the midst of the throng of men. "Seems to me he's trying mighty hard to prove something to you."

Lara instinctively reached across the table and clasped the other woman's hand. In the midst of this tragedy, Lara had found a friend.

Just then Lara heard her name being shouted by a familiar voice.

Leaping to her feet, she saw Tommy and Megan coming toward her. Afraid to anticipate their reaction to her, she took a hesitant step forward then waited. Then Tommy opened his arms, and she ran into them.

"How is she, Sis?"

"Steven says she's okay. He refuses to give up hope."

Tommy's eyebrows rose fractionally. "Steven?"

Lara nodded. "I'll take you to him." She grasped Megan's hand, and with Tommy on the other side of her, they crossed the stretch of land to the rescue site. Steven broke away from the cluster of men as soon as he saw them. He held out his hand and after an instant's hesitation, Tommy shook it.

Quickly and unemotionally, Steven brought them up-to-date on the efforts to free Kelly. "I've got someone down there now bringing out rocks. It's tedious work, and all we can do in the meantime is wait."

"Can I talk to her?" Megan asked.

Steven and Lara exchanged glances. It was Lara who responded. "She's been asleep for a while now. I think all of this wore her out."

Megan's eyes widened. "Are you sure…are you really sure she's asleep?"

Lara swallowed her own doubts and embraced her sister-in-law. "I believe that with all my heart."

"What about Jennifer?" Tommy asked. "Who's taking care of her?"

"She's at my house," Steven said. "Mrs. Marston, my housekeeper, is with her."

He settled the two women just beyond the work area while he and Tommy went to check on the progress that had been made. Lara found herself taking her strength from Steven's quiet self-confidence.

Watching him work with the men from town, she realized with a start that he was no longer an outsider. At some point since his return, the bold hit-and-run developer of eleven years ago had become an accepted, even respected member of the community.

At last he came over to the two of them and held out his hand. A smile played across his lips.

"Come with me."

Megan was already starting forward. He led them back to the well.

"Listen," he said softly.

Lara strained to hear, and when she did, tears welled up and spilled down her cheeks. Megan's cheeks were similarly damp. The sound was weak and came from very far away. The words were halting, but Lara had no doubt about what she heard: Kelly was singing.

Lara lifted shining eyes to Steven.

"Thank you."

Megan nodded. "You have no idea how bad I needed to hear that."

"I think maybe I do," he said, and gently brushed away Lara's tears as Tommy came to hold Megan. "It won't be long now," he promised.

Still, the tedious process seemed to drag on interminably through the morning and afternoon.

When the sun began to set on the second day of the ordeal, Megan was with Tommy, and Lara was once again alone with only her thoughts for company. Terry lingered nearby, but as if she understood Lara's unspoken need for solitude, she waited for some sign that she was needed again.

Floodlights lit the scene, giving it an eerie sense of unreality. The sound of drilling had ceased, and only the low murmur of conversation and hushed directions penetrated the silence.

Steven donned his hard hat and draped cables and tools around his waist. Just before he stepped to the opening, his gaze swept the perimeter of the crowd and found her. He gave her a jaunty thumbs-up gesture, which she returned with a trembling hand. An ambulance and a team of paramedics stood by.

She folded her arms across her middle and held on for dear life. Nervously her fingers bit into the soft flesh of her upper arms as the wait dragged on.

A quiet stirring of excitement drew her attention. She saw the fire chief smile, then heard an eruption of sound at his announcement. "He's got her. He's bringing her out."

A cheer arose. Lara saw the flash of his bright yellow hat as Steven began to emerge. And then she could see Kelly, blinking at the bright lights, rubbing grubby hands across her dirt-streaked cheeks.

Steven placed Kelly carefully into Megan's arms. Even the normally stoic Tommy had a suspicious glimmer of dampness at the corners of his eyes.

"Mommy! Daddy!" Kelly exclaimed in a tired but excited voice. "I not like it down there."

Steven spoke up then. "I think it might be a good idea if you took her to the hospital to get checked out. She seems just fine, but it's best to be sure."

Tommy nodded. "We'll take her right away." He paused. Lara knew he was struggling with mixed emotions about owing such a debt to a man he'd come to hate on her behalf. "You saved our little girl. We owe you."

"Just make sure she grows up to be as lovely as her Aunt Lara," Steven responded, his eyes never leaving hers. "That'll be thanks enough."

Tommy apparently caught the heated look passing between Lara and Steven, because he frowned. "We'll see you back at the house then," Tommy told Lara.

Steven's gaze, sending a clear, urgent request, made Lara tremble. "No," she said to Tommy. "You and Megan need to be alone with Kelly tonight. I'll stay at Steven's. We'll bring Jennifer back in the morning."

Tommy started to argue, but Megan again intervened. "Fine. We'll see you all in the morning. Come over in time for breakfast."

When they had gone, Steven cast her a rueful glance. "I don't think your brother approves."

"He's always been very protective of me. He'll come around."

Steven smiled. "I guess if I can win you over, Tommy should be a piece of cake." He draped an arm around her shoulders. "Let's go home."

Home. The word sent a thrill through her.

*

STEVEN found himself singing in the shower later that evening. Exhaustion vanished under the hard, steamy spray of water. He hadn't felt this alive in years. He knew Lara was responsible. His sweet, sensuous, spirited Lara. This time he would never let her go. He would give her back the spirit and laughter he had taken from her. At the very least he would spend a lifetime trying.

Anxious to be with her, he yanked on clean jeans, then pulled on a shirt that he didn't bother to button as he walked barefoot down the hall to the guest room.

Jennifer was drawn up on her side under a sheet, her blond hair a halo of wispy curls. Lara was sitting on the floor beside the bed, her head resting against the edge, her own blond hair spilling over her shoulders. One hand rested on Jennifer's shoulder in a tender caress.

As he drew closer, Steven realized Lara had fallen asleep. He found himself staring at her. How had he ever walked away from her?

Blue eyes blinked open. Then her lips curved into an enticing smile. "Hi," she murmured sleepily.

The gleam in her eyes was pure seduction. She rose and came to him, standing before him tall and proud. "I've been waiting for eleven years. Love me, Steven. Please."

A groan tore through him. His blood surged, hot and swift. He swept her into his arms and carried her upstairs.

When they reached his room, Lara anxiously stripped away his shirt, then ran her hands lovingly over his chest. When she touched the snap on his jeans, his control reached its limits. He brushed her hands aside and fumbled with the buttons of her blouse, not satisfied until it had been swept away and her breasts were spilling into his hands. She gave a low moan as he urged the rosy nipples into hard peaks.

He slid her jeans and bikini briefs down her long legs, lingering to taste the creamy softness of her thighs. Her flesh grew more heated, her cries more anxious.

He placed her gently on the bed. When she held out her arms to him, his last shred of control vanished, and he stripped off his remaining clothes and stretched out beside her.

"You are so beautiful," he whispered as he touched a finger to the pulse at the base of her throat, then drew a delicate path to the tip of her breast. Her eyes closed as a tiny gasp escaped before she could hold it back.

His hands caressed her, lingering where he seemed to be pleasuring her the most. As she rose above him, he felt her hot tears fall on his shoulder, but when he would have stopped to comfort her, she pleaded with him to go on.

"Just love me, Steven. I need you. Please."

Unable to stem the flow of her tears or to deny her plea, he poised above her, then met the upward thrust of her hips with a long, deep stroke that plunged him into the center of her warmth. His body rejoiced in the joining, leading her, then following, until they both exploded in a glorious fury of fire with the promise of eternity.

ONCE the farmhouse was in sight the next morning, Lara could hear the angry voices all the way across the yard.

"Stay out of it, Megan!" Tommy snapped, his voice carrying clearly. "You don't know what that man did to her. He very nearly destroyed her."

Lara gazed at Steven in mute apology.

"He's only saying what he feels," Steven said. "Besides, it's true. I did hurt you terribly."

Megan's equally furious voice cut through the air.

"I see what he's doing for Lara now. If you'd really wanted

to help her, you'd have spent the last years trying to get them back together, instead of encouraging her anger. For the first time since you brought me here to live, your sister actually seems ready to live life again. If you can't be supportive, you're the one who ought to stay out of it.''

Jennifer turned a distraught face up to Lara. "Why are Mommy and Daddy fighting?''

"It's just a disagreement, baby,'' she said, then set her chin at a defiant tilt. "And I think it's just about time it ended.''

Lara threw open the screen door and marched into the kitchen. "Enough!'' she declared. "I will not have the two of you fighting over the way I live my life.''

Tommy's gaze went from her to Steven and back again. Some of the tension went out of his shoulders. "I just don't want you to be hurt again, Sis.''

"It won't happen, Tommy,'' Steven said, putting an arm possessively around Lara's waist. "I'm back in her life to stay, if she'll have me.''

Lara waited with bated breath as Tommy gave Lara an intense perusal. "You're really happy, Sis?''

"This is what I always wanted. Even Megan could see that.''

Tommy scanned her face, then nodded. "Then I guess I'll have to accept it.'' He shot a warning glance at Steven, but the gaze was returned evenly. Message sent and received. Finally he held out his hand. "I hope things work out this time.''

"I'm going to do my best,'' Steven promised.

Jennifer sat on her father's lap while Megan and Lara fixed a huge, farm-style breakfast. When the food was ready, Megan brought Kelly out. Lara looked around the table and felt an abiding gratitude for the blessing of their togetherness. Steven caught her eye and smiled, a slow, tender smile filled with understanding. Her heart felt as though it might burst with happiness.

There was a tap on the back door.

"Logan,'' Lara called to her farm manager. "Come on in and grab some coffee. Would you like breakfast?''

"No, thanks, Ms. Danvers. I just wanted to get a look at the little one and see how she's doing."

"I fine," Kelly announced, still basking in her role as the center of attention. "Only one boo-boo." She pointed to the adhesive bandage on her arm. "See."

"My goodness," Logan said with a shake of his head. "That's a very impressive injury."

Kelly nodded seriously. "It get better. Mommy kissed it."

"Yes, indeed. That's the very best medicine," Logan concurred. Then he glanced at Tommy. "Thought maybe you'd like to take a look around, long as you're here. The corn's doing mighty well this year."

"I'd love to, Logan. Sis, you want to come along?"

Though Tommy's enthusiasm seemed sincere, Lara couldn't help but recall their arguments about the farm before he and Megan had left. Was he looking for a chance to reinforce his position that the time had come for her to sell the farm?

"Absolutely," she said. "I love showing this place off."

STEVEN was waiting by the gate when she came into view after showing Tommy around the farm. Her expression gloriously happy. She came straight to him, slid an arm around his waist and placed a kiss on his cheek.

"Miss me?" she inquired.

"Forever."

She studied him closely and apparently saw beyond the smile. "Are you sad about something?"

He held her hand, rubbing his thumb across the knuckles, then lifting it to his lips. He kissed the callused tips of her fingers. "We need to talk."

Her eyes widened, and her hand tightened around his. "Is it Kelly? Is there some aftereffect from her fall?"

"No," he said promptly, furious with himself for frightening her. He struggled to find the right words. "You know, this trip was an unexpected expense for Megan and Tommy," he began finally. "With a new job and the move, they can't have a lot of extra money right now."

"Good heavens, is that all?" she said, her relief painfully obvious. "I have a little money put away. I'll pay for their tickets."

He touched a finger to her lips. "No, love. That's not the point. There's been the time away from their new home, too."

Her voice went flat. "They want to take the girls back with them, don't they?" Her eyes grew misty when he nodded. "It's because of what..."

He gathered her close. "Don't even think that. It has nothing to do with what happened to Kelly. They just feel that as long as they're here, it makes sense for Jennifer and Kelly to leave with them now."

"Oh, Steven," she whispered, resting her cheek against his chest. "What am I going to do?"

"You're going to say goodbye and promise that you'll come to Kansas City very soon to visit."

"But then what?"

"Then you and I will start talking about making a life for ourselves."

BITING her trembling lower lip and blinking back tears, Lara insisted on saying her goodbyes at the farm that afternoon. She stood on the front porch and waved until the car that was to take her brother and his family to the airport was out of sight.

Then she turned and with a tiny cry of dismay buried her face against Steven's chest and sobbed as though her heart had broken.

Witnessing her desolation gave Steven a tangible image of what his own departure must have cost her. So many goodbyes for such a young lifetime. It was all he could do to keep from weeping with her.

*

THE rain began after midnight. Lara heard it pounding rhythmically on the tin roof and felt it was a fitting accompaniment for the dull throbbing in her head and the heaviness in her heart. She had anticipated with dread the time when Jennifer and Kelly would leave, but she had thought she could prepare herself for it. Steven's presence kept her from drowning in her misery.

She rolled over and caught him looking at her.

"Can't sleep?"

She shook her head.

He began kneading the muscles of her shoulders and she let the soothing sensations wash over her.

"Sweetheart, this isn't forever. You can visit Jennifer and Kelly. They'll probably be back for Christmas and again next summer. And there is one positive benefit you're ignoring completely."

"What's that?"

"This." He dropped a kiss on her shoulder. It sent a predictable tingle dancing down her spine as he added, "You and I would not be able to be together quite so easily with your watchful little nieces around."

He closed the distance between them then, his lips claiming hers with such absolute tenderness that it took her breath away. Then with unending gentleness he swept her away to their own private island of dreams, where magic caressed her flesh and brought her a blessed relief from the anguish of her thoughts.

At last, with Steven's arms around her, she slept.

In the morning, though, her depression returned, magnified by the rolling clouds that masked the sun and threatened yet more rain. Steven found her at the kitchen table, a cup of coffee clasped in both hands, staring off into the distance. He brushed a kiss across her forehead.

"What shall we do today?" he asked, his attitude determinedly upbeat.

She faced him guiltily. "Would you mind if I go out and help Logan with the harvesting? Maybe the exercise will help me shake off this rotten mood."

"I'm not complaining."

She gave him a weary smile. "No, you're not." She put

her cup down so hard the coffee splattered across the table. "I've got to get out of here."

She hadn't gone ten yards when she realized how impossible she was being. She was not going to sulk forever. She'd snap herself out of this. In the meantime she went back to the kitchen and gave Steven the lingering, breath-stealing kiss he deserved. "I'm sorry. I'll try to be in a better mood by tonight."

"No problem," he said, forgiving her so readily it made her heart ache. "If you're not, I'll just have to dream up some extraordinary means of cheering you up."

Despite the promise of an enjoyable evening ahead of her, her day went from bad to worse. She was so distracted that Logan finally ordered her away from the equipment. "The mood you're in, you're downright dangerous out here."

She knew he was right, but the dismissal did nothing to improve that awful feeling of being abandoned and useless. She walked down to the stream, kicked off her shoes and waded along the edge but couldn't seem to work up the energy to go for a swim.

The sky grew darker, the air oppressively still. Finally the ominous signs registered.

"Oh, dear heaven," she said softly.

Surely Logan and the others had left the fields by now, she thought. Fat drops of rain began to fall, scattered at first and then with more insistency. Her hair was drenched, her shoes soaked through and caked with mud.

She heard the loud roar that could have been a train rattling along nearby tracks. But there was no railroad, and she knew well what the ominous sound meant. She whirled around and scanned the sky and found exactly what she feared: a huge, dark funnel cloud, twirling debris up from the land. Where it skimmed the earth, it was a tight, black column. But as it reached toward the sky, it expanded into a wide swirl that dipped and swayed like some evil prankster.

"Dear God," she breathed in horrified fascination. Terrified, she raced to the house. The sound of the approaching tornado increased to ear-shattering levels.

In the basement she found a stack of old blankets and sat down. She drew her knees up to her chest, her pulse beating erratically. What little light penetrated the darkness from the two high windows on the opposite side of the room began to fade until the room was pitch black. The whole earth seemed to tremble then. The house creaked on its foundation.

She thanked God that Jennifer and Kelly were not here. She prayed desperately that Steven was someplace safe, that Logan and the men had reached safety. And she prayed that she would survive to experience once more the depth of Steven's love. She suffered another pang of regret that she had allowed her black mood to spoil even one moment of their time together.

She saw occasional flashes of lightning through the windows, heard echoing cracks of thunder. There was a rumbling, then another. There was another explosion of sound, the shattering of glass and then...nothing.

STEVEN drove along the winding road that led from his house to the Danvers's farm, his eyes wide. While there had been a few broken branches scattered about his own property, there had been nothing to suggest the devastation he found as he drove past Lara's fields. A large, tangled path of destruction had been cut through the middle, leaving raw earth and broken stalks in its wake. Tree limbs and debris were everywhere.

With the road blocked by a fallen tree, Steven pulled onto the shoulder and set off on foot. His heart hammered with fear as he made his way through the destroyed field. Was this where Lara had been working this morning? Had she made it back to the house? He began to run, oblivious to the mud that sucked at his shoes.

When he reached the back door to the house, he called out to her. The shout echoed back to him.

Choking back a terrible sense of panic, he found the door

to the basement. He threw it open and descended into pitch darkness.

"Lara!"

His call was greeted by silence. As he moved on, a hard knot of fear formed in his stomach. He was halfway around the room, when he saw her lying in a crumpled heap on the floor, rain pouring in on her through the broken window.

He was at her side in an instant. "Lara," he said softly. "Sweetheart, can you hear me?"

Gently he felt her head, locating a bump just over her temple, then a cut along her cheek.

Her eyelashes fluttered against her cheeks. After what seemed an eternity, her eyes blinked open.

"Steven, is that you?" She tried to sit up. "Are you okay? You aren't hurt, are you?"

He laughed. "No, sweetheart, I'm not the one who's hurt. I almost went crazy, though, when I couldn't find you."

She put her hand over his. "I'm fine."

The next thing she knew, she was in his arms being carried up the basement stairs.

Lara's hands were shaking, and there was a sick feeling in the pit of her stomach as she and Steven walked outside. And then her heart seemed to stop. Her hand closed urgently on Steven's forearm. The look she gave him was stricken.

All around her was chaos. A screen, apparently ripped from one of the windows—or perhaps even from some other house—lay twisted at the base of a tree. Bits of unidentifiable metal, pieces of farm machinery, no doubt, glinted in the sunlight that was breaking through the clouds. Tree limbs had been tossed around like so many pick-up-sticks. The shrubs along one side of the house had been uprooted and were scattered in every direction. Two windows in addition to the one in the basement were in jagged pieces. A child's tricycle she'd never seen before was half buried in the mud.

Lara swallowed hard as Logan hurried toward her.

"You okay, Ms. Danvers?"

"I'm fine. How are the rest of the men?"

"They're okay. We got everything we could into the barn before the worst of it hit. I've sent 'em on home now to check on their families."

"How'd the cows and horses do?"

He gave a lopsided grin. "Bessie's got a scrape on her rump, but that's the only injury as far as I can tell. You ready to go out and take a look at things?"

She glanced up at Steven, and his grip on her hand tightened. She gave Logan a jaunty smile, determined to make the best of whatever hand fate had dealt her. "Let's do it. I'm as ready as I'll ever be."

"Come on then. I've saddled the horses."

"I'm not sure about riding the horses, Logan," Steven said. "Not with her head injury."

"We won't be able to get around in the truck," Lara protested. "There are too many trees down. I'll be okay. If my head starts to bother me, I promise we'll turn back."

Steven didn't look pleased, but he gave in.

As they guided the horses around the scattered debris, Lara felt her determination begin to flag. Not a single field had been left untouched except, ironically, the one they had just harvested. When she saw that, she almost sobbed.

"Can we save any of this?" she asked Logan, her heart heavy, her expression hopeless.

The farm manager shoved his hat to the back of his head and regarded her sympathetically. "Hard to say, Ms. Danvers. I suppose it's possible that some of the corn may be okay for feed. When the men get back, we'll start doing what we can."

"Thanks, Logan." She took a deep breath. "I suppose once you've finished cleaning up, we'd better pay the men off and let them go."

"I hate to say it, missy, but I think you're right. I'm real sorry, ma'am."

Steven had remained silent throughout the exchange, but as they rode back to the barn alone, he said, "This is going to make things rough for you, isn't it?"

"I have enough to live on and to pay Logan, but I'll probably have to ask for an extension on the loan on the farm, and I'll need to borrow money for next year's seed.'' She bit her lip to keep from crying out in frustration. She tried to hide her mounting distress with a nonchalant shrug. ''Hey, this is just one of the hazards of farming, right?''

She swung down from the saddle and straight into Steven's arms. They encircled her waist and held her in place. ''Don't give me that unconcerned act, Lara.''

''All right,'' she exploded suddenly, all of her anger at the injustice of it spilling out. ''I hate it! I hate being beholden to the bank again. I hate knowing that no matter how well I run this place year after year, it takes one short storm to destroy it. I hate living on the edge, never being able to get ahead.'' She faced Steven, eyes blazing. ''Do you know I actually had begun to set money aside so I could make you an offer on your land someday? I was so damn proud of that. I wanted the Danvers's property to be whole again.'' She waved her hand in the air in an angry gesture. ''Whoosh! A storm blows through and it's all gone. Just like that.''

''You could walk away from it,'' Steven said quietly.

Her head snapped around, and she stared at him. ''What?''

''I said you could give it all up, end the uncertainty. You could go back to school, become a doctor. That's what Megan and Tommy want for you.''

Her brow knit in a puzzled frown. ''You discussed it with them?''

''Only Megan. She's worried about you.''

''Is that what you think I should do? Do you think I should give this up and go back to school?''

''I didn't say that. I said it's an option. Have you considered it?''

''No,'' she said heatedly, suddenly angry with him and not entirely sure why. Perhaps it was simply that he was pushing her in a direction that had been closed to her for too long. ''I gave up that idea years ago. It's too late.''

He placed his hands on her shoulders and forced her to look at him. ''Think about it, Lara. Don't waste your life doing something you hate. Tommy and Greg are on their own now. If you want out, now's the time.''

She looked around and tried to imagine walking away from the farm. She couldn't do it. "It's been in my family for generations," she protested. "I can't just leave it."

His gaze was unrelenting. "Is that your sense of duty talking or genuine caring?"

Her voice faltered, her determination suddenly less certain. "I...I don't know."

He tilted her chin up and smiled at her. "Think about it. Okay?" He gave her a gentle nudge in the direction of the house. "Now, let's go get this place cleaned up."

They worked for hours. Steven started by making the repairs to the windows and hosing down the outside of the house, while Lara worked in the yard. She hauled limbs into a pile near the barn, planning to chop them later for kindling and firewood. Then she raked the debris into piles to be put into garbage bags and hauled away.

She worked with a savage intensity. The sun, mocking them now with its brightness, beat down on her shoulders and brought sweat to her brow. At times she paused to watch Steven. The bunching of the muscles in his shoulders, the gleam of perspiration on his bare chest stirred a sharp pang of longing in her heart.

By sundown the worst of the damage around the house had been cleared away. She turned the hose on and rinsed the traces of grime off her hands and face. Then she sank down on a bale of hay in the shade.

"Well, if it isn't Farmer Danvers," Steven taunted, coming upon her. Blue eyes glittered dangerously as he propped a dusty boot on the bale beside her. "This sight reminds me of the way you looked that night at the stream, the night we made love for the first time." He leaned forward and ran a finger lazily along the line of her jaw as his gaze captured hers and held. "Want to go swimming?"

"Now?" Her voice came out as a husky whisper.

Steven nodded.

WHEN he stood before her by the stream's edge, magnificently naked, she reached out to touch him, then hesitated, awed that he was hers. Then she watched in wonder as he trembled in wait of her touch. At last her fingers were upon his chest, tangling in the wiry whorls of hair, then moving daringly lower to the sweetly throbbing core of his desire. He groaned in pleasure at that most intimate caress, before gathering her to him and plunging them both into the cool water of the stream.

With ripples lapping at their flesh, he settled her in place, filling her, completing her. Rocking slowly, he began a motion that was sweet torment, as he found the tip of her breast with his mouth. Her fingers dug into his flesh as her head fell back, and his lips left her breast to plunder the tender skin she'd exposed.

The past came back to her in a rush of vivid sensations. This was the way it had been for them before, yet different. The climax that was rushing at them with a sense of wild abandon carried with it the knowledge that they had endured. Steven's name was torn from her lips, a hoarse cry in the night's stillness. Ecstasy followed.

When she could find the breath to speak, Lara murmured, "We should go back. It's getting cool."

"And I'm starving," Steven admitted with a rueful laugh.

They hurried into their clothes and strolled back to the farmhouse. In the kitchen they worked in companionable silence, stopping only for stolen kisses as they chopped vegetables and grated cheese for omelets.

His hand came to rest at the base of her spine, and he turned her until he could drop a kiss on her lips. Lara felt her senses stir again.

"You'd better not distract me," she warned. "Or you really will starve to death."

Forcing her attention back to the stove, she sautéed the vegetables, then added them to the eggs. In no time the food was on the table, and even more quickly it was gone.

"That's ridiculous," she said with a laugh, looking around

at the empty plates. "We ate as though we were afraid some-one would come and steal it away from us."

His eyes twinkled. "There is one hunger that isn't satisfied."

"Oh, really. I thought we'd taken care of that one first."

"That was the appetizer. I was thinking of dessert."

"Is this insatiable side to you something I need to worry about?"

"I was rather hoping you'd find it one of my better qualities," he taunted. Then his expression suddenly turned sober. "There's something we should talk about."

She waved her hands in a gesture of truce. "Please, no serious talk tonight. I just want to get some sleep."

"No. This can't wait. It's something we touched on this afternoon."

"This afternoon?"

"Yes. About your going back to school."

"Steven, it's out of the question."

"Because you don't want to go?"

"I didn't say that. As you well know, I'm a little short on fortunes these days."

"I'm not."

Her eyes widened. "Forget it! It's bad enough being in debt to the bank. I won't start borrowing money from friends."

"Aren't I more than a friend?" he inquired with a wry expression.

She waved aside the argument. "You're missing the point. If I can't do it on my own, I won't do it."

"Does that mean you want to, though?"

"Dammit, leave it be. I didn't say that."

A silence fell between them, and she thought that was the end of the matter, but not meeting her eyes, Steven said slowly, "There's another alternative."

"What?"

"Sell me the farm."

Those four words echoed off the walls, pounding into Lara's head as violently as unexpected blows. *Sell me the farm.* Was that what all this had been about? Betrayal, so recently dismissed as a thing of the past, came surging back to choke her on its bitterness.

Her whole body trembling with anger, she got to her feet. "Get out," she said very, very softly.

Steven stared at her in shock. "What?"

"You heard me. I asked you, no, I ordered you to get out of my house." Her voice rose. "Leave! Now!"

He stayed right where he was. "Let's talk about this. Why on earth are you so angry?"

"I think you've said quite enough."

Faced with her stubborn determination, he finally stood. But when he got to the door, he turned and tried one last time. "Lara," he began, his voice a plea.

She turned her back on him.

Only after she heard him leave, heard the finality of the door closing, did she give in to the sobs that seemed to well up from deep inside.

*

WHEN the phone began ringing the next morning, as it had all through the night, she ignored it. It continued incessantly, until finally she snatched it up and snapped, "Leave me alone!"

"Lara?" The gruff, distinctive voice of Terry Simmons sounded uncertain.

Lara sighed. "Terry, I'm sorry."

"Are you okay?"

"I've been better," she replied honestly.

"I heard the storm hit pretty hard out your way. How are things?"

"The house and barn are okay. The fields took the worst of it."

"Is there anything I can do?"

"No, thanks. I should be able to see from Mr. Hogan's reception at the bank how much trouble I'm really in."

"Why don't we meet for lunch? It sounds as though your spirits could use a little boosting."

Lara hesitated, then realized she needed Terry Simmons's unquestioning comfort and perhaps even a little motherly advice. "Beaumont's at noon?"

"I'll see you there."

"WHO put that stormy expression in your eyes?" Terry inquired when Lara joined her.

"Isn't losing most of my crop justification for gloom?"

Terry nodded. "Would be for some folks, but I'm guessing this has to be a man-woman thing. What's he done?"

Lara considered whether or not to laugh off Terry's incredibly accurate guess, then decided against it. Finally she took a deep breath. "He wants me to go back to medical school."

Terry's brown eyes widened dramatically. "What an awful man!"

Lara stared at her, then caught the twitching of her lips. "Okay. I know that doesn't sound like much, but there's more. Since I refuse to accept money from him to do it, he offered to buy the farm."

"I think I'm beginning to see the problem. You don't want to sell, not even if it means getting the career you always wanted."

Lara shook her head. "I'm not so sure I even want that anymore," she said slowly, surprised herself by the admission. "I mean, becoming a doctor was real important to me at one time, but I think the truth of the matter is that I really like farming. In spite of everything, I like the challenge of it."

"If you can say that after nearly getting wiped out yesterday, then I've got to believe it's true. So why don't you just tell Steven that?"

Unbidden, tears sprang to Lara's eyes. She swallowed hard, forcing the words past the lump in her throat. "Because I'm not so sure whether it's my happiness Steven wants or the farm."

"Oh," Terry whispered softly. "Oh my."

"Exactly."

Suddenly Lara felt a hand on her shoulder. She hadn't a doubt in the world as to its owner.

"Lara," Steven said. To her amazement there was anger underlying the smooth tone of his voice. She dared a glance up.

He nodded politely at Terry. "Would you mind if I steal Lara away?" he said, already urging her from the booth.

"I'm not going anywhere with you," Lara snapped.

"Oh, yes, you are." The words were spit out through clenched teeth. "Or we will have one hell of a scene right here."

Lara jerked free of his touch and marched from Beaumont's. Once on the street she whirled around.

"Don't you ever, ever try that with me again," she seethed.

He clasped her hand and started walking. "It seems I'm always dragging you off to the town square to talk."

He gestured to an empty bench. She kept a careful distance between them.

"Let's start with last night," he suggested. "Why did my offering to buy your farm send you into such a tizzy?"

Lara sat stubbornly silent.

"Lara!" His voice rose ominously.

"All right!" she shouted right back. "It's your motive that worries me. Why did you make the offer?"

"So you'd have the money to go back to school." There wasn't even a flicker of hesitation in his eyes. "Do you have a problem with that?"

"Oh, yes," she said with barely concealed fury. "For starters, I don't believe it."

He appeared honestly stunned by her attitude. "Why on earth not? It's the truth."

She hesitated for just an instant. If he was acting, he was doing a good job.

"Don't insult my intelligence," she retorted. "You don't go around buying up land for some altruistic reason. You're a businessman. You wanted my land so badly eleven years ago, you seduced an innocent kid to try to get it. Why should

I believe for one moment that things are any different now? Your tactics certainly haven't changed.''

His complexion paled, except for two spots of color high on his cheeks. He rose to his feet, towering over her. The cold look on his face made her quake inside.

''That's what you think of me?'' His voice was low, but it cut through her like the lash of a whip. ''You think I'm capable of using you to get what I want?''

Despite a sudden wave of uncertainty, she met his furious gaze boldly. ''Yes.''

''I see.'' He shook his head. Suddenly the anger was gone, replaced by sorrow. His voice fell to a ragged whisper. ''You don't know me at all.''

His leaving had a quiet air of finality about it that shook her far more than his angry words. Beyond all else, it penetrated her righteous indignation and left her in doubt. He hadn't exactly denied her charges. He had disdained to acknowledge them at all.

With her own anger fading, she was left with doubts and a terrifying yearning emptiness that she knew from experience only Steven could fill.

LARA brought the car to a squealing halt in front of Steven's house, sending gravel flying. She got out and raced up the steps. When Mrs. Marston opened the door, Lara demanded, ''Where is he?''

''On the terrace.'' As Lara started through the house, Mrs. Marston called out to her. ''Be careful, Ms. Danvers. He's in a foul mood.''

Adopting an air of bravado, Lara grinned. ''I know.''

Steven was sitting in the sun, his head bowed, rubbing his temples. He looked utterly defeated.

''Steven.''

He lifted his head at the whisper of his name and stared at her.

''Can we finish that talk?'' she asked quietly.

''I thought you were finished this afternoon.''

"So did I," she said. "It's possible, though, that I jumped to a hasty conclusion."

"It is possible," he concurred, a wry twist to his lips.

"I want to go back to what happened eleven years ago." She lifted her chin and met his gaze evenly. "Why did you seduce me in the first place?"

"Would you believe me if I told you it was because I couldn't help myself?"

His eyes never left hers as he spoke. Breathless, she whispered, "What about the land?"

"It had nothing to do with that. When I first saw you, I didn't have the vaguest idea of your name or where you lived or anything else about you."

"But there came a time when you did know who I was," she persisted.

Steven sighed. "Lara, I am not going to deny that I came to this part of the state looking for land. Speculating in land is what my company does, in addition to putting together development deals and doing engineering studies."

"So you stole from the farmers to make yourself rich." She was unable to restrain the bitterness she'd felt for so long.

"I stole nothing," he retorted. "How many of those families did you ever talk to?" he asked. "How many did you ask if they could have survived another year without financial collapse? They got money and an opportunity to build new lives. There's not a farmer among them who would say otherwise."

It was true, she realized suddenly. She had never heard the farmers speak negatively about Steven.

"You tried to get my father's land."

"He and I discussed it, yes. He didn't want to sell. He felt very strongly that it was the only legacy he had to leave to you and your brothers."

Tears sprang to Lara's eyes as his words recalled her mother's deathbed wish that she save her father's legacy. "Why did you insist on buying part of it three years ago?"

"Because I'd heard the kind of financial trouble you were in, and I knew you'd never accept a loan from me. It was the only way I could think of to protect the land for you."

"And now?"

"I only offered to buy it, so that you could go back to school. In fact, my intention was to keep it and…" His voice trailed off uncertainly.

"And what?"

He lifted her hand to his lips and brushed a kiss across the knuckles, all the while keeping his eyes steadily on hers. The pace of her heart picked up as she waited.

"I was going to give it back to you—all of it—as a wedding present."

A mist of tears clouded Lara's vision, and her hands trembled.

"I was hoping that someday, after you became Dr. Lara Danvers, you'd also consent to becoming Mrs. Steven Drake."

"And what if I stay plain old farmer Lara Danvers?"

"You, my love, will never be plain," he said, drawing her onto his lap. Her arms instinctively circled his neck, and she took a leisurely survey of his face as he added, "As for your occupation, I don't care if you take up beekeeping. I still want you to be my wife."

Lara's pulse raced out of control then, and fire danced through her veins.

"I would be proud to marry you, Steven Drake. Very proud."

With that he swept her into his arms and carried her up to his room. Their room. It was hours before Lara was aware of anything except the fire that raged in her body, the sweet throbbing that rose to an impatient demand before sending her off into aching ecstasy.

As she sighed and curled herself into his waiting warmth, his breath whispered across her cheek, the words soft, but spoken without hesitation.

"I'll love you, Lara. For always."

For always.

SOUL MATES

Candace Schuler

Victoria Dillon stood bareheaded under the scorching Arizona sun, silently debating. Should she use her last bottle of Perrier to quench her own thirst or in the radiator of her overheated Mercedes?

She'd pulled off the road for the third time, trying not to let the steam billowing from under the hood of the sleek white car throw her into a dither.

She shaded her eyes and peered down the road both ways for the fourth time in as many minutes. Nothing. Just a two-lane blacktop highway stretching into infinity and a barren red-dust desert.

She was stranded in the middle of the Navajo reservation, with no water, no knowledge of the high-powered car she drove and not a service station in sight. She did have a six-ounce bottle of orange-flavored Perrier, about a quart of warm Diet Coke and an owner's manual for the Mercedes. Somewhere.

"Glove compartment," she mumbled, flipping through maps, motel brochures and gas receipts.

When she finally found it, the manual listed several possible causes for the engine to overheat, aside from no water in the radiator. But she knew that wasn't the problem.

A leak in the hose was listed, but it looked fine to her. Fat, smooth and black, presumably connected at both ends to whatever it was supposed to be connected to.

She straightened, lifting the heavy sheaf of midnight hair off the back of her neck with one elegant hand.

"Check the fan belt," she read. Victoria squinted under the open hood of the car again.

Where was the fan belt? What did it look like?

She stuck her head farther under the open hood. So engrossed was she that she failed to hear the soft crunch of tires as a truck stopped behind her.

JOHN REDCLOUD pulled up behind the disabled Mercedes, wondering if the rest of the woman would live up to the promise of those gorgeous legs. Wondering, too, what she was doing out here all by herself.

The desert was no place for people who didn't know how to take care of themselves. One look told him that she didn't. The gauzy white summer skirt, the flimsy sandals, the flashy gold-trimmed car all said, *city woman.*

Grabbing his straw cowboy hat, John shouldered open the door of his dusty Chevy pickup. His booted feet hit sunbaked earth with the soft thud of a cat.

Shading his eyes from the blazing sun, he slammed the door of his truck. The woman jumped and jerked upright, turning toward him.

The promise of her legs had not been an empty one.

She was reed slender, elegant and delicately built. Her shiny hair, raven black and almost Indian straight, fell from a precise center part to brush against her shoulders. The classic pageboy style and feathery bangs framed the sharp elegant bones of her face.

John sighed heavily. He had a weakness for such women, despite a lot of hard-learned lessons about them.

At his first step Victoria dropped her oversize sunglasses into place on the bridge of her nose and tented her hand above them to see past the glare of the sun.

The man walking toward her was tall. He wore faded dusty jeans and a dirt-smeared denim workshirt, unbuttoned and hanging open over his smooth coppery chest. The sleeves were rolled halfway up his forearms, and he wore old leather work gloves. A beautiful silver buckle set with a large square of polished turquoise glinted just below his navel.

Ranger buckle, Victoria said to herself. *Late 1800s. Probably Navajo.*

He stopped less than two feet in front of her. "Need some help, miss?" he asked softly.

Victoria could make out the curve of his jaw and a hint of firm lips, but his eyes were hidden by the brim of his hat.

It didn't matter, she decided. Help had arrived. And who'd have thought to meet a Greek god here?

"Boy, do I! I was beginning to think I'd driven into the twilight zone and there was no one left in the world but me."

"The desert's a big place," he agreed, then motioned toward the car. "What's the problem?"

"I'm not real sure." Victoria smiled up at her rescuer. *I know you can help me* that smile said. It made most people want not to disappoint her.

It made the small hairs rise on the back of John's neck. He also had a thing about beautiful women who thought a smile was all it took to get through life. His ex-wife had been one.

"Something's wrong with the cooling system, I think," Victoria said then. "The temperature gauge keeps climbing into the red."

He nodded and pulled off one of his gloves. Stuffing it into his waistband, he ducked to lean over the engine. A small silver pendant dangled from a leather thong around his neck.

"Here's your problem," he said finally, and waved his hand toward the engine. "No fan belt."

"What happened to it?" Victoria asked.

"I imagine it fell off somewhere," he said dryly. "I'll have to rig up something that'll get you as far as the gas station in Chinle." He rubbed his chin, thinking. "Got another belt besides the one you're wearing?" he said, pushing up the brim of his hat.

His eyes were as Greek-god perfect as the rest of him. That indefinable color known as hazel, they glittered like pale jewels against his smooth coppery skin.

It took all her suddenly scattered concentration to answer his question. "Yes, I have another belt," she said. "In my luggage. But what for?"

"To use as an emergency fan belt. It'd have to be narrower

than the one you've got on, though. Then again..." He reached out and clasped her waist in both hands.

Victoria stiffened in surprise.

"Hey. Whoa, there." John steadied her. "I'm not going to hurt you. I just wanted to measure—"

What he just wanted to do, he realized, was exactly what he *was* doing. Touch her. He wanted to cup the tempting swell of her breasts, to run his fingers slowly down the length of her gorgeous legs. He wanted... John yanked his hands away as if he'd been burned.

"Never mind. It'd be too small, anyway. Your waist isn't any bigger than a skinny twelve-year-old's." He turned away. "I'll see if I have anything in my truck I can use."

Victoria stood where she was, stifling the urge to look and see if his hands had actually left burn marks on her outfit. She sighed almost regretfully. He was one of the most beautiful men she had ever laid eyes on. *Does he come by that body naturally,* she wondered, *or does he have to work at it?* She wondered if he worked out at a health club, pumping iron like her brother Conrad.

Honest labor, she decided. His muscles weren't the over-developed kind. Besides, she doubted that the Navajo reservation would have an organized health club. She could picture him chopping wood, though, or digging post holes or hoisting bales of hay.

He would be shirtless, his bare arms and shoulders and back gleaming with the sheen of healthy exertion, his chestnut brown hair curling damply around his ears.

She would tiptoe up behind him, she decided dreamily, and run the tip of her fingernail down the hollow of his spine. He would drop his hay hooks and turn. His hands would envelop her waist, pulling her to him. His head would bend toward hers, his mouth— "There. That ought to hold it."

Victoria snapped out of her daydream. He wasn't looking at her. *Thank God!* "Is it fixed?"

"Temporarily." He cut the trailing ends of the rawhide he'd used and tossed them into his toolbox. "It'll get you as far as

Chinle. And I'll be right behind you in case you have any trouble," he added.

Victoria averted her eyes. "That really isn't necessary."

He looked at her. "Yes, it is. You could break down again before you get to the gas station. Watch your fingers." The hood slammed shut. "Besides, there's only one road. And we're traveling in the same direction."

"Oh, yes. Of course. I guess we'd better not waste any more time, then."

"Guess not," John agreed easily, but the hairs on the back of his neck bristled at her lady-of-the-manor tone. *Spoiled little twit. Doesn't she know how to say thank you?* He fastened the toolbox locks and stood up—just as Victoria rounded the front of the car.

His shoulder brushed against her thigh, the rough denim shirt snagging and lifting the gauzy material of her skirt as he straightened. She gasped and stepped back, reaching out with both hands to push it down. But not before John had caught a fleeting glimpse of a slender thigh, a bare hip and the rounded curve of a firm buttock.

All she had under her skirt was a scrap of white lace and the longest, most gorgeous legs he had ever seen.

Altered images of her long bare legs and tiny lace panties began flickering through his mind with lightning speed. Different poses. Different positions. Different settings. But all with the same theme.

"Sorry about that," he mumbled. "I hope I didn't get you dirty."

"No...no, it's fine." Their eyes met.

For Victoria it was like looking into the golden-hued eyes of a mountain lion. A *hungry* mountain lion.

For John it was as frustrating as hell. She was still wearing her sunglasses. God, he hated sunglasses!

City woman, he reminded himself sternly, as if the words were an incantation.

"Well, let's get a move on," he said gruffly. "Get in."

Victoria's murmured "Thank you" was barely audible as she settled gingerly into the driver's seat.

"Chinle is about ten miles straight down the highway." He bent to speak to her through the open window. "Keep it under fifty and don't use the air conditioner, and you'll be fine."

Eyes straight ahead, Victoria nodded. "Okay, fine. And...and thank you," she added belatedly.

She put the car into gear, stepped on the gas and shot out onto the highway. A small cloud of dust and gravel rose from beneath her rear tires.

John stood still for a second, staring at the rapidly receding car. *Spoiled, ungrateful little twit,* he thought, and turned toward his pickup. As he steered back onto the highway, the Mercedes was already little more than a white blur. She might be holding it to fifty, but he doubted it. *Drives like a bat out of hell,* he thought, and somehow it didn't surprise him. Women like her—driving cars like that—usually did.

Victoria had covered several miles before she remembered to slow down. "The fan belt, Victoria," she mumbled to herself, fighting the urge to speed. The last thing she needed was to break down and have to accept his help again.

The man was pure Neanderthal, she fumed silently. Running around with his chest hanging out like that. Showing off his muscles. And no doubt expecting her to drool all over him.

Which, to her embarrassment, was exactly what she had done. Had he seen her doing it?

A sudden graphic picture formed in her mind of the two of them lying on the front seat of his pickup, their clothes half off and tangled around them, their passion-slicked bodies straining toward fulfillment.

She shook her head, denying the fantasy—and the rush of heat that had pooled between her thighs.

"Forget it," she said out loud. "The car's fine. There's a gas station up ahead. You never have to see or speak to the man again."

She slowed the car, turned left into the service station and put her hand out the window, thumb and forefinger circled to show that everything was okay; he could drive on.

But he slowed to turn in behind her.

"Fill 'er up?"

Victoria turned as a service-station attendant peered into her window, his round face shaded by a Dodgers baseball cap, his expression unsmiling.

"No, I don't need any gas, thank you," she said shakily, wondering if Navajo men ever smiled. "Well, actually, I guess I do. But my main problem is the fan belt. It's broken." She reached down and popped the hood release. "I'll show you."

A large brown hand settled over her door handle, pulling it open. "What the lady is trying to say, Willie—" he cupped her elbow, lifting her out of the driver's seat "—is that she's operating with a jerry-rigged fan belt and she needs a new one." He glanced down at her. "Isn't that right, little lady?"

"Yes, that's right," Victoria agreed tightly. *If he calls me "little lady" just one more time...* She eased her elbow out of his hand, turning to the station attendant.

"Well, I dunno," he said slowly. "That's not exactly a Chevy you're drivin'." He looked up. "Whaddaya think, John? Is there a Mercedes dealer in Flagstaff?"

"Probably. If not, you could always call Phoenix."

"Yeah, Phoenix for sure. Might have to wait two, maybe th—"

"Excuse me...Willie, isn't it?' Victoria's voice, soft, low and icy broke between them.

"Yes, ma'am. Willie Salt."

"Well, Mr. Salt, I am entirely capable of handling a discussion about the repair of my car myself." She was being rude, but enough was enough. "Am I making myself clear?"

Willie Salt nodded.

"Good." She turned. "As for you, Mr....?"

"John'll do."

Victoria nodded and held out her hand.

John enclosed it in his own. It was soft and small but surprisingly strong.

"Thank you for your help, John. I appreciate it." She withdrew her hand and turned to Willie Salt.

He had been dismissed. By an expert. *The little twit dismissed me as casually as if I were her butler.* He couldn't let her get away with it. "Little lady?"

Victoria's head snapped around. "Yes? What is it?"

John grinned. "I'll be at the café across the street when you need me."

"Need you?" Her chin rose. "I won't need you."

"Oh, I think you will." He turned and sauntered back to his pickup.

Twenty minutes later, from her perch atop her suitcase by Willie's soft-drink machine, she watched him drive back. He pulled up. "Need a ride, little lady?"

For a moment Victoria considered telling him what to do with his ride. But she was hot. And sweaty. She wanted an aspirin. And a bath. And a turkey club sandwich.

Willie Salt had told her it would be a couple of hours before he could give her a lift to the motel. And three days, at least, before a fan belt arrived from Phoenix. Since Chinle didn't have a taxi service, she eyed the man in the pickup. "Does that thing have air conditioning?"

He grinned. "Sure thing, little lady."

Victoria gritted her teeth and got in.

*

"ARE YOU SURE no one's left a message for me?" Victoria asked the smooth-faced Navajo woman behind the counter of the Thunderbird Lodge.

"I'm sorry. There have been no messages for you, Miss Dillon. There are no phones in the canyon, you know, so someone must come," the receptionist said.

She wasn't dealing with the hustle and bustle of Phoenix, Victoria reminded herself. Her sister-in-law, Lindsay, had warned her about the difficulties of communicating with the residents of the Canyon de Chelly before she left on this buying trip. But it was already after ten o'clock, and business was business. Or should be.

You'd think Mrs. Redcloud would have found a way to get a message to me by now, she thought, plopping herself down in her chair.

"Life moves at a slower pace in Navajoland," Lindsay had warned. "So relax and enjoy it."

Easy for Lindsay to say, she thought. *Of course! Lindsay!*

That was why there was no message. Maria Redcloud wasn't expecting Victoria. Lindsay was the expert—the one who drove here from Phoenix every summer to buy handmade rugs and blankets for the family department store's Indian Arts Boutique. But Lindsay was pregnant with twins. And Victoria, at loose ends since her divorce eight months ago, had volunteered to make the trip in her place. She hurried toward the desk. "Do you have a message for Lindsay Cullen?"

But the receptionist's black eyes were focused just beyond the glass-paned doors. And a smile was curving up the corners of her generous mouth.

It was him. The white knight with the Greek-god physique and the condescending manner. And he looked just as perfect in clean jeans and a buttoned shirt as he had yesterday all dirty and bare chested.

"Good morning, John," the Indian woman said to him. "What can I do for you?"

Victoria heard his boot heels click against the floor as he crossed the lobby behind her. She shifted sideways, edging around a tall, potted cactus, wishing that she hadn't been quite so outspoken about his manners when he'd dropped her off at the lodge yesterday.

He'd called her "little lady" once too often with that half-amused look in his hazel eyes, and she'd given in to the urge to tell him exactly what he could do with his male superiority. She might have been a tad more diplomatic if she'd known she'd run into him again.

"Mornin', Ruth," he said. "I'm looking for one of your

guests. Lindsay Cullen. Grandmother was supposed to meet her here this morning.''

Grandmother? Victoria thought. *His* grandmother?

The Indian woman flipped through a card file. "She's not here, John. Sorry."

"Well, darn it all. Grandmother wanted me to fetch her out to the canyon."

Victoria sighed, accepting the inevitable. "Excuse me," she said, and stepped around the cactus.

Both heads turned toward her.

"I'm Lindsay's sister-in-law. I'm here in her place, to see Mrs. Redcloud," she added, still not looking at the man she could sense was staring intently at her.

"Oh, yes. Yes." The receptionist looked up at John. "This lady's been waiting for a message since a little after nine."

Steeling herself, Victoria turned to meet his gaze.

"Well, well," drawled John. "If it isn't the little lady with no fan belt. I didn't see you there," he said, hazel eyes running over her appreciatively.

She was dressed all in white again: a crisp, sleeveless white dress that made her smooth, tanned skin look like honey; a wide white leather belt that wrapped snugly around her tiny waist; strappy white sandals. He wondered if she was wearing those scanty scraps of white lace underneath her ladylike little dress.

"So," he said, "how're you feeling after your— What was it you called it? A 'thoroughly unpleasant experience at the hands of a caveman,' wasn't it?"

Victoria's chin lifted. "I believe *Neanderthal* was the word I used."

"Yeah, that was it. I don't believe I've ever been called a Neanderthal before," he said easily.

"Really?" she murmured. "I find that hard to believe." Her eyes held his with a level, challenging look.

"You gonna start calling me nasty names again?" John said lazily.

Victoria's low laugh bubbled out then, taking her temper

with it. "No, not this time." She smiled up at him. "Shall we start over?" She held out her right hand. "I'm Victoria Dillon," she said formally, "and I'm pleased to make your acquaintance."

John took her hand in his. "John Redcloud. I'm pleased to meet you, too, Miss Dillon."

"Victoria, please," she said.

They dropped hands quickly, both of them denying the quick, hot flash of feeling that sizzled between them.

Spoiled city woman. John cleared his throat. "We'd better get a move on." He nodded a farewell to the receptionist. "See you around, Ruth."

"Tell Grandmother I'll drop up later this afternoon," the woman responded.

"I'll tell her."

"Your sister?" Victoria asked as they crossed the lobby.

"Cousin." He pulled open the door. "What happened to Lindsay that she couldn't come herself?"

"Impending motherhood," Victoria said. "Twins. She just found that out a couple of weeks ago, and my brother Conrad—her husband—decided he didn't want her driving all over Arizona by herself."

He nodded, his eyes drawn to the gentle lift and sway of her breasts under the white dress. She wasn't wearing a bra. "You'll have to change your clothes, you know."

"Why?" She looked down at herself, then back up at him. "What's the matter with my clothes?"

Arrogant little twit, he thought, admiring the aggressive thrust of her chin. He moved a step closer.

"Well?" she demanded, all but tapping her foot.

"You sure do fire up real easy," he said. "It makes your eyes go all sparkly and..."

"And what?" she prodded.

"Hot," he said, low.

Victoria felt herself flush. "That's all men like you ever think about, isn't it?"

"What?" He brushed his fingertip over her lashes. "Your eyes?"

She swayed toward him slightly, her lids drifting closed. "No, se—" She caught herself before she said it. Sex. It was what *she* was thinking about. *What's the matter with you, Victoria?* But it was too late.

Instinctively, John reached out and his hands closed over her bare arms, lifting her to him. His head bent. His mouth covered hers.

Victoria gasped, her hands rising to push him away. But his tongue slipped between her open lips, hot and sweet, and she lost all will to resist. Her head fell back under the bruising pressure of his kiss.

My God, she thought. Where had all this come from? This hunger? This searing heat? She was humming—*throbbing*—with needs and desires she'd never felt before.

But then, suddenly, his mouth lifted from hers, his hands let go of her arms, and it was over.

"Well, now that we've got that out of the way," he said, "I guess we'd better get a move on."

Victoria couldn't move. *Out of the way?*

"Grandmother's waiting," he said tersely.

His grandmother, yes. "I have to change my clothes first," she said. It was the only thing she could think of that made any sense. "What should I change into?"

"Jeans, if you own such a thing." His voice was gruff, almost angry, but she didn't notice. "You go change, and I'll meet you out front."

"Okay," she agreed, turning toward her room.

"Try not to take all day about it!" he hollered after her, enraged by her total lack of response—and his own lack of restraint.

He hadn't meant to kiss her at all, he fumed. She was exactly the kind of woman he'd promised himself never to get involved with again.

THERE WAS a whole group of people milling around in front of the gift shop when she got there, but Victoria didn't see John.

"Would you like to buy a ticket for the canyon tour, miss?" a young Indian girl asked.

"No, thank you. I'm looking for John Redcloud."

"You might check down by the corral. His truck was parked there earlier. Just on the other side of those trees."

Victoria nodded. "Thank you." She slipped her sunglasses back on, making a concerted effort to tamp down her rising annoyance as she followed the girl's directions. He'd told her not to take all day, then wasn't where he said he'd be. She could see his pickup truck, but no John.

And then, suddenly, all her annoyance disappeared as she caught sight of the corral and the horses. Most of them were run-of-the-mill riding-stable horses, though three or four of them showed promise of more spirit. One was a real beauty, a gleaming bay mare with more than a trace of Arabian ancestry.

"Oh, you beauty, you," Victoria crooned, climbing onto the lowest rung of the fence. Leaning over, she held out her hand, palm up. "Come here."

The horse approached with a mincing sideways step, wheeled away with a nervous snort, then pranced back.

The velvet nose just touched Victoria's fingertips. Warm breath blew across her palm. Victoria let the mare smell her, then stroked the horse's velvety-soft muzzle. "Sorry, girl," she apologized. "I haven't got anything for you."

"Here, try this." A strong brown hand appeared over Victoria's shoulder, but the horse shied away. John dropped a half apple into Victoria's palm. "Oh, come on, Scarlett," he chided. "Quit being such a flirt and take it."

The horse pranced back, took the apple and then crowded against the fence, looking for more.

"Is she yours?" Victoria asked.

John nodded. "Picked her up at auction four years ago. She came as a package deal with her mother." He scanned the corral. "That roan over there."

Victoria looked where he pointed. The roan mare was nothing special. "Her sire must have been something else."

"Must have," John agreed. "I take it you know something about horses?"

Victoria climbed higher, then turned and sat, balancing on the top rail. "I have an Arabian of my own. Ali." She patted Scarlett's neck. "I ride almost every day when I'm home."

"Would you like to ride now?"

"Now?" Her hand stilled on the mare's red hide. "I'd love to ride into the canyon. Is Scarlett for hire?"

"Not on your life." John waved toward the corral. "Pick any other horse you want, though."

Victoria scanned the horses. "That one," she said finally. "The buckskin gelding."

John was impressed. Rover was second only to Scarlett. "Fine" was all he said, oddly disturbed to realize that she was a good judge of horseflesh. It didn't fit with the image he wanted for her. "Now let's see if you can saddle him by yourself."

"No problem," Victoria said.

"IT'S SO BEAUTIFUL here," Victoria said almost reverently. "Lindsay's always said you had to see the Canyon de Chelly to believe it," she said. "It's magnificent. The colors, the trees, the smell." Her arm swept out in a wide arc. "Everything. Pictures just don't do it justice." Saddle leather creaked as she twisted around to look at John. The excited smile of a child curved her glossy lips. "How soon do we get to one of those famous ruins?"

John couldn't help but respond to her eagerness with a smile of his own. "Another five minutes at most if we—"

"Get a move on," Victoria finished for him.

She pulled her mount up sharply when the first of the Anasazi ruins came into view. The crumbling remains of a culture long dead held her silent for a moment, awestruck that an ancient people could build a whole village on the seemingly inaccessible ledges of the canyon walls. "It's incredible, isn't it?'' she said. ''And sad, too. I wonder what happened to them?''

''Drought seems the most likely answer.''

''Tell me about the canyon,'' Victoria said as they guided the horses into the center of a wide, shallow stream. ''The canyon as it is today, I mean. What crops grow here besides corn?''

''Squash and beans, mostly. Pumpkin.'' He gestured at a tree. ''Peaches.'' A big six-wheel sight-seeing vehicle lumbered into view, heading for the ruins. ''Tourists,'' he said.

''You don't like having them here, do you?'' she said, sensing something beneath his easy words.

He shrugged. ''It's not a question of liking or disliking. Tourists are necessary to the economy of the canyon. They're a fact of life,'' he said.

''Well, I wouldn't like them here if this were my home.''

John grinned at her tone. *Spoiled little twit,* he thought again. ''The canyon isn't exactly my home.''

''You don't live here?''

''Uh-uh. I visit. Have done every summer since I was six.''

''Is that when you were sent away to boarding school?'' she asked.

''No.'' John shook his head. ''That was when my parents got divorced and my mother moved us to Flagstaff.''

''You grew up in Flagstaff?'' Victoria peered at him. Divorced parents. Flagstaff. He wasn't all Navajo. ''Your mother isn't Indian,'' she surmised.

''Italian mostly. With a little Swiss mixed in.''

''Ha! I knew it!'' Victoria crowed. ''No Indian alive ever had goldy green eyes like yours.''

''Goldy green?'' he repeated. He hadn't thought she'd looked at him long enough to notice.

''John. Hey, John.'' A young Indian boy, about seven years old, hailed them from a stand of cottonwoods.

''Hey, Ricky!'' John hollered back. ''What's up?''

''Grandmother sent me to look and see if you were comin' yet.'' He loped toward them. ''She said I could be the sentry.

Christina, too,'' he added, speaking of his younger sister. ''But I'm the *head* sentry. I sent her back to tell Grandmother you were coming as soon as I saw you.''

The child scrambled up, balancing easily on the horse's rump, his arms around John's neck.

''Grandmother said to tell you she made tea for the 'part-ment store lady.'' He looked over at Victoria, whose smile widened.

She extended her hand. ''My name's Victoria Dillon. What's yours?''

The boy hesitated, but John nudged him. ''Richard Red-cloud,'' he said, his hand darting out to shake hers. ''Grand-mother's made some corn cakes for you, too,'' he told her. ''With honey and pinyon nuts. But we can't have any till you get there.''

''Then you'd better sit down so we can—'' John began.

''Get a move on,'' Victoria finished.

''That's three,'' John said.

''Three!'' Ricky shrieked. ''You have to run,'' he told Victoria.

''Ricky, sit down,'' John ordered, reaching behind him to pull the child down.

''But she has to run!''

''Why?'' Victoria said.

''Because if you get three, he tickles you,'' Ricky said.

Victoria set her heels into Rover's sides and ran.

She heard Ricky's excited shriek, a muffled shout from John, and then the furious splashing of hooves through water as he came after her. His horse was faster, but she had a slight head start.

The splashing behind her got louder.

She whooped wildly, the thrill of the chase tingling along her spine.

''We're catching her, John!'' Ricky shouted.

Victoria turned her head slightly, to check his position. He was closing in on her.

''Come on, Rover. Come—''

One minute she was in the saddle, the next she hit the ground, and everything went black.

*

"OPEN YOUR EYES, Victoria," a voice demanded.

She struggled to obey. Her ebony lashes fluttered open, revealed only a blur and drifted closed again. Something cold and damp wiped across her forehead. Victoria opened her eyes.

Above her, a face floated into focus. It was a woman's face that had been carved by time. Black eyes, wise, inquisitive, stared down at her.

"Awake now?" the woman said in accented English.

"Yes…yes, I'm awake. I think." Victoria lifted a hand to her head. "What happened?"

"Your horse stumbled and threw you." The deep, musical voice came from outside her line of vision.

Victoria turned toward it. John. His Greek-god face wore a frown instead of a smirk, and his eyes were serious.

"Grandmother wants you to lie still and let her make sure you haven't broken anything."

"I'm sure I haven't," Victoria began, but Maria Redcloud's weathered old hands were already running over her body.

"Okay," Maria said. She sat back on her heels. "You stay," she ordered Victoria sternly, then turned to the others behind her. A quick instruction sent a wide-eyed little girl racing across the clearing. Another had John and Ricky backing out of the open shelter where Victoria lay.

"Grandmother wants to get you out of those wet clothes," he said. "And she doesn't want us to watch. Come on, Ricky. Let's go see if we can round up the horses," John said, turning away as the girl returned and handed Maria some dry garments.

With a deft maneuver, Maria dropped a faded red calico tunic over Victoria's head, then pulled the white blouse off her shoulders beneath it. She handed the damp garment to the waiting child to drape across the branches of a nearby bush.

After divesting her of her wet sneakers, Maria stood and helped Victoria to her feet. The calico tunic fell almost to midthigh. Victoria took off her jeans, too, stepping into a wide cotton skirt.

"All," Maria said, motioning toward her hips, and the girl took the tiny scrap of lace and hung it up to dry with the rest of the clothes.

"Thank you…Christina, isn't it?" Victoria said, sinking back down on the sheepskins she'd been lying on. She felt much better sitting down, and took in the scene before her. It was as if a picture in a history book had come to life: the open-sided structure made of four upright poles and a leafy, latticed top that sheltered her from the sun, the upright loom, the six-sided hogan across the small clearing, the old Indian woman leaning over the camp stove.

Maria wore the same sort of clothing Navajo women had worn since the early 1860s. A deep green velveteen tunic, long-sleeved and high-collared, was tucked into a full, ankle-length calico skirt. A lavish silver-and-turquoise-embellished concha belt cinched her waist. A many-stranded necklace of turquoise beads hung around her neck, along with a delicate silver-and-turquoise cross. Her heavy gray hair was smoothed back into a traditional knot. And on her feet—

Victoria blinked. Yes, on her feet Maria Redcloud wore black Converse high-tops. But the Navajo were known for adapting the ways of other cultures to the needs of their own.

"Take," Maria said then, thrusting an enameled tin cup under Victoria's nose.

The scent of herbal tea wafted up. "Thank you." She took a cautious sip. Hot but not too hot. Liquid comfort. "Thank you," she said again, smiling. "It's just what I needed."

"The horses are all taken care of, Grandmother," Ricky said as he came running up ahead of John. "Can we have our corn cakes now?"

In answer, Maria opened a covered basket and took out what

looked like two large, thick sugar cookies. She handed them to Ricky with a few quick words.

"Aw, Grandmother—" Ricky began.

"Don't argue, Ricky," John admonished. "Grandmother wants to talk to her guest alone. So give Christina her corn cake and take off."

Ricky stood there for a moment.

"There was a load of tourists at the ruins when we rode by," John said. "Maybe one of them will give you a quarter to pose for a photo."

Both children squealed and scampered off as John stood watching, a fond smile on his face. Then he crouched in front of Victoria.

"How're you feeling?" he said softly.

"Fine."

"No headache or blurred vision?"

She shook her head.

"Dizziness?"

"A little at first, but only for a minute. And it's gone now," she said, looking at him over the rim of her cup. She held it out. "May I have some more tea?"

"Any more tea, Grandmother?" John rose.

Maria nodded. "Just half," she said to him in Navajo. "Too much will make her sleepy. It has a mild sedative in it."

John looked over at Victoria. She gave him a sweet, dreamy smile. "I think she's already had too much."

VICTORIA AWOKE to the muted music of the breeze rustling through the leafy roof above her head and a soft, scraping sound that she couldn't quite place.

It was Christina. She sat cross-legged in a corner, head bent, attention focused on the fluffy bundle in her lap. Victoria propped herself up on an elbow, fascinated to realize that the child was carding wool.

"Hello," Victoria said softly.

Christina looked up. A friendly smile curved her lips. "Oh, you're awake. I'll go get Grandmother."

Victoria stretched, arching her back. She felt so good, so...euphoric almost. She didn't even have a twinge of the aches that should have rewarded her carelessness on Rover. She wondered how long she'd been asleep—and where John was.

She'd dreamed about him, she remembered suddenly, as images of their entwined bodies filled her waking mind. Scandalous dreams that made her fantasy of heated, frantic lovemaking in the cab of his truck pale by comparison.

Had he really left her here, all alone?

It seemed so, for there was Maria, walking toward the shelter with Christina.

"Better?" Maria asked.

"Yes. I'm fine," Victoria said.

"I look," Maria said, obviously not trusting her patient's judgment. She bent over and peered into Victoria's eyes as if she were trying to see into her soul. "Okay," Maria said. "Hungry now?"

"Yes, I am. Ravenous," she said, meaning it. "But I'd like to use the bathroom first."

Maria gestured to Christina.

"I'll show you where it is," the child said, reaching for Victoria's hand. They started down a well-worn path that led away from the family's living quarters.

"There," the child said, pointing toward a small outhouse.

Victoria entered it cautiously. The inside was scrupulously clean, and the chemical toilet had a flush mechanism. Victoria used it quickly and emerged.

"You can wash here," said Christina, motioning toward a large earthenware jug suspended from a metal bracket on the outhouse. A wide shallow bowl sat on a wooden shelf beneath it, a bar of soap beside it.

When Victoria had finished, Christina took her hand with the air of an adult about to lead a child across a busy street. "Now we go back to the ramada."

"Wait a minute," Victoria said. "My skirt's too long," she explained, bending down to lift the hem. Giving it a couple of twists to gather in the material, she tucked it into the waist-band.

That was how John saw her—being dragged up the path from the outhouse by Christina, her raven hair in a bewitching tangle, her skirt tucked up around those tantalizing legs, her bare feet dusty. At first glance, she could have been mistaken for an Indian herself, if a slightly untidy one.

But a second, closer glance revealed her for what she was. The smooth, manicured hands, the gleaming red nails, the aristocratic elegance and air of pampered wealth. Most certainly not for him.

He didn't want her, John told himself, in any way that really mattered. But, Lord, he'd love to have her in every other way!

He'd sat there, watching her while she slept, and *ached* to lie down beside her. If they'd been alone, he might have done just that.

"Ricky! Ricky!" Christina called then. "Guess what! I'm going to have my rugs in a store!" She released Victoria's hand to run ahead.

John pulled himself up sharply. Fantasizing again, he thought, disgusted. He'd been doing too much of that—ever since pulling up behind that flashy little Mercedes. He vowed to stop it.

"You look fully recovered," he said.

"I'm fine, thank you," Victoria said, willing herself not to smooth her hair. She just knew it was a rat's nest of tangles.

"I'm glad you're back," she said to John as she walked into the shade of the ramada. "I need someone to interpret. For your grandmother and me. Mrs. Redcloud," she said, coming up behind the woman at the camp stove. "I'd like to thank you for your kindness and find out when we can discuss our business. I—"

Her words were cut off as Maria turned and thrust a plate of lamb stew into her hands. "Eat first," she said. "Talk after."

"Need me to interpret that for you?" John asked.

Victoria ignored him. *Smart-ass,* she thought, and followed her hostess. John watched her with a smirk on his face, waiting for her to attempt the cross-legged position with a full plate in her hand. But she made it look easy, sinking gracefully to the ground between Maria and Christina. The skirt puffed out around her. It covered her right leg completely, but the other leg, where her skirt was tucked into the waistband, was bare nearly to the top of her thigh.

Luscious thigh, he thought, scooping up a bite of stew with a tortilla.

He looked up into her face. Their eyes locked. Hot amber burned into bittersweet chocolate, a tangle of warring emotions sizzling between them. Speculation. Desire. Denial. They both looked away.

"I have decided that I must know this Victoria Dillon better," Maria said in Navajo. "I must know her soul before I can entrust her with my rugs."

John's head snapped up. "Why? You never wanted to know her sister-in-law's soul."

"I could see what kind of woman she was." She looked over at Victoria. "I cannot see this one so clearly."

"What's she saying?" Victoria asked. She could tell that the conversation was about her, and that John didn't like whatever Maria was saying.

John waved her to silence. "What difference does it make?"

"I must know if she will treat my rugs with the reverence they require."

"Reverence?" His grandmother was up to something. *Reverence, my ass,* he thought.

"What's going on?" Victoria said again.

"Grandmother wants to know your soul."

"My soul?" Her glance flickered back and forth between the two of them. "Please tell her I don't understand. I'll be happy to tell her what I can, of course, but…" She shrugged. "I'm not sure what she wants from me."

"Grandmother?" John said.

"Tell her I wish to know nothing specifically. But I would

like her to stay in the canyon as my guest, for a day or two so that I may know her. Perhaps even a week.''

"A week!'' John said in English. A week of looking at Victoria would turn him into a raving maniac.

"A week?'' Victoria echoed. "A week what?''

"She wants you to stay here for a few days while she gets to know you.''

"Stay…?'' Victoria wasn't on a schedule, and she was stuck here, anyway, until her car was fixed. "I guess I could extend my reservations at the lodge,'' she said hesitantly. "I'd have to call home but—''

"Not at the lodge,'' John said. "Here.''

"Here?'' Her eyes widened. "You mean right here? In the canyon?'' That put a whole different slant on things.

Ignoring John and his gorgeous body would be impossible in the confines of the Redcloud hogan. "Wouldn't it be kind of crowded?'' she asked finally.

"Damned crowded,'' agreed John. He didn't live in Maria's hogan, as Victoria obviously thought. He had a small one of his own that he used when he stayed overnight in the canyon. But it would still be crowded.

"Well, then…?''

"You see the problem, Grandmother?'' he said in English.

"She can have a tent of her own. From the lodge. You can put it up for her,'' Maria said in Navajo. "I do not think she can do it for herself.''

"Grandmother suggests that you should have your own tent during your visit. The lodge rents them.'' He paused. "Or I could bring my camping gear from home.''

Yes, that's right, she thought then, relief storming through her. He'd told her earlier that the canyon wasn't his home. That he only visited. He probably wouldn't be here at all while Maria was "getting to know her soul.'' She could handle an occasional meeting with him, she told herself. So long as he kept his shirt on…

She turned and looked directly at Maria. "I'd love to stay,'' she said. "For as long as you'd like to have me.''

*

THERE WERE ONLY women in Maria Redcloud's ramada as Victoria approached it next morning. Maria, her granddaughter Nina, who was visiting, and her great-granddaughter, Christina. Only seven o'clock, Victoria marveled, and already they were busy. Maria sat at her loom, stringing it for a new weaving. Christina was carding wool. Nina sat cross-legged, plying a needle through the mound of white fabric in her lap.

"Good morning," Victoria called.

Nina and Christina looked up and smiled. Maria nodded. "Good morning," Nina greeted her. "Did you sleep well?"

"Like a baby," Victoria lied. She'd spent the first night in her tent fighting dreams of John. "Am I too late for coffee?"

"I will get it for you," Christina offered.

"No, stay where you are. I can get it." Victoria set the borrowed skirt and tunic she was carrying on top of a large covered basket. "One of these cups okay?"

Nina nodded. "There is sugar and powdered creamer there—" she pointed "—if you want them."

"Black is fine," Victoria said, pouring a cup. She came over to sink cross-legged onto the sheepskin next to Nina. "Is that suede you're working on?" she asked.

"Yes." Nina held it up. It was a white tunic with a long fringe on the hem. Embossed silver, coinlike buttons decorated the long sleeves and outlined the split collar. An intricate pattern in tiny blue and coral beads would cover three-fourths of the bodice.

"Oh, how beautiful!" Victoria gasped.

"My wedding dress," Nina said proudly. "I am to be married next week."

"Congratulations," Victoria said warmly. "Or is it good luck one wishes the bride?" She smiled at Nina over her coffee cup, recalling that she had seen her extend her hand to her mother and grandmother last night after greeting them. Showing off her engagement ring, of course.

"Your ring—" Victoria nodded "—may I see it?"

Nina held out her hand. The ring featured a highly polished, intensely blue turquoise at its center, surrounded by diamond chips.

"It's exquisite."

"Thank you," Nina said proudly. "My fiancé made it especially for me. It is one of a kind."

Maria Redcloud spoke to her granddaughter.

"Yes, Grandmother. I'm sorry," Nina said in Navajo. She turned to Victoria. "I haven't offered you any breakfast. I can prepare you—"

"No, nothing," Victoria interrupted her. "Coffee is enough. I never eat in the morning."

Maria spoke again, a rapid string of Navajo, scolding in tone. Nina replied in the same language.

"Humph," Maria said.

Nina laughed. "Grandmother says you are too thin," she told Victoria. "I said it is the fashion to be thin. You can see her response."

Victoria smiled and put her empty cup aside. "What can I do to help?"

Maria spoke again.

"Grandmother suggests that you might like to help Christina card her wool," Nina said.

"Oh, yes, I'd love to." Victoria scooted across the sheepskin rug. "If Christina would show me how."

Christina transferred the wooden cards to Victoria's lap and patiently showed her the motion to make. Victoria flubbed it; Christina laughed and showed her again, until she was finally doing a credible, if painfully slow, job of carding the wool.

"In a little time," Nina said approvingly, "you will be nearly as good as Christina."

They whiled away the morning that way, talking and sewing. Victoria learned that the rest of the Redcloud family had risen with the sun. Nina's mother, Dolores, her sister, Rose, and her brother-in-law, Luis, all worked at the lodge. Her father, Matt, was off on council business. John and Dan and Ricky were mending a fence. Victoria heard about Nina's fiancé, Bob, who was a teacher like herself, as well as being a skilled silversmith.

"I don't know when I've enjoyed myself more," she said when Nina set her beadwork aside to start preparations for the noon meal.

"But you must have many good times," Nina said.

"Yes," Victoria agreed. "But not like this." She spread her arms wide. "The canyon is so beautiful. So peaceful. And the company so congenial. It's like a better world, maybe."

"You sound like John," Nina said. "Every summer when we Navajo move back into the canyon, he says the same thing."

Victoria got to her feet. "Don't you live here all year?"

"No, only in summer. It gets too cold here in winter. And the children must go to school."

"So where do you live?"

"In Chinle. At least, most of us do." Nina poured oil from a large can into the skillet, then lifted the lid of a large ice chest. "As John did until four years ago. He has a ranch outside of Chinle now." Chunks of chicken sizzled in the pan. "He is building a fine herd of horses. They are his first love. More than his precious computers, even."

Maria commented then.

"Yes, Grandmother," Nina agreed in English. "Horses are much better. We Navajo," she said to Victoria, "have historically counted our wealth in sheep and horses. Grandmother is slow to give up the old ways."

AFTER THE FAMILY had assembled for a lunch of fresh corn tortillas, sliced garden tomatoes and fried rabbit—which tasted a lot like the chicken Victoria had thought it was—it was time to wash up.

And then she broke a nail. Reaching into the soapy bucket of water for a plate, she snapped the nail off all the way to the quick. The plate clattered to the ground and Victoria clutched the wounded fingertip, trying not to howl at the sharp, stinging pain.

"What is it, Victoria?" Nina asked, alarmed. "Did you cut yourself?"

"No, no." Victoria waved her finger in the air as if to cool it. "It's nothing."

John looked up from the leather strap he was repairing.

"Let me see," Nina said. "How bad is it?"

"Grandmother!" Christina hollered. "Victoria has cut herself."

John rose to his feet and assisted Maria to hers as he headed toward the commotion.

"It's nothing really," Victoria insisted. "I didn't cut myself. It's just...a broken nail," she finished sheepishly, feeling like a prize fool.

The nail on the index finger of her right hand was gone, torn off just below the quick, among four long, perfectly manicured red ones.

"All that noise for a broken fingernail?" Maria said in Navajo, slanting a pleased glance up at her grandson to see if he had seen how silly the Anglo woman was acting. He had.

"Looks like you'll live," he said dryly.

Nina was more sympathetic. "Here." She handed Victoria the dishtowel. "You dry. It will probably sting if you put it in the water."

SHE BROKE the second nail pulling weeds in the garden. It wasn't a painful break this time, just annoying. Her manicurist was going to have a fit when she finally got back to Phoenix.

At this point it was anybody's guess as to when that might be. Maria had steadfastly refused to discuss the sale of her rugs, claiming, when Victoria had tried to talk to her through Nina, that she still did not properly know her soul. And then she had sent her off with Christina to be shown how to weed a garden.

That evening after dinner, when the members of the Redcloud clan had retired to their respective hogans, Victoria sat alone just inside the open flap of her tent with a pair of nail clippers, calmly cutting the rest of her nails. She'd already taken off the red polish. When she got them all filed smooth, they'd be fine. Not glamorous, but serviceable, which she'd begun to think was better.

She had never known such tranquillity, she thought, sighing as she filed. Never had such a sense of satisfaction from a day's work. Which might be because she'd never *done* a day's work before. Not really.

As the beloved only daughter of Emily and Thomas Cullen of Cullen's Department Store and the cherished baby sister of Conrad Cullen, she'd found life had always been effortless and easy. Friends had been easy; both sexes seemed to seek her out. Love and marriage had been easy; she'd met Brad Dillon during her junior year in college, become engaged in her senior year and married him in the wedding of the Phoenix social season after graduation. Even the divorce had been easy.

And none of it had given her the same sense of satisfaction that she'd gained today. The only thing that would have made it more wonderful was someone to share it with. Someone like John.

She hadn't seen him since the embarrassing incident of the broken nail. He had not even returned for dinner.

"John and Dan have gone into Chinle for more fence wire," Nina had said, explaining their absence.

Victoria had spent the evening wondering if it took all day and half the night to buy fence wire. She wondered, too, if he were avoiding her.

"You're looking very pleased with yourself," John said, making her jump.

Well, speak of the devil, she thought, looking up to find him standing just outside the tied-back flap of the tent.

"Where'd you come from?" she said, trying to sound cool and unruffled.

"Chinle." He tried not to look at her bare knees. Her bare shoulders. The little lace ruffle that adorned the sleeveless bodice of her white nightgown. "I saw your light when I came down the path," he said a little defensively, "so I thought I'd deliver a message from Willie Salt."

"Oh, yes. My car." She stopped filing as a terrible thought occurred to her. "Is it fixed?"

"Yeah," John said, wondering why she was looking at him like that—as if he'd just taken away her favorite doll. "You can pick it up tomorrow. I thought you'd be pleased."

"Well, I am...I guess. I mean, I'm glad the car's fixed. But—" She brightened. "I can't get it tomorrow. Your grandmother and I haven't come to an agreement on her rugs yet."

"Grandmother will come to an agreement fast enough if she knows you're set on leaving."

"But I'm not! I mean— She wants to 'learn my soul,' doesn't she?"

John snorted. "You don't really believe that, do you?"

"Well, yes, I do. Why else would she want me here?"

"Why else, indeed?" he said dryly, turning to leave.

Victoria jumped up. "Hey, wait a minute." She stepped outside the tent, heedless of her bare feet. "You can't say something like that and then walk away."

He looked down at her hand on his arm. "I think it would be better if I did," he said.

"Well, I don't! I want to know what you meant."

"You do, do you?" he responded. *What the hell,* he thought. *Tell her.* It would give her something to think about besides herself. "My grandmother," he said, "wants you here to prove to me that you're no good."

"What?" She bristled. "What do you mean?"

"No good for me," he elaborated. And, unable to resist, he caught her chin between his thumb and finger. "It's very simple, really," he said, staring down into her eyes. "My grandmother knows I'm attracted to you. The good Lord only knows how, but she does. And she knows what happened the last time I was attracted to a woman like you."

"A woman like me?" Victoria whispered.

"A city woman. A pampered Anglo woman." He shook his head. "Grandmother thought a little reminder of how unsuitable a woman like you is to this life—my life—was in order.

So she decided to keep you around for a few days to show me just how poorly a woman like you fits in.''

"Stop saying 'a woman like you'!" Victoria said. "I'm an individual. So don't try to shove me into some pigeonhole, because I won't fit."

"No," he agreed softly, fighting the need to take her in his arms and kiss away her frown. "My ex-wife—an Anglo—didn't fit into my life at all." He was quiet for a moment. "Nina said that you enjoyed yourself today, that you actually seemed to get a kick out of weeding the garden."

"I did," Victoria assured him, touched by his honesty. "I liked it a lot."

"It doesn't change anything." He ran the back of his finger wistfully down her cheek. "I still can't have you."

Something stilled in Victoria's chest. Her heart, she thought. And her lungs. All the vital functions ceased for one incredible second. And then they started up again. Beating harder, taking in more air than ever before. *"I still can't have you,"* he'd said.

But he could. Oh, he could!

"John, I..." she began.

"No, don't say it," he cautioned. "I know you want me, too. But it wouldn't work. We're too dif—"

"No, that's not it at all! Well, it is, partly. But—"

He put his finger over her lips. "No," he said. "Just go back inside your tent. I told Willie I'd get you over there tomorrow afternoon to pick up your car," he said gruffly. "Forget we ever had this conversation."

Victoria went, but there was no way she was going to forget. Forget the most wonderful thing that had ever happened to her? Not likely. One little no wasn't enough to discourage Victoria Dillon when she finally knew what it was she wanted in life.

"Just you wait, John Redcloud." She smiled to herself. "Tomorrow you won't know what hit you."

WELL, thought Victoria, *alone at last in the front seat of John Redcloud's blue pickup truck with only his hat on the seat between us.* She looked over at him, half hoping that he'd make her fantasy come true. More than hoping. Wanting. Desperately.

"What?" he asked, feeling her stare.

Victoria forced her eyes forward. "Nothing," she said, a small, secret smile curving her lips.

He could sense the feelings radiating from her like heat waves in the desert. The same feelings that sizzled through him. *Lust,* he reminded himself. *Just lust.*

He should have brought Christina along, he thought then, shaking his head to dislodge the image of their two bodies locked together in heated abandon. A child sitting on the seat between them would have kept these feelings, these fantasies, at bay.

Thank God the service station was only a few miles on. He could drop her off, be rid of the temptation to ravage her for the rest of the afternoon.

The garage was closed. And Victoria's flashy little car was locked inside for safekeeping. A young teenager was tending the gas pumps.

"Willie had some kinda emergency," he informed them. "I don't know where he keeps the key to the garage or when he'll be back. He didn't say."

"Damn it all," John swore. "Now I'll have to take you back to the canyon before I can go out to my place."

"Your place? The ranch Nina told me about?"

"Yeah, I need to go out and check on a few things. I was going to drop you off, let you drive back to the lodge."

"I'd rather go out to your place with you," she said.

"My place?" Not a good idea. "What the hell for?"

"I'd like to see it. Nina said you raised horses."

"Yeah. So?"

"Well." Victoria shrugged. "Is there some good reason I shouldn't see your ranch?"

He could think of a dozen good reasons, all of them

about...this *feeling* they had for each other. "No, I guess not. Okay, we'll go out to the ranch."

THE HOUSE WAS low and rambling—typical of the southwestern United States. The outside was native stone and timber with a wide, rough-hewn plank deck and a double carport with a big yellow van parked under it. This must be John's "traveling classroom." Nina had told her that he taught computer literacy at three schools on the reservation this way. A hay barn, horse barn and neat network of corrals were spread out behind the house.

Victoria was delighted. "This is wonderful, John," she said, slipping out of the truck. "Can I see the horses? The house?"

"There's the house," he said. "The horses are down this way."

"I meant the inside."

"What do you want to see inside the house for?" he asked. He didn't want her in the house! If he saw her standing in his house—there wouldn't be any corner of his life left that he didn't associate with fantasies of her.

"Well, it's usually considered polite to invite a person inside your house."

"In the Anglo world, maybe."

"Oh," she said softly.

Damn! Now she looked as if he'd stolen her doll again. "Look, if you want to see inside, it's fine with me," he said. "What'll it be? Horses first, or the house?"

"Horses," she said, sensing that would please him.

"That's my latest acquisition," he said, pointing her toward a corral set off by itself. A dappled gray yearling colt trotted up to the fence. "This is Hi," he said, reaching out to scratch the young stallion's velvety muzzle. "Yahiya ibn Abdu," he added. "He's going to sire a lot of prizewinners when he's a little older."

"Why, he looks just like Ali," Victoria said, climbing up on the lowest rung for a better look. "Ali's a little darker now." She studied the animal. "Did you say his name was Yahiya ibn Abdu?"

John nodded.

"Sired by Morgan Breckle's Royal Abdu from Las Vegas, right?"

"Yeah," he said slowly, respect showing in his eyes. She knew a lot about horses!

"So was Ali!" she said with a pleased smile. Another link had been forged between them. "Out of Fatima." She patted the colt. "Who was his dam?"

"One of my own mares. Gray Pigeon."

"Well, he's beautiful." She sighed. "Your whole herd is beautiful. Can I see the barn now?"

"I thought you wanted to see the house," he said quickly. If he took her into the barn now, he'd be all too tempted to take her, period. And he wasn't going to do that. She wasn't the woman for him, not by a long shot. "Just keep telling yourself that, Redcloud," he muttered.

"I'm sorry?" Victoria said. "What did you say?"

"One of the mares in there is only a couple of weeks away from foaling," he said. "Strangers make her nervous. Let's go up to the house."

"Fine," said Victoria.

They walked across the planked deck silently, both of them caught up in their own feelings, poised on the edge of something they couldn't define. This was a turning point and they both knew it.

The brass knob turned under his hand, the heavy oak door opening inward. Almost holding her breath, Victoria stepped onto the large Mexican tiles of the entryway.

The first thing she noticed was the coolness, the kind of coolness that came from an air conditioner. That was definitely Anglo. The next was the magnificent rendering of a sandpainting on one whole wall of the living room. Definitely Navajo.

"That's from the Blessing Way ceremony," he said. "It's meant to ensure good luck or to celebrate a happy event. Nina and Bob will have Blessing Way songs at their wedding, 'for good hope.'''

"It's beautiful." She took a closer look. "Did you paint it?"

"My father did. He was in training to be a Singer. But he gave it up after the divorce."

"Singer?" Victoria said over her shoulder.

"What you Anglos would call a medicine man."

"Does he live here with you?"

"He died six years ago. Cirrhosis of the liver."

Victoria turned from the painting. "Oh, John. I'm sorry." Those few words explained a lot. His wariness of her was more than just an Anglo wife who couldn't accept his life. His father's marriage to an Anglo hadn't worked out, either.

"It'd been a long time coming. He was ready," John said. "Would you like to see the rest of the house?" The subject was closed.

"Yes, please. Is that the kitchen?" She walked to a door.

It was. The room was sparsely but pleasantly decorated with a few pieces of Indian pottery, furnished simply with a long trestle-style table and modern electrical appliances. It would take only a few feminine touches to make it really homey.

"What's through there?" she asked, eager to see the rest of it. She was learning a lot about John from his house. He was tidy. He had a good sense of color and design. And he was lonely. He didn't really live in this house, he just occupied it.

"Just the bedrooms and my office. Nothing that would interest you."

"But they do," Victoria said. "Can I look?"

He shrugged. "Be my guest."

The first room was his office. Filled bookcases lined two walls. Most of the center of the room was occupied by a large desk-height table with two computer terminals, two printers and several stacks of computer paper, technical journals and school textbooks.

"Looks like control central," Victoria said lightly.

The next two rooms were presumably meant to be bedrooms; they were empty. The last room was his. A king-size bed set against the longest wall was covered with a spectacular Navajo blanket. A natural-stone fireplace occupied the entire north wall. Sliding glass doors draped with loosely woven fabric led out to the deck. A chest of drawers stood opposite. And that was it.

During the drive he'd told her that he'd built this house, or had it built, for the Anglo wife who hadn't wanted it. *Stupid, stupid woman,* Victoria thought.

But *she* was going to live here with him. *She* was going to be the woman to banish the loneliness and fill this house with warmth and laughter and love and the children so obviously intended for those empty bedrooms. She turned to tell him so and found him standing right behind her.

"It's a beautiful home, John," she said, looking up at him with her heart in her eyes.

"I'm glad you like it."

She put her hand on his chest. "I like it very much."

His heart started to thud. "Victoria." Somehow his hands were on her shoulders. "Victoria."

"Yes?"

He groaned and pulled her to him. "Damn," he said softly, lowering his mouth to hers. "I promised myself I wouldn't do this."

*

VICTORIA MOANED in helpless delight and melted against him. Her arms tightened around his neck, pulling him closer. Her lips closed around his tongue, sucking. Her fragrance surrounded him.

Night-blooming flowers and forbidden sex; the thought broke through his frenzied rapture. Only she wasn't forbidden now. She was his. Every hot, silky, responsive inch of her, yearning for him as passionately as he yearned for her.

He slid his hand up her side and ran the heel of it over the swell of her breast.

"Yes." She sighed into his mouth, as he slid his hand inward to cover her breast. It was as soft, as sweet, as delicate as he had known it would be. The nipple was a hard little pebble, pressing against the sensitive center of his palm through her clothes.

"Victoria." His voice was a whisper of wood smoke. "Victoria, let me undress you."

"Oh, yes." Her hands fell to her belt. "Yes. I want to be naked with you."

"Let *me* undress you," he said, brushing her eager hands away. "I've dreamed of this," he said softly, unbuckling her belt. "Daydreams, night dreams. Every time I looked at you I wanted to do this." He lowered the zipper.

Victoria's throat worked. Her eyes closed.

"From that first day, when your skirt came up— Remember?"

Victoria nodded.

"And I got that tantalizing little glimpse of that scrap of lace you call underpants—" He slid his hands inside the parted cloth. Lace brushed his palms as he pushed her baggy shorts away. They fell, unimpeded, down the long silky length of her legs, and he cupped her heels to pull off her tennis shoes as she lifted each foot out of the shorts.

The honey-colored stretch-lace teddy she was wearing under her discarded T-shirt fitted her like a second skin. He could see the outline of her nipples and the soft black shadow of the hair between her thighs.

"Lord, Victoria," he groaned, reaching for her again. "Why do you even bother?" His mouth covered hers before she could answer.

He bent without removing his mouth from hers and lifted her in his arms, making his way over to the bed. He lowered her to the striped blanket. Their mouths finally separated then as he drew back and looked down at her.

She looked so damned *right,* he thought almost despairingly, lying there on his bed with her silky ebony hair spread out against the deep blues and greens of the blanket his grandmother had made for him. If he forgot about where she came from, it would be easy to believe that she was Indian herself—that she could belong here.

She smiled up at him softly, sweetly. "What is it?" she whispered, raising her hand to touch his cheek. "Why have you stopped?"

He turned his lips into her palm. "I haven't stopped," he told her. "I was just taking a minute to look."

Her smile deepened. "I'd like to look, too."

"You would, would you?"

"Mm-hmm." Her hand slipped inside the collar of his shirt, to the first pearl-headed snap. A gentle tug had it open. The small charm around his neck swung forward on its short leather thong. "I've had a few fantasies of my own about what you look like under your clothes, too." She tugged the second snap open, then came upright on the bed, and knelt in front of him to finish unsnapping his shirt. "That very first day, when you stopped to help me and came strutting up to my car—"

"Strutting!"

"With your shirt hanging open and your chest all hard and gleaming with sweat. I kept hoping you'd take your shirt off so I could get a better look at all that virile beauty."

"Well, now," he drawled. "Is that any way for a little lady to talk?"

Victoria gave him a playful, narrowed-eyed glare. "That's the way this little lady talks," she informed him. "And I didn't want to just look. I wanted to touch you, too...rub my hands all over your chest to see if all those gorgeous muscles were as hard as they looked." She smoothed her palms over him. "They are."

"There's another part of my anatomy that's pretty hard right now," he said.

"Yeah?" Head tilted, she gave him a flirtatious, seductive look. "Would it help if I rubbed it, too?"

"Victoria!" He pressed a hand over her teasing fingers, flattening them against his stomach before they could curl around his hardness.

"John!" she said back, then giggled. "I'd never have thought you'd turn out to be such a prude."

"Prude?" he said, and stood. "I'll show you prude, little lady." He dropped his shirt to the floor and reached for the buckle on his belt.

"Take it off," sang Victoria. "Take it all off."

John stopped undressing, his hands on the waistband of his jeans. "This isn't the way you acted in my fantasies," he accused.

"No?" She came up on her knees and wrapped her arms around his lean hips. She pressed her cheek to his stomach, her chest to his hips. "Is this better?" she whispered fiercely.

"It'll—" John cleared his throat. "It'll do for a start."

She lifted her head. Their eyes met and held for an endless second, all teasing gone.

"Victoria," John said, sinking onto the bed with her in his arms. He touched her face with wondering fingertips, buried his lips against the pulse above her collarbone, his hand skimming down to cup her breast.

Victoria moaned softly, and reached out to touch him in turn. *So smooth,* she thought, caressing him as he caressed her. *So warm. So wonderful.* Was any other man so perfectly made in both body and spirit?

She felt languid, all liquid and warm, as they lay there together in the quiet room; then John was looming over her, naked, his big hands tugging at the lace straps on her shoulders. Victoria lifted her body, assisting him as he peeled her out of the teddy.

Her body was more perfect than any fantasy could possibly be. It hadn't occurred to him that the honey gold color of her silky skin owed nothing to the kiss of the sun. He hadn't realized that the tangle of black curls at the apex of her thighs would be the softest thing he had ever touched. He reached down to cup that feminine delta.

They both sighed.

And then his fingers began to move, seeking even softer, creamier flesh, gently stroking the little nub hidden there, and Victoria's sighs turned to moans. Then to whimpers. And finally, to a muffled scream of fulfillment. Almost before she had her breath back, he was moving over her, positioning himself for entry.

"Victoria," he moaned, sinking into her warm, welcoming moistness.

As if she knew exactly what he wanted, she lifted her legs and locked her ankles behind his hips. Matching him thrust for thrust, breath for ragged breath, she held his strong, trembling body in her arms and poured out her love.

"Oh, John," she moaned when her second climax took her. "John, my love." She sighed when passion finally claimed him, driving his body into hers with one last mighty thrust.

JOHN HAD HEARD her whispered endearment; just as he had heard every moan and sigh and soft murmur she had uttered before that. He told himself that it was only a word spoken in the throes of passion. So how could she have meant it? The terrifying thing was that he wanted her to mean it.

"John?" Victoria's soft voice broke into his thoughts. Her hand stroked gently through the damp hair on his forehead. "John, have you fallen asleep on me?"

He raised his head. "Would I be that impolite?" he asked, smiling at her.

"Probably," she said, smiling back. "But I wouldn't mind. I just thought maybe you could shift over a tad."

He levered himself off her, cradling her in one arm. "Better?"

She snuggled into his shoulder and put her hand on his chest. "Perfect," she said. But she lied.

Oh, physically everything was perfect. It had never been more perfect. But where were the words of love? Or the endearments, at least, if he wasn't ready to say the big *L* word yet?

"You have the softest, silkiest skin," he said then, "and you smell so damned sexy."

Victoria's heart turned over, her touch of postcoital sadness disappearing.

"What do you call that perfume you wear?"

"It's called Victoria. I have it specially blended."

"That figures," he snorted, smiling up at her lazily. "What's in it?"

"Tuberose and musk. With a touch of sandalwood."

"Well, I like it."

"I'll wear it for you always," she promised, scattering soft little baby kisses over his smooth flesh. Her lips touched the charm around his neck. "Does this have some special significance?"

"Not really," John hedged. "It's Changing Woman. She's the major female god figure in Navajo mythology."

"I know who she is," Victoria interrupted. "But why are you wearing her around your neck?"

"To protect me from women like you."

"What?" Victoria pushed herself upright.

John smiled at the outraged look on her face. "My grandmother had it made when I came back to the reservation after my divorce. Her reasoning was that Changing Woman should keep away unsuitable Anglo floozies like you."

Victoria grinned, a wicked, seductively feminine grin. "Didn't work very well, did it?" she said, and stretched out on top of him.

THEY MADE LOVE again, then stripped back the bedspread and slept and woke only to make love a third time. Each time, they revealed a little more of themselves, a little more of what made them uniquely them.

"I've had this one recurring fantasy," John confessed in a hoarse whisper, his thumbs stroking her nipples as she rocked above him.

"Which is?" Victoria prompted.

"You'd stride me just…oh, that's so good!…just like you are now, except…except, ah, Victoria!"

"Except what?" she panted.

"Except that you'd have all your clothes on. Not your panties. You'd have taken them off already and—yes, like that." He put his hands on her hips, urging her on.

"And?"

"And I'd still have my jeans on, but…but opened. We'd be parked on the side of the road in the truck and—"

"In the truck?" Victoria said, laughter and passion in her voice. "You…you too? I had a fantasy about the truck."

"You did?" He dropped his hand to the place where their bodies joined and found her with his thumb. "Did I do this in your fantasy?"

"OH, VICTORIA," John groaned, tangling his hands in her hair. "You never did *that* in any of my fantasies."

She lifted her head for a moment. "Do you want me to stop?" Her voice was husky, thick with the wonder of loving him, the power she had over his big body.

"No…no.…"

THEY WERE in his kitchen. Victoria stood at the stove in one of John's shirts, stirring soup. John sat at one end of the trestle table, wearing only jeans and carefully spreading Skippy peanut butter and Smucker's blackberry jam on bread. They had missed lunch.

"I have a teaching degree," Victoria was saying, "but I haven't ever taught school."

"Because you got married right after college?"

"Mostly. Brad didn't see any reason for me to work. But lately—" *Very lately.* "I've been thinking of looking into getting a teaching position. Maybe—" she stared down into the soup "—maybe here on the reservation."

John was silent for a moment, wrestling down the surge of

joy her statement brought. If she taught on the reservation, then they could— But, no, she wouldn't stay.

"I would've thought some classy, private girls' school would have been more your cup of tea," he said mildly.

"They don't need me." *You need me.* "Nina said there's always a need for good teachers on the reservation."

"And you, with all your experience, are a good teacher?"

"I could be," she said, stung. She stirred the soup harder, biting her lip to stop the tears.

John stood up. She looked so damned dejected all of a sudden.

He put his hand on her shoulder and turned her around, "Victoria, I'm sorry. I didn't mean that the way it sounded."

"Yes, you did," she accused him. "But you're wrong."

He shook his head. "This isn't the place for you."

"Yes, it is," she said evenly. "This is exactly the place for me. Mostly...mostly because I want to be where you are, but—"

"Victoria, don't say—"

"But I'd want to stay here, anyway," she went on firmly, "even if I weren't in love with you, because I can make a difference here. I can be useful."

"You're not in love with me, Victoria," John said desperately. "It's lust. That's all. Just lust."

"You don't feel anything else for me?"

"Affection," John said reluctantly. "A great deal of liking. That's all you feel, too."

"That's *not* all I feel," she said stubbornly. "I'm in love with you, John Redcloud. So you're just going to have to learn to live with it."

HE AVOIDED HER for the next two days. Two days in which Victoria was busier and worked harder than she ever had in her life, with all there was to do in preparation for Nina's wedding. Victoria found herself harvesting vegetables, hauling water and grinding corn—by hand—as if she'd been doing these things all her life. But she opted out of watching Matt

Redcloud slaughter Christina's sheep—the girl's gift to Nina and Bob—electing to stay at the ramada when it was being prepared for the wedding feast.

John showed his face the following day. He had to—the whole family had come for Nina's wedding day. He arrived during the lull after breakfast had been eaten and cleared away.

Christina's sheep, looking more like a main dish now, was roasting over the embers of a slow-burning fire. Huge pots of garden-fresh beans, squash casserole and tamale pie were being kept warm in round brick ovens. Cakes and pies snuggled safely in covered baskets. The corn pudding had been made. The ceremonial corn mush simmered on the camp stove.

The bride was in her mother's hogan, attended by her mother and sister, taking a ritual bath in yucca suds. Maria was poking the cook fires. The men of the family were gathered under the ramada, engaged in discussion. Ricky and Christina were squatting in the dust, playing a game of cat's cradle. Victoria sat on a flat rock in the sun, watching them.

"John, John!" Christina said suddenly, abandoning her game. "Do you see my sheep being cooked?" she shouted.

"I smell it," he said, licking his lips. "Smells great."

"I gathered the wood for the fire," Ricky said, unwilling to be left out. "And I helped with the butchering. It was neat, John," he said with the ghoulishness of most little boys. "Grandfather cut the—"

"I've seen it done before," John interrupted. He didn't like it. Weak stomach.

"We have missed you these past two days," Maria said in Navajo. "Where have you been?"

"Thinking," John said in English.

"You are troubled?" Maria asked, with a quick look at Victoria. "You are unsure about something?"

"No, nothing," he lied, glancing over at Victoria.

She looked back at him with a particularly martial light in her chocolate eyes.

"I'm glad you're here, John," she said. "Your grandmother and I have business to discuss. I'd like you to translate."

"What does she say?" Maria demanded in Navajo.

"You know very well what she says," John said in the same language. "Why don't you talk to her yourself?"

Maria snorted and waved her hand dismissively.

"Did you tell her what I said?" Victoria asked.

"You haven't said anything yet."

"Well, tell her—" she took a deep breath "—I know that she doesn't approve of me. And tell her I know why. Because she's afraid you'll get hurt."

"What?"

"Tell her," Victoria demanded.

John shrugged. "You heard her," he said to his grandmother in Navajo.

Victoria waited for him to translate the rest. "Is that it?"

"That's it. Navajos say a lot with a few words." He looked down at her. "You finished now?"

"Not by a long shot." She looked Maria square in the eye. "Mrs. Redcloud," she said earnestly, "I know you're worried about your grandson. But I won't hurt him because—" She stopped, realizing that she had the undivided attention of every person present. "Because I'm in love with him, too."

Too? John thought, fighting panic. *Where'd she get this "too" stuff?*

"Very much in love with him," she repeated. "And when we're married I want to live here on the reservation, teach school here and—"

"Married!" John exploded. "Who said anything about marriage? Dammit! It's just lust!" he shouted.

"Marriage?" Maria said in English. "You have asked this young woman to marry you?"

"It's not just lust!" Victoria shouted back. "I'm in love with you. And you're in love with me."

"I never said anything about love!" But he'd thought about it. "And I won't!"

"You don't have to say it. As long as you feel it, that's all I care about," she lied.

Maria's voice broke between them. "Do you propose to

take another bride without consulting me first?'' she demanded of her grandson in English.

"I didn't consult you the first time, Grandmother." John ground out the words.

"No, you did not," Maria agreed. "And look where it got you."

"Grandmother, please!" John began. "I am *not* going to marry this woman."

"So you say, Grandson. But this woman—" Maria lifted a hand at Victoria "—thinks differently. What have you done, that she should think this?"

"I've done nothing!"

A suspicion of a twinkle appeared in Maria's eyes. But it was gone just as fast.

She reached out, took Victoria's chin in her gnarled hand and turned the smooth, honey gold face to her own. She stared intently. "Has my grandson promised you marriage?"

Victoria didn't flinch at the question. "No," she said.

"Has he spoken to you of love?"

"No," she said. "He hasn't *spoken* of it."

"But you have spoken of it to him?"

"Yes." Victoria's eyes went to John's face, then back to Maria's. "Yes, I've told John I love him."

Maria nodded, released her chin and reached for her hands. "You have worked hard," she said, touching the small scratches Victoria had earned with four days of work. "You have given a willing hand to whatever was asked of you. You have respected our ways. You have learned your tasks quickly. And you have done all with a joyful spirit." She looked into Victoria's eyes again.

"You will make your home here, on the reservation?" Maria asked.

"Yes." The word was a mere whisper.

"You will learn our ways and our customs?" she said.

"Yes."

"You will give my grandson children?"

"Yes," Victoria said fervently, triumph blazing in her chocolate eyes. Maria Redcloud approved of her. "Many children."

Maria patted Victoria's hands, then put them away from her. "You have my blessing on this marriage."

"Now, wait just one goddamned minute!" John exploded. "I haven't heard anyone ask me about all this!"

Victoria turned to him with her heart in her eyes. "Will you marry me, John?"

"Lord, Victoria!" he said, tamping down the surge of joy her words brought him. It wouldn't work. "You're not even Navajo!"

Victoria blinked. "What's that got to do with anything?"

"I swore I'd never marry another woman who wasn't at least part Navajo, that's what it's got to do with it."

"Oh, well..." A slow smile spread over Victoria's face. "Then there's no problem. My great-grandmother on my father's side was a Navajo," she said. "My great-grandfather was Conrad Cullen. He had a trading post near Fort Defiance," she continued when he said nothing. "They met when he..." She trailed off, realizing that everyone was staring at her. "What?" she said, looking around. "What have I said?"

It was Matt Redcloud who answered her. "Your great-grandmother was Navajo?"

"Yes, of the Bitter-Water clan."

"Why did you not say this before?" Maria asked.

Victoria shrugged. "It's not something I think about very often. No more than I think about my mother being half French. And, to be totally honest," she said to Maria, "I wanted you to judge me for myself."

Maria nodded, satisfied with her answer. John was another matter.

"Well, don't think it makes any difference," he warned her. "You're still a pampered twit as far as I'm concerned." He turned and stomped off before she could stop him.

"Do not worry," Maria said. "He is stubborn, but he will come to his senses soon. Come." She gave Victoria's hands a little pat. "We must dress for the wedding."

NINA MADE a beautiful bride. Standing under the sun and trees in the loving circle of her family and friends with her hand in that of her groom, she glowed with the special radiance of all brides. The fringe of her white tunic fluttered over the matching suede skirt. Her wide silver-and-turquoise concha belt was a gift from her parents. Turquoise earrings dangled from her ears.

The couple and the bride's father, who was performing the ceremony, stood in the center of the circle. There was an exchange of rings, then the recitation of the wedding vows, and then the bride and groom fed each other a fingerful of cornmeal mush from a Navajo wedding basket with its traditional black-and-white-and-red starburst design.

Victoria looked across the circle of that moment, seeking the face of the man she loved. She found him staring at her with an intent, furious expression on his face. She held his eyes, staring back, while the concluding speech was delivered.

She's so damned beautiful, John was thinking. So damned *right,* standing there with his grandmother on one side and Christina on the other, looking more Navajo than many of the guests. It didn't help that Maria had dressed her in borrowed Indian finery.

Victoria lost sight of him at the conclusion of the ceremony when everyone pressed forward to congratulate the bride and groom. She pressed forward herself, and touched her cheek to Nina's.

"Be happy," she said.

Nina's eyes twinkled. "You, too, my friend." She squeezed Victoria's hand. "Keep after him."

Victoria's eyes widened.

"Grandmother told me," Nina said, smiling. "That means she approves."

She had Maria Redcloud's approval, but she'd lost John's. If, she thought despondently, she had ever had it in the first place.

"What can I do to help?" she said to Maria, as she went to check on the roasting sheep.

"You can help Rose set out the food," Maria began. "On those tables under the trees. Rose—"

Her words were cut off by the sound of pounding hooves splashing through water. Every head lifted at the noise.

"What is it?" Maria began. She shaded her eyes, looking toward the rider. "Who is disturbing this wedding celebration with such foolishness?"

The horseman, riding bareback, was adroitly maneuvering his mount through the throng of guests.

"It's John, Grandmother," Rose said. "And I think he means business."

"You!" John said, bringing Scarlett to a halt in front of the three women. He pointed his finger at Victoria.

"Yes?" she said, feigning a calm she didn't feel. "Was there something you wanted?"

"You," he said again, amber eyes blazing. "I want you."

"For what?" she challenged, her chin up.

"Yes, Grandson," Maria interrupted sternly, but a wide grin split her face. "What do you want with this woman?"

"I want to marry her," he said. "I want to give her children." He leaned down. "I want to love her," he said softly.

Victoria was speechless with delight and joy and love.

He pushed his hat back. "Well, little lady?"

"Yes," she said, lifting her arms to him as he hauled her onto the horse. "Oh, John, yes!"

LAUGHING breathlessly, they rode pell-mell through the trees that separated his hogan from those of the rest of the Redcloud clan. John dragged her off his horse and ducked through the hogan door with Victoria in his arms. She squealed as he tossed her onto the low-slung bed.

"Laugh at me, will you, woman?" he growled playfully, on the edge of laughter himself. And then he covered her mouth with his, and tangled his hand in the black silk of her hair, as he told her silently, eloquently, endlessly of his love for her.

"Victoria," he breathed raggedly, when he could. "I didn't

mean it when I said I didn't want you," he confessed. "I do. I want you desperately." Their tongues touched lightly. "I need you." He nipped at her bottom lip. "I love you."

Her arms tightened around his neck in sudden, unbearable joy. Happy tears gathered in her tightly closed eyes. "Say it again," she demanded.

He laved her bottom lip with his tongue. "I love you. And I want to marry you."

Her smile was warm and teasing and full of love.

As if he sensed her need—because it echoed his own—his hand smoothed down her torso to the fringed belt at her waist and pulled at the knot. It fell away easily, and his hand slipped under the soft fabric, over the softer skin beneath. They both sighed.

"Are you wearing anything under this outfit?" John asked, his fingers feathering slowly up over her stomach toward her breast, teasing them both.

"Just panties," she said, gasping as his hand covered her breast. He cupped it tenderly. "Pale pink lace with—" his thumb strummed over her nipple "—with little ribbon ties at the sides."

"Yeah?" Gently he rolled her nipple between his finger and thumb.

"Uh-huh. All—" She licked her lips and tried again. "All you have to do is untie them."

"Yeah?" he said again. His eyes had gone from hazel to amber to gold. His hand was on her thigh when a shout of laughter disturbed the still, warm air of the hogan.

Victoria stopped his hand with hers. "The wedding," she said. "They'll be wondering where we are."

"No, they won't. They know where we are."

"John." She grabbed at his hand again. "It's Nina's wedding. We should probably go back."

"Don't want to." He yanked at the tie on her left hip.

"But someone might come looking for us."

His fingers drifted over to her right hip. "They won't," he assured her, and looked down into her face, his fingers holding on to the second ribbon tie. "Do you want to go back to the party?"

Victoria hesitated, shoulds and wants warring in her.

"Last chance." He gave the ribbon a tug.

"No," she said, wants winning hands down.

He pulled the knot loose. "Good choice." He grinned wickedly. "Because I wasn't going to let you up no matter what you said."

"No?" Victoria looked up at him. "Well, in that case..."

"In what case?" he prompted, tugging the panties away.

"Well, I've always had this fantasy..." She pulled his head down and whispered in his ear.

"Yeah?" He pulled back to look at her. "A sweet little lady like you with a fantasy like that in your head?"

Victoria nodded.

"Well," he said, reaching for her again, "let's get to it, then."

A scrap of pale pink lace, trailing crumpled satin ribbons, fluttered gently to the floor of the hogan.

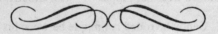

DESIGNING WOMAN

Candace Schuler

"Now that's what I call a gorgeous man." Elaine Prescott turned from the gap in the stage curtains. "There's a tall blond hunk out there among all those doctors," she announced above the noise of the models and technicians scurrying around backstage.

Daphne Granger was used to her assistant's frequent exclamations regarding the opposite sex and didn't even bother to look up from the loops of corded silk and beads she was arranging around the waist of a volunteer model.

"Is he over six feet?" asked Suzie, one of the professional models. She stood an even six feet tall in her stockings.

Elaine peeked out. "At least," she affirmed. "And he has shoulders like a football player. Great hair. Terrific tan," she reported. "And a smile to *die* for."

Daphne half listened as she gave a final tweak to the belt she was arranging and stepped back. "You look terrific, Mrs. Danvers," she pronounced.

The woman nodded and walked to her place in the line of models who were about to stage a charity fashion show for Children's Hospital of San Francisco.

Daphne had been roped into this by her oldest, best and most endearingly eccentric friend, Sunny McCorkle. Not that she minded, since the proceeds were earmarked for new equipment for the hospital. And, besides, it was fun—almost like the old days when she and Sunny had both been protesters on behalf of a cleaner environment, as well as sisters in the fight for equality of the sexes. Now, as then, Daphne worked in the background while Sunny held center court with a microphone in her hand.

Pulling her thoughts away from Sunny, Daphne glanced at

Elaine and Suzie, giggling and whispering, their eyes still glued to the gap in the curtains.

"Come on, you two, quit drooling and get to work. We're on in less than five minutes."

"Who goes on first?" someone asked.

Daphne glanced down at her clipboard and back up at the empty place in the line of beautifully dressed women in the silks and satins and glitter of evening wear. "Kali should be first in line." She looked around the room.

"I'm here, Daphne. Don't panic." A strikingly beautiful black woman rushed to her place, the pale pink silk of her bat-winged dress billowing as she moved.

"Now when have you ever seen me panic?" Daphne smiled and cocked her head, holding one hand up for silence. The squeal of a microphone being adjusted was clearly audible. "Oh, damn! Sunny's announcing me already." Daphne thrust her clipboard at Elaine.

"Just take a deep breath, Daphne," Elaine advised.

"Makeup okay?" Daphne tilted her face to the light.

"Gorgeous," Elaine assured her.

Daphne always looked gorgeous. There was no way that anyone with her cheekbones could be anything else. That she also had wide golden-brown eyes, a delicately chiseled jawline and a neck like Audrey Hepburn didn't hurt, either.

"And my dress?" Daphne's soft apricot silk evening dress with its wide boat neck and long, full sleeves gathered at the wrist with a narrow ring of crystal beads suited her peaches-and-cream skin to perfection. A corded belt of bright coral silk and more crystal beads accented the simple dress beautifully.

"The dress is lovely. Your hair looks great," Elaine said, eyeing the short, gently tousled hairdo, its color somewhere between aged bourbon and pale golden sherry. "Your notes are on the podium," she added.

Daphne entered from stage right to polite applause and took her place. Surprisingly, Sunny didn't mouth any of the pleasantries that were usual on such an occasion. Instead, she gave

Daphne's hand a squeeze, winked one huge chocolate-brown eye, and scampered offstage before Daphne could thank her for the lovely introduction.

Daphne thanked her anyway, then took a deep breath and smiled, willing the butterflies in her stomach to settle down. She really hated this part of a fashion show, preferring to manage things backstage and let her designs speak for themselves. But this was a charity function and the audience expected to see her.

"Good evening, everyone," she began, her husky voice made more so by nervousness. "Tonight you'll be seeing some of the newest evening designs from my Night Lights collection. The gowns are—" Daphne stopped suddenly in midspiel.

Elaine's "gorgeous hunk"—it could be none other—was sitting almost directly in front of the podium. His eyes were fastened intently on Daphne's face.

She blinked once and looked again. *It can't be,* she thought, her eyes wide. But she knew beyond a doubt that it was Adam.

No wonder Sunny had been in such a hurry to get off the stage! She had probably invited him.

"Daphne!" Elaine hissed at her from the wings.

Daphne glanced toward stage right, focusing on her agitated assistant. "And, uh, now," she improvised, "here to describe the fashions is my very capable and, uh, lovely assistant, Elaine Prescott." She motioned for the other woman to join her.

Elaine hurried out, automatically smiling at the crowd as Daphne introduced her again.

Daphne mimed confusion as she turned away from the audience, and thrust the cue cards into Elaine's hands. Then she walked backstage.

"Daphne, are you all right?" Suzie was the first to reach her.

"Where's Sunny?" Daphne demanded. "I want to wring her neck."

"Huh?"

"The tall busty redhead in the gold lamé," Daphne said.

"Oh, Mrs. McCorkle. She went that way." Kali pointed toward the backstage exit. "Fast."

"Coward!" Daphne muttered. Then she turned, glancing at the models. "Why are you all just standing around? You're on, Kali," she instructed, nodding toward the stage.

The black woman instantly assumed the haughty, elegant expression of the professional runway model and glided onstage.

"Our next model this evening is Mrs. Beth Garwood, the wife of Dr. Arthur Garwood..." Elaine's voice was well modulated and professional but Daphne barely heard it.

She peered around the edge of the curtain. Adam's golden blond hair made him easy to pick out. Dr. Brian McCorkle, Sunny's husband, was at the same table. Sunny's seat was empty.

Suddenly, as if feeling her eyes upon him, Adam half turned and looked over his shoulder. There was a puzzled expression on his handsome face as Daphne hastily tucked herself farther behind the concealing material.

He still looked the same, she thought, daring to peek again. Oh, he was older, of course. Who wasn't? But his hair hadn't changed at all. It was still thick and straight and the color of ripe, golden wheat. From what she could see, he had managed to keep his physique, too. He still looked more like the football player that Elaine had tagged him than a successful doctor.

It was those shoulders and that build that had first attracted her to him. He had just been coming out of the entrance of Harding Park, near the university, clad in battered running shoes and blue shorts. A sweat-soaked terry headband had held his hair out of his face, and there was a gleam of hard physical exertion covering his body. He was as beautiful as a young Greek god and Daphne had been so enthralled by the sheer male beauty of him that she actually ran into him with her bicycle.

Lord, but he had been angry! For the first few minutes, anyway. She had, after all, knocked him down and left tread marks across the toe of his right sneaker. It had taken half a dozen apologetic smiles and the promise of a date before he forgave her.

Daphne sighed. Where had all the time gone? *Adam will be thirty-seven in a couple of weeks,* she thought. *I turned thirty-one this year.* And in just two months it would be eleven years since their divorce.

"Daphne, what happened out there?" Suzie put her hand on Daphne's arm. "Are you all right? You look like you've seen a ghost."

Daphne smiled a little wryly. "I guess I have, sort of." She nodded toward the audience. "See that blond hunk of yours out there?"

Suzie peeked around the curtain. "Uh-huh. Yummy."

"He's my ex-husband."

The model's head snapped around. "Really? I didn't know you'd ever been married to anyone but Miles." Her look became frankly curious. "You must have been awfully young."

"I was eighteen," Daphne said softly, thinking of the way they had eloped.

It had been her idea. Adam had wanted to wait until they could "afford" to get married, until he was out of med school and into his internship, at least. But Daphne didn't want to wait. And, in the end, neither did he.

Maybe it would have been better if they had waited, she thought. But it was too late now.

"I was twenty when he filed for divorce," she added softly.

"Oh," Suzie said. "Gee, I'm sorry, Daphne."

"Oh, don't be." Daphne shook off her reverie. "It was a long time ago."

"Did you know he was going to be here tonight?"

Daphne shook her head. "I'd heard that he was doing his residency in plastic surgery at some hospital in L.A. But that was, oh, five or six years ago. He always said he intended to establish his practice in San Francisco.'' She sighed softly and picked up the clipboard, her mind back on the business at hand.

"You have one more dress after that, right, Suzie?'' she said.

The model nodded and Daphne turned to watch her parade out onto the stage. The tall, lanky model seemed to float down the runway.

"And that, ladies and gentlemen, concludes our fashion show for this evening,'' Elaine said finally. "What do you say we give a big round of applause to our lovely models?'' she continued as they all began to file out for the finale.

"Let's get the designer of these fabulous clothes out here, too, shall we?'' Elaine continued.

Daphne had known the words were coming, as Elaine turned to the wing where she was standing, adding her applause to that of the audience.

Daphne fixed her assistant with a threatening glare and walked out on stage. She forced herself not to look at the table where Adam was sitting.

"Thank you, ladies and gentlemen,'' she said. "I hope you enjoyed the show. I know we enjoyed putting it on for you.'' She paused, smiling warmly as the applause began again, and now her eyes were irresistibly drawn to Adam's table.

His golden head was tilted slightly as he gazed up at her and there was the hint of a question in his pose. Then he raised his glass and smiled. It was that sweet, slow, utterly charming smile that she remembered far too well for her own good.

Daphne felt her knees turn to mush and it was all she could do to finish her little speech and get off the stage.

IT WAS CHAOS backstage, technicians dodging models who scurried about in various stages of undress as they struggled to get into the gowns they would wear for that evening's charity dance in one of the hotel ballrooms.

"Hey, Daphne." Elaine hurried over. "Suzie just told me the most *amazing* thing."

"I'll just bet she did," Daphne said dryly as she continued to match the dresses against the list on her clipboard.

"Well," Elaine prodded. "Is that gorgeous blond hunk really your ex-husband?"

"Modesty forbids me to comment on the 'gorgeous' part," said a voice from behind them. "But I *am* her ex-husband."

Daphne turned to face him. "Hello, Adam."

"Hello, Daffy," he said, calling her by the nickname no one else had ever dared use. "It's been a long time."

"Yes," she agreed. And yet, Daphne felt as if it hadn't been any time at all. He was having the same effect on her that he'd always had.

They stood there, silently staring at each other, seemingly oblivious to the models and stagehands swarming around them, even to Elaine, standing wide-eyed by Daphne's elbow.

"So," he said softly, reaching out to gently grasp her shoulders. "Let me look at you." He held her away from him as his eyes ran over her. "You cut your hair."

Whatever she had expected him to say, it hadn't been that.

"Yes," she said again, and before she stopped to think, she reached up and touched the thick lock of blond hair that fell over his forehead. "So did you," she said, smoothing it back with an almost wifely gesture.

She didn't seem to hear his swift intake of breath as wonderingly, she touched the tiny crow's-feet at the corner of his left eye. Her fingers whispered over one of the twin creases that ran from nose to mouth in either lean cheek. His lips had lost that youthful look of vulnerability and sweet sensuality. He had the mouth of a virile, passionate man now; he looked experienced and knowing.

An infinitely more interesting face, Daphne thought again, marveling at the healthy, golden glow of his skin. He looked as much like a Greek god as he ever had, all big and golden and glowing with health.

Suddenly, Daphne became aware of what she was doing. Her hand dropped abruptly to her side. "I'm forgetting my manners," she said, drawing her composure around her like a shawl. "Adam, this is my assistant, Elaine Prescott." She turned. "Elaine, this 'gorgeous hunk'—" her eyebrows arched slightly when Elaine blushed "—is Dr. Adam Forrest."

"Dr. Forrest." Elaine bobbed her head in greeting.

"Call me Adam, please." He smiled at her, and her blush deepened as he released her hand. "Will we see you at the charity dance tonight?"

"Not if she doesn't get busy now, you won't." Daphne broke into the conversation. "I want these dresses covered before we leave," she continued. "And all the jewelry collected and put into the hotel safe. Elaine?" She waved her hand in front of her assistant's face. "Earth to Elaine. Come in, please."

Elaine's eyes refocused. "What? Oh, the dresses. Sure. I'll do it right now." She smiled up at Adam and her usual brand of brashness seemed to return. "Save me a dance, okay, gorgeous?" she quipped, bouncing away.

Adam laughed. "Is she always like that?"

"Oh, no." Daphne's expression was deadpan. "She's just shy because she doesn't know you yet. Wait until she gets warmed up."

"No thanks. I think I'll pass." He sighed. "A kid like that makes me feel about a hundred years old."

"Well, you *have* gotten older," Daphne agreed. "But experience looks good on you."

"On you, too." He smiled and his bright blue eyes ran over her again. "You're even more beautiful than I remembered."

A faint smile curved Daphne's lips. Compliments from the closemouthed Adam, she thought. He had never called her beautiful before, except in bed. Words had always been hard for him.

"Why, Adam," she said lightly. "I didn't know you noticed such things."

He grinned in acknowledgment of her gentle barb. "Are you coming to this charity dance?" he said then.

"I haven't decided yet." Daphne's husky voice was casual, belying the sudden quivering of her stomach.

"What's to decide?" Adam smiled that sleepy, inviting smile of his. "We could have a dance for old times' sake. It'll be fun."

"Well…" Daphne hesitated. It would be more than just fun, it would be…what? Exciting? Thrilling?

Try dangerous, she thought, dangerous and foolish. He still had the power to stir her deepest emotions. Still, she thought, why not? What could it hurt? She wasn't married anymore…but was he?

Her eyes flickered to his left hand. There was no ring but that didn't mean anything.

"Won't your wife object to all these free dances you're passing out?" she said, before she could stop herself.

Adam's eyes captured hers. "I'm not married." There was a brief pause as he tried to read her expression. "Are you?"

Daphne shook her head slowly. "Not anymore." She glanced downward. "I was, but Miles—my husband died three years ago."

"I should say I'm sorry, shouldn't I?" Adam reached out and lifted her chin. Daphne felt his touch sizzle down to her toes. "But I'd be lying."

"Lying?" Daphne echoed.

"I make it a rule never to make love to married women," he explained softly. "And I've suddenly discovered that I want, very much, to make love to you."

"Oh." The single word came out as a whisper. This new, older Adam was certainly full of surprises, she thought. The Adam she once knew would never have said anything like that, especially in a room full of people.

"Well?" he said, his gentle smile mocking both of them. "Am I going to make love to you? With you?" His voice was a husky whisper.

Where had he learned all this, she wondered. His new technique was devastating. "But I thought…" She made a vague gesture. "The charity dance, aren't you supposed to be there? Don't you have a date or—something?"

Adam shook his head. "I came with a large group of people," he told her. "The fashion show was a duty appearance." He grinned. "Actually, Sunny threatened to picket my office if I didn't come. Now, any more excuses?"

"I have to supervise things here. No, really," she added. "There's a fortune in jewelry that has to go in the hotel safe." She paused. "Insurance won't cover it if I keep it in my room."

"You're staying at the hotel?" The words seemed to rasp out of his throat.

"Yes," she said, low. "I always stay here when I'm in town, which is every few months of so. More often, lately." She knew she was babbling, but she couldn't seem to stop. "Business is getting so good, I've been seriously thinking of opening up a West Coast office. It would—"

"Daffy." His fingers pressed her shoulder, silencing her. "When I said I wanted to make love to you, I didn't mean that I was going to throw you down and ravish you the minute we're alone, you know."

Her eyes grew wide. "You didn't?" she said softly.

Adam uttered a strangled sound. "No, I didn't." His free hand came up to grasp her other shoulder gently. "Although I'd like to, I also like to think I've developed more finesse than that. Besides, I'm not so thickheaded that I can't see the idea scares you."

"Oh, no. It—" Daphne began and then stopped, lowering her head to hide the light blush that touched her cheeks.

"All right, it doesn't exactly scare you," he amended. "But it makes you a little nervous, right?"

Daphne nodded.

"Well, it makes me a little nervous, too. Hell, it makes me a lot nervous! It's been quite a shock seeing you again like this without—" he paused "—without any warning. I had no idea that tonight's fashion guru and my ex-wife were one and the same. And I certainly didn't expect—" His hands dropped from her shoulders. He shoved them into his pockets and half turned away from her. "I didn't realize that you'd have such a strong effect on me." He looked up at her then, a sheepish, almost embarrassed expression on his face. "But I'm as hot for you right now as I was when you ran over me with your bicycle," he admitted, his eyes blazing into hers. He was blushing under his tan.

"Adam!" she said softly. She didn't know what else to say. It was how she felt, too, but she'd had the advantage of *knowing* that's the way she would feel if she ever saw him again.

"Daphne!" He mimicked her shocked tone as he stared back at her. Then he shrugged and his chest lifted in a deep sigh. "Maybe we should just forget that...dance," he said. "It's probably better to let sleeping dogs lie."

"I was sort of looking forward to it," Daphne murmured.

Adam paused. "So was I," he said softly, "but—all right," he said like a man casting caution and good sense to the wind. "We'll have that dance. And then maybe we'll go somewhere quiet for a drink. Talk about old times and catch up with each other's lives. How does that sound to you?"

Daphne nodded her approval. "Sounds fine."

"All right, then. Why don't you do whatever it is you have to do and I'll meet you in the main lobby in, say—" he glanced at his watch "—thirty minutes?" Adam hesitated for the barest instant, indecision on his face, and then he cupped Daphne's cheek in his palm and bent his head, touching his lips lightly to hers.

Taken by surprise, Daphne responded as naturally as if there hadn't been eleven years between this kiss and the last one they had shared. What Adam had intended as a brief, experimental meeting of lips turned into something more.

He took fire immediately, molding his palm to the base of

her skull, splaying his fingers through her pale golden-brown hair, taking full possession of her willing mouth.

They stood like that for a few endless seconds, connected only by the heat of their clinging mouths and his hand at the back of her head. It was Adam who broke the kiss, tearing his mouth from hers with difficulty. He pulled back to look down into her face and his eyes had the heavy-lidded, sleepy expression that Daphne recognized as a sign of his desire. Her own eyes, she knew, had probably lightened to gold as they always did when she was aroused.

"Don't keep me waiting, Daffy," Adam said then.

*

DAPHNE STOOD in front of the bathroom mirror in her hotel room, lipstick pencil in hand.

I'm as hot for you right now as I was when you ran over me with your bicycle. Had Adam really said that? And had he meant it?

"Oh, God, I hope so," Daphne said out loud, surprising herself with the fervent sound of her voice. Then "Fool," she said to her reflection. "You're an idiot to even *think* of going to bed with him. The man divorced you, remember?"

She closed her eyes as the memories assailed her. The last— the final—time Adam had kissed her, had loved her, was the night before she was to leave for New York. His lovemaking had been tinged with a barely controlled anger because he didn't want her to go.

"You can design clothes right here in San Francisco," he'd argued. "You *are* designing clothes here. Why do you have to run off to New York?"

She'd tried to explain it to him; a big-name department store had expressed an interest in her designs and she was flying back East to pursue the matter. She'd only be gone for a month or two. Why couldn't he understand? Her career was as important to her as his was to him.

The argument had come to an abrupt halt when he had become impatient, and thus inarticulate. With a strangled oath, he had grabbed her, kissing her into silence, covering her body with his as they sank to the floor of their tiny studio apartment.

Their arguments always ended that way. In bed, with Daphne whimpering and writhing beneath the heated thrust of his golden body, willing to forget her side of the argument and give in. But this time it was too important to her and the next morning she had been on that plane for New York. Her ticket, paid for by the department store, was round-trip with an open return. She had never used it because, one month later, Adam had filed for divorce, charging her with desertion.

And now he has the gall to think I'm going to fall into bed with him, as if nothing had happened!

"If you had any sense at all," she said to her reflection, "you'd lock yourself in this room and forget you ever saw him tonight."

Obviously, though, she didn't have any sense. With another resigned sigh, Daphne scooped up a tiny gold mesh bag as she passed the bed and left the room.

Adam stood by one of the rounded Doric columns near the hotel's impressive front desk. The set of his shoulders was rigid. She had seen him stand exactly that way more times than she could remember, waiting for her. Punctuality had not been one of her virtues in the old days.

"Adam?" Daphne touched his shoulder.

He whirled around. "Daphne," he began. "You're on time," he said disbelievingly.

"Well, don't look so amazed," Daphne's husky voice teased.

As if by mutual consent, they paused just short of the entrance to the ballroom. The dance floor was full to overflowing, music and laughter spilling across the threshold as smiling couples dipped and swayed to the Big Band sound of the orchestra. It was a gay, inviting scene but neither of them made a move to join in.

"Yoo-hoo, Adam! Oh, A-a-a-dam," Sunny McCorkle called out as she danced past in the arms of her husband. One hand fluttered in the direction of the tables. "We're sitting over—" She broke off when she caught sight of Daphne, then her face split with a self-satisfied grin. "Come join us after this dance," she said, giving them a thumbs-up sign.

"I'm beginning to smell a rat," Adam said softly.

"Only just beginning?" Daphne glanced up, eyes twinkling.

Adam considered that. "Didn't someone mention a quiet drink somewhere? *Away* from all this noise and confusion?"

"Yes, I think someone did." Together, they turned and silently, arm in arm, crossed the wide lobby and entered a dimly lit cocktail lounge on the other side.

Adam guided Daphne to one of the tiny tables in the farthest corner of the room, silently signaling to the waitress. "I'll have a Chivas on the rocks," he said when she hurried over to take their order. "Daphne?"

"I'll have a Brandy Alexander, please." She laid her mesh purse on the table. "This is nice," she said to Adam when the waitress had gone. "Cozy and quiet."

"Think we'll be safe here? From that lovely redheaded rat?" Adam grinned at her over the flickering candle flame. "She'll go crazy wondering where we've gone," he said. "You know, you could have knocked me over with a feather when I saw you walk out onto that stage." He fell silent as the waitress set down their drinks. "Biggest damn surprise of my life," he continued when she left. He picked up his drink.

"Well, here's to old times." He paused for just a heartbeat, his glance catching Daphne's over the rim of the glass. "And to new ones," he added softly.

Daphne sucked in her breath. "To new ones," she said diffidently, feeling suddenly like a young girl on her very first date. She stared down into her glass for a moment, then,

"So," she said, determined to break the silence. "Tell me what you've been doing for the past eleven years."

Adam eyed her for a brief moment, then shrugged. "Studying," he said. "Working."

"Be more specific," Daphne ordered.

"After my state boards, I did two years of rotating internship, three years of residency in general surgery, a year in orthopedics, and then, two more years residency in plastic surgery," he said, summarizing eight years of hard work into one sentence.

"All at the same hospital in L.A.?"

"Yes, how did you know?"

Daphne smiled sweetly. "A little rat told me. So…how long have you been back in San Francisco?"

"Almost six months now." His voice sounded hoarse, and he paused to clear it. "A position opened up here on the staff of Children's, Brian McCorkle recommended me and—here I am, back in my old hometown."

"And loving it."

"Yes," he admitted. "There's no place quite like it."

"Hmm," Daphne agreed.

"Why don't we talk about you now?" Adam suggested. "What does it take to become a successful fashion designer?"

"Work, work, and more work. In that order."

"Well, it has obviously paid off," he complimented her. "From what I saw tonight, it looks as if you've become a raging success—"

"Only fair to middlin'," Daphne interrupted.

"Just like you always said you would," he finished. "You didn't stay with that department store very long."

"No," she answered. "Those quilted jackets I was doing for Bloomie's were only a flash in the pan. In one season." She snapped her fingers. "Out the next."

"So what happened?"

"Oh, I got a job with a design house and…learned more there in one month than I had in the whole two years of fashion college. In less than a year I was doing a few designs on my own—under the house name, of course. I did that for almost three years. And then—then Miles and I decided to go into business for ourselves and, well, the rest is history.''

Adam's smile disappeared. ''Miles,'' he said. ''He was your husband.''

''Yes,'' she said softly. ''Poor Miles.'' She sighed.

''I'm sorry, I shouldn't have brought it up.'' Adam's voice was tight. ''It upsets you to talk about it.''

''No, I—'' she began. It didn't upset her in the way Adam meant. It was just that she had never really loved Miles, not in the way she had loved—still loved—Adam. The thought always made her feel a little guilty.

''No, it doesn't upset me to talk about him,'' she assured Adam. ''It's been almost three years since the accident. He was driving up to a friend's place in Connecticut,'' she told him. ''It was a Friday night, very late, and he was hit head-on by a drunk driver. The doctors assured me that he died almost instantly.''

''Daphne, I'm sorry. Sorry, and terribly ashamed.''

''Ashamed? Why?''

''For that crack I made backstage. I had no right dismissing another man's death so...so callously. Even if—*especially* if it would give me something I wanted.''

She reached across the table, covering his hand with hers. ''Please, Adam, don't. I know you didn't mean it.''

He looked up at that, and his hand tightened on hers. She couldn't quite read the message in his eyes. Desire, of course. That had never been far from the surface between them. But there was something else there, too. Relief?

He stood, pulling her to her feet. ''Why don't we go have that dance now? It's time.''

Yes, Daphne thought. *More than time.*

As they reached the threshold of the ballroom the orchestra began a slow, sweet number, and without a pause Adam swung her onto the crowded dance floor. His right hand settled on the small of her back, pulling her close to his body. His left hand reached for hers and their fingers linked, palms touching. He brought her hand to his chest, turning her wrist slightly so that it was resting snugly against the black satin lapels of his jacket.

She moved more fully into Adam's embrace, settling into him without even thinking about it, the way they had always danced together. Her head nestled beneath his chin, her left hand seeking the soft, short hairs at the nape of his neck. The movement caused the wide neckline of her dress to slide down, baring the opposite shoulder, but Daphne didn't notice. She burrowed more deeply into him.

Sighing, his eyes closed, Adam lowered his head to rest his cheek against her hair. The back of his hand pressed against the top of her breast as they swayed to the slow, soft music.

Daphne's eyes closed, too, and her heart began to beat a little faster. She had to make a conscious effort to keep her breathing even. She needn't have bothered. Adam's breath was just as uneven, his heart was beating just as fast.

"Daphne." The word was a caress. A question. "Daphne, look at me." His voice was low, intense with emotion.

Daphne gazed up at him. His eyes were blazing: a bright, burning, scorching blue. It was like looking into a raging inferno of long-suppressed desire. Daphne melted.

"Yes," she said, answering his unspoken question.

Adam stopped dancing, oblivious to the other couples. "When?"

"Now." Daphne's eyes closed again. "Please."

Adam touched his mouth to the exposed curve of her shoulder. Then he led her from the ballroom.

They were still holding hands when they stepped off the elevator on Daphne's floor. Their palms were pressed tightly together, fingers intertwined like two frightened, lovesick teenagers who have finally, irrevocably decided to do something about their feelings for each other.

Only I wasn't this scared the first time, Daphne thought,

taking two steps to every one of Adam's as they hurried down the corridor. *I wasn't this excited. And, oh God, I wasn't nearly this hungry!*

Daphne's room was in shadows, illuminated only by a narrow wedge of light from the bathroom. Before Daphne could even find the light switch, Adam hauled her into his arms.

"Oh, Daphne," she heard him say, just before his mouth found hers in the darkness, claiming it with a savage hunger. She stretched on tiptoe, her mouth answering his, her arms clinging to him.

The thrust of his tongue was almost manic, seeking, searching, as their mouths twisted and turned upon each other. His hands roamed her back while he kissed her, kneading the curves of her spine and shoulders, sizzling over apricot silk as he sought a way to the warm soft skin beneath the dress.

Daphne, too, began seeking bare flesh. Her hands dropped to his neck, whispering over the skin of his nape, and slid under the collar of his evening jacket. With her mouth still sealed tightly to his, she managed to ease the jacket off his shoulders. It dropped, unheeded, to the carpeted floor.

Her arms circled his waist then, as his went back around her, and her hands tugged impatiently at the fabric of his shirt until it came free of his slacks. With a muffled cry, she pressed her palms flat against the smooth bare skin of his lower back, pulling him even more tightly to her.

Obligingly, Adam arched, thrusting his hips forward as he sought the soft cradle of her thighs. But their heights were too disparate for either of them to feel the pressure where they most wanted it. Adam bent his knee, insinuating it between her parted thighs, and slid his hands down to cup her buttocks, lifting her into his aroused body.

Daphne whimpered softly, deep in her throat, and began to move against him. Her hands flexed rhythmically against the bare flesh of his back, her thighs tight against the welcome intrusion of his.

Adam's tongue thrust deeper into her open mouth, blatantly

imitating the more subtle movements of his hips. His hands feathered over her pliant body, frantic now as he looked for a way to get her out of the dress without letting her go. He managed to loosen the belt enough so that it slid to the floor, but that was as far as he could go.

In answer, Daphne withdrew her hands and, in two quick movements, unfastened the small crystal buttons at either wrist. Then, crossing her arms in front of her body, she grasped the elastic waistline, pulled the dress up over her head and dropped four hundred dollars worth of pure silk inside out on the carpet.

"There," she said matter-of-factly. "It's off." She stood before him wearing only a pair of expensive high-heeled shoes, very sheer French panty hose and a strapless bra the color of heavily creamed coffee. Her breasts rose softly above the satin bra, and Adam reached for her again.

But Daphne stepped back, then grasped the end of his bow tie with trembling fingers and tugged it loose. She drew it out from under his collar, tossing it to the floor with one hand, reaching for the topmost button on his shirt with the other.

Adam put his hands on her waist then, over the lace band of her panty hose, as if to steady her. His long hard fingers curved around to the small of her back. His thumbs rested against her hipbones, rotating slowly.

Daphne gasped softly but continued with her task. At last it was done and she slipped her hands under the shirt.

So soft, she thought. *So warm. So exactly as her hands remembered him!*

She straightened her fingers, threading them up through the tangle of silky hair on his chest and then down again, until she could feel one hard male nipple against the center of each sensitive palm. She sighed deeply, savoring the feel of the man she had thought she would never touch again.

Adam's hands slid up her back and deftly released the clasp of her bra. She lifted her arms from her sides, letting the bra fall away from her body. Her breasts were full and firm and aching, the nipples pale brown and hard as little pebbles, puckered tightly with desire. She moved forward until her breasts were touching his chest, until the little golden whorls of hair were tickling her sensitive skin.

Adam crushed her to him, his mouth taking hers in a quick hard kiss that seemed designed to brand her lips with his passion. Then he lifted and carried her across to the bed.

Daphne's shoes hit the carpet with soft little thumps. Then Adam laid her gently on the turned-down bed and straightened up to remove the rest of his clothes.

Daphne half sat up, intending to shimmy out of her panty hose, but Adam bent over her, gloriously naked now, and pressed her back into the pale green sheets. Hooking trembling hands in the waistband of her one remaining garment, he drew them past her hips and down her legs. Standing there beside the bed, her panty hose dangling inside out from one hand, he gazed down at her.

His eyes made a visual feast of her ankles and calves and smooth creamy thighs, leaving ripples of sensation fluttering across the softly rounded belly, and the full, taut breasts that rose and fell with each quick breath.

Daphne, lying so still under his heated gaze, was making a survey of her own, taking inventory, remembering...

His legs and arms were still corded with the long, lean muscles of a regular runner, still dusted with that sprinkling of soft blond hair. His shoulders were still those of a football player, his chest still deep and broad. Avidly, her eyes starved for the sight of him, she followed the narrowing arrow of chest hair down the flat-muscled wall of his stomach to where it widened again. He was full and hard and straining eagerly toward her.

Her eyes skittered back to his face and found his eyes waiting. They stared at each other for a full thirty seconds without saying a word.

"You're so damn beautiful," he said finally.

"So are you." Daphne lifted her arms, opening her body to his. "Now," she whispered huskily. "Please."

He came to her in one swift movement, thrusting forward into her willing moistness. Her body arched as he entered her, both of them moaning in satisfaction as he buried himself deep inside her. He pressed his hips down and forward, trying to hold her still as he fought for the control that her eagerness had taken from him. But Daphne continued to move, her legs wrapping around his waist, her hips bucking rhythmically under his.

"Daphne." His voice was ragged, breathless. "Oh, baby, slow down. I…" His hands slid down her torso to hold her. "I'll be too fast for you if you don't slow down."

"No." She panted. "No, you won't…not this time…" She pressed her nails into the hard curve of his buttocks. "Oh, Adam, *please*," she urged.

Assured that he wasn't going to leave her wanting, Adam slipped his hands under her hips, fitting her body even more closely to his, and began to move. His hips pumped strongly against her. One minute…two, and then Daphne's body stiffened like an overstrung bow and she gave a low moan of ecstatic pleasure that was echoed a moment later by a deep cry from Adam.

It took several long minutes for their breathing to slow to near normal and several more before Adam reluctantly raised his head from the warm sweet space between her neck and shoulder. He stared down into her eyes and the look that passed between them was somehow hesitant, almost shy.

Well, Daphne thought, *what do you say to an ex-husband when you find yourself in bed with him after a separation of eleven years?*

Before she could come up with a suitable answer, Adam lifted himself from her body and rolled over onto his back. He lay beside her, silent and still, not touching, as if waiting for her to speak first.

Daphne turned her head and found him staring at her in the darkness. His eyes seemed to reflect every bit of the confusion she felt, but in the dim light, she couldn't be sure.

"Daphne, I—" he began.

His words were cut off by a series of sharp staccato beeps. They both jumped as if a whip had been cracked over their nude bodies and then Adam jackknifed to his feet. "Damn beeper!" He scooped his tuxedo up off the floor, found the small rectangular metal box and shut it off.

"I'm sorry." He gestured at the beeper in his hand, his expression registering something that looked suspiciously like relief. Daphne recognized it because she felt it, too.

"Probably the hospital," he said then, sitting on the edge of the rumpled bed with his back to her. He switched on the bedside lamp and reached for the phone. "I have to call my service," he mumbled. "Could be an emergency."

Daphne nodded and scurried under the covers, listening to his side of the phone conversation.

"Umm-hmm. When?" he said into the phone. His voice was cool, professional. "How long has she been complaining of pain?" He found his white jockey shorts and, phone wedged between his ear and shoulder, used both hands to pull them on. "Umm-hmm. No, I realize she can be difficult to deal with, and I left instructions to call me if— No, you didn't interrupt anything important. Fifteen minutes." He dropped the receiver into the cradle. Now he was zipping up his slacks.

"That was one of the hospitals," he said unnecessarily. "One of my patients seems to be experiencing some unusual pain after an abdominal tuck. I don't want to take any chances." He sat down again to put on his shoes and socks. "I hope you understand."

"Yes, of course," she said, understanding only that he couldn't get out of the room fast enough.

Dressed now, Adam leaned across the width of the bed and touched Daphne's shoulder. "I'm sorry about this, Daffy. About leaving you like this right after..." He hesitated, not knowing what to say.

Daphne stopped him. "It's okay," she said. "I really do understand. Duty calls."

"Maybe we could get together for lunch tomorrow," he suggested. Rather halfheartedly, Daphne thought.

She didn't want any part of any "mercy lunches." *You didn't interrupt anything important.* "I don't think so," she stated.

"But—"

"No, really, I can't." She forced herself to smile. "I have to catch an early plane home tomorrow." She slid from the bed, wrapping the bedspread around her as she rose. She pulled open the door, shielding her half-clad body behind it. "Well, it's been lovely seeing you again, Adam," she went on. "We must do it again sometime."

Adam hesitated for a moment, then tossing his tuxedo jacket over his shoulder, he strolled toward Daphne. He stopped at the open door and lifted her chin with his free hand. Daphne clutched the bedspread tighter.

"Give me a call next time you're in town and we will," he suggested, dropping a quick, careless kiss on her astonished mouth before he left.

*

"MRS. GRANGER, you have a call on line one," Elaine's assistant shouted across the busy workroom.

Daphne's head snapped up at the words, a half panicked, half inquiring look skittering over her face.

"It's Mrs. McCorkle," the girl added, as Elaine picked up a couple of Daphne's sketches to study them.

The panic receded instantly. "Sunny, you traitor!" Daphne said without preamble as soon as she picked up the phone. "I ought to strangle you! If you were here right now I *would!*"

"It's nice to hear from you, too," Sunny said cheerfully.

"The lowest, sneakiest trick you've ever pulled," Daphne accused. "You *knew* Adam was at Children's Hospital. You *knew* he was going to be at that charity benefit. Why didn't you tell me?"

"Oh, is *that* what this is all about?" Sunny's voice was innocence itself. "If I'd had any idea that just *seeing* him again was going to upset you this much I would have said something."

"I am not upset."

"Whatever," Sunny agreed absently. "So, listen—the reason I called is to invite you to a party next week. Now before you say no, Daphne," she hurried on, "remember that you did tell me you'd be back in town then. That meeting at I. Magnin. And as long as you're going to be here anyway, why not come to our party? It'll be a real hoot! All the old gang's coming."

"Adam, too, I suppose?" Daphne interrupted.

"Well, of course! It's his party."

"I thought it was your party."

"Well, I'm *giving* it," Sunny said patiently. "But it's *for* Adam. His thirty-seventh birthday, remember? It's sort of a welcome home, too, to San Francisco. Brian thought—"

"And you expect me to come?" Daphne could hardly believe her ears.

"Well, yes. That's exactly what I expect." Sunny paused. "Oh, come on, Daphne. I know you're terribly busy and everything, and this trip to San Francisco is business, but it would be so much fun if you could make it. Say you'll at least *try* to stop by?"

Daphne, realizing that she had been manipulated by a master, said she'd try. "But don't count on it," she warned.

"Terrific!" Sunny squealed. "See you on the twenty-eighth. And wear something drop-dead sexy," she ordered, hanging up before Daphne could remind her that she'd only said she'd *try* to make it.

That Sunny, she thought. Well, she had no intention of going to Adam's birthday party. Why ask for trouble? That night with Adam had been a mistake. But with him right there in the flesh, she hadn't really cared.

Well, now she cared. Because now it hurt. And now she

missed him as deeply as she had eleven years ago. For the past week, she had been weaving crazy, impossible dreams.

No, she told herself. *No, I'm not going to that party.*

"I think you should go." Elaine's words made Daphne start with surprise.

She looked over her shoulder, realizing that Elaine was only responding to the conversation she had overheard and not answering Daphne's unspoken comment. "Oh, you do, do you?" she said.

"Yes, I do," Elaine stated. "And if you promise not to bite my head off, I'll tell you why."

"I have a feeling I'm not going to like this," Daphne said. "But go ahead." She cocked her head, forearm resting against the edge of the drawing board. "Why should I go?"

"Because…" Elaine paused then rushed ahead. "Because, ever since he kissed you," she said, "you've been moping around like some lovesick teenager, that's why. You practically jump out of your skin every time the phone rings. You're irritable and cranky. You snap at people for no reason."

"I know I haven't been a joy to be around lately," she admitted. "But I *don't* know how you think my going to Adam's little party is going to change things. The way I see it, it will only make it worse."

"No. Just think about it a minute," Elaine urged. "If you stay away from him you'll think about him all the more. But if you go out to California, see him again, even have an affair, maybe… Well—it'll give you a chance to get him out of your system. See? And you'll probably realize that your relationship wasn't as good as you remembered."

"My God, Elaine," Daphne said. "How do you know so much?"

"Well, Suzie told me what you'd told her," she admitted.

"No, I didn't mean that," Daphne murmured. "I meant how did you know…" She shook her head as if to clear it, then smiled. "Do you think you could stand taking care of my cats for a couple of days?" she asked.

"You're going, then?"

"Yes," Daphne said decisively. "Yes, I'm going."

DAPHNE'S RESOLVE wasn't quite so firm as she sat in her rented LeBaron, trying to work up the nerve to go in.

It looked like a fairly big party, she thought, eyeing the cars that lined both sides of the steep street for half a block in either direction. *Oh, come on,* she scolded herself. *There's nothing to be afraid of. Be brave,* she told herself, her fingers fussing with the red satin ribbon on Adam's birthday gift.

After much thought, she had decided on a one-pound box of gourmet chocolate chunk cookies; soft and chewy and rich with Hawaiian macadamia nuts. They were homey without being homemade, extravagant without being expensive, friendly without being intimate. And they said absolutely nothing about how she felt.

After all, *she* might have come to San Francisco with the idea of starting up an affair with her ex-husband as a way to get him out of her system for good, but there was no telling what he might have in mind.

Daphne finally got out of the car and, mindful of the height of her heels, carefully made her way up the steep incline of the street and the even steeper angle of the stairs, to the front door. Taking one last deep breath, she rang the doorbell.

"I'll get it!" A high-pitched, childish voice rang out.

"*I'll* get it," another, older voice said. The door was yanked open. "You go back upstairs before I blister your rear," Sunny threatened cheerfully, shooing the oldest of her three children back up the wide stairs.

"Daphne!" she cried, swooping to enfold her in a Giorgio-scented hug. "You look great! Elegant as all get-out, dammit!" she exclaimed, taking in Daphne's loosely belted ivory silk big shirt and shiny, formfitting brown leather pants.

"I'm so glad you came," she said. "I knew you would." She turned her head, speaking over the noise of the stereo. "Brian, come look who's here. It's Daphne."

He ambled over to greet her.

"Daphne, honey," he said warmly, as he leaned down to kiss her. "It's good to see you again. Where've you been keeping yourself?"

Daphne returned his kiss warmly. "New York, mostly." She answered him literally, her eyes darting past his shoulder to the crowded room beyond. Adam wasn't anywhere to be seen. "Dallas and L.A. during the markets. And San Francisco every month or so." She grinned up at him. "You're just never around when I drop by."

"That's because nobody ever tells me when you're dropping by," he grumbled good-naturedly.

Sunny ignored his teasing. "I'm going to take Daphne into the living room and reintroduce her to everyone," she stated.

Daphne wandered from group to group after that, reacquainting herself with the friends of her carefree, radical youth. The music throbbing from the stereo was from that era, too, an eclectic mix of the Rolling Stones, Steppenwolf, the Beatles, the Beach Boys, Dylan, the Righteous Brothers, Peter, Paul and Mary.

"Oh, and do you remember that 'Save the Otters' march? The one Carl arranged. It rained all over us, remember?"

"...that time Sunny chained herself to the door of the student union building and then lost the keys to the handcuffs and the janitor had to saw them off her."

"...Daphne was marching down Market Street in the feminists' Sunrise Protest. Remember how she hit that cameraman with her sign and ended up on the six o'clock news?"

Laughter, including Daphne's own, filled the air.

"Adam got so mad I thought he'd bust a gut," another voice said.

Yes, Adam, Daphne thought. Where was he?

"I called the hospital a few minutes ago," Brian told them. "They said he was still in surgery—"

There was a unanimous groan.

"So we're going to go ahead and eat without him—"

Good-natured cheers filled the air.

"No one had better lay a finger on that cake, though," Sunny warned. "We're not cutting it until Adam gets here."

Everyone trooped toward the laden dining room table, filling their plates with triangles of shrimp toast, steamed pearl balls, finger-size egg rolls, five spice chicken, sweet and sour pork and fluffy boiled rice. Chinese food used to be Adam's absolute favorite, Daphne remembered, reaching for a plate. Apparently, it still was.

"IF EVERYBODY'S finished eating, let's push back the furniture and dance." Sunny picked up her plate with one hand and reached across for Daphne's with the other. "I'll just take a few of these things out to the kitchen first. You all start moving the furniture."

Daphne rose as some of the others began to do as Sunny had suggested, and approached a young woman who had earlier been defending the practice of vivisection. "I know this sounds like a line from an old movie," she began, smiling, "but don't I know you?"

"You used to," the younger woman said. She paused, a cool unfriendly smile on her lips. "I'm Marcia Forrest."

"Oh, my God, of course! Marcia. No wonder you looked so familiar." *And are so unfriendly,* Daphne thought. Adam's baby sister had never liked Adam's wife. "The last time I saw you, you were what? Twelve? Thirteen?"

"Thirteen," Marcia acknowledged.

"So, what are you up to these days?"

"I'm in my second year of medical school at UC San Francisco. I intend to specialize in cardiovascular surgery. Surgery on the heart," she added, as if Daphne might not know what it was.

"How…admirable. Adam must be very proud of you," Daphne said sincerely.

"Yes, I believe he is," Marcia said.

"Well, it was nice talking to you again but I—think I'll just go see if Sunny needs any help.'' She hurried off to the kitchen.

"Marcia Forrest certainly has a charming bedside manner, doesn't she?'' Daphne said a few minutes later, as she helped Sunny load the dishwasher.

"The original Miss Iceberg,'' the redhead agreed dryly.

"And Gracie and Art? How are they?'' Daphne asked, referring to Adam's parents. "As I remember, they weren't all that crazy about me, either.'' Her eyebrows quirked upward. "I'm sure they thought I was going to lead their future doctor away from the straight and narrow.''

"They're fine, too, as far as I know,'' Sunny told her. "Still living in the old neighborhood, even though Adam was all prepared to buy them a big new house. But they did accept a trip to Hawaii last summer. As an anniversary present.''

"That must have made Adam happy.''

"Tickled him pink,'' Sunny agreed, turning on the dishwasher. She leaned back against the kitchen counter.

"Do you know,'' she said, "this is the first time I've ever heard you willingly mention Adam's name since the divorce.''

"Is it?''

"Yes,'' Sunny said softly. "Why is that, I wonder?''

"Because,'' Daphne replied firmly, "this will be the first time I've seen him since the divorce. Well, not counting the, uh, charity thing. Since he's…back in the Bay Area now I'll probably run into him once in a while. Here, anyway and…it's only sensible to try to be civil.''

"Hmm'' was all Sunny would say. Then she cocked her head slightly, listening. "Well, you'd better prepare to be civil. I think I hear Adam's voice.''

Daphne followed her friend out of the kitchen, hanging back as Sunny hurried up to greet her latest guest, watching as Adam kissed Sunny's proffered cheek.

He laughed at something she said, his eyes crinkling up at the corners, and extended his hand toward Brian. Then he moved away from the door to greet Marcia with a brief, brotherly hug.

"I take it you knew about this little surprise," he said.

Marcia nodded. "Of course. How else do you think I could make sure that Ginny would get you here?"

"So, Ginny was in on this, too, hmm?" He glanced back over his shoulder. "Well, come here and take your medicine, woman." He circled the shoulders of a small, dark-haired woman. Laughing, she stood at his side. As he turned back to his sister, he caught sight of Daphne.

He went stock-still for a moment, his eyes on hers as the quick color came and went in his face, but Daphne wasn't looking at him. She was looking, instead, at the woman who stood so securely in the circle of his arm. She was, Daphne thought despairingly, quite lovely.

Daphne felt all her plans go down the drain. It just hadn't occurred to her that Adam—*her* Adam—might have another woman. Not after the night in her hotel room.

Her eyes lifted to his face then, a half-accusing expression in their golden-brown depths. *Well, don't worry,* she telegraphed silently, her pride stung. *I want to keep that night a secret, too.*

What happened next was that Daphne smiled, a lovely, utterly false smile, and crossed the room to him. "Happy birthday, Adam," she said evenly, extending her right hand as she spoke.

He took her hand. "Thank you," he answered, his voice just as even.

And then their hands dropped back to their sides and they stood there like two people who had never been more than casual friends.

"Aren't you going to introduce Ginny to Daphne?" Marcia prompted.

"What?" He shook his head slightly as if coming out of a trance and met his sister's eyes. "Oh, sure. Sure."

The two women nodded at each other, exchanging cool smiles, neither sure of the status of the other in Adam's life.

Marcia was quick to fill in the gaps. "Ginny is a nurse. The best OR nurse he's ever worked with, Adam says."

"Yes." He gave Ginny's shoulders a halfhearted little squeeze and dropped his arm. "The best," he added.

"They've been a team practically since the day Adam started at Children's. And—"

"Marcia, please," Ginny interrupted. "You're making me blush."

"Sorry," Marcia said, but she didn't look sorry.

"Well, it's been lovely to meet you, Ginny," Daphne said then. "But, if you'll excuse me, I have to find Sunny and say my goodbyes."

"You're not leaving already?" Marcia's tone was victorious.

"'Fraid so. I've got an early meeting at I. Magnin tomorrow," she lied. "And, unfortunately, I need to go over my presentation one more time."

Sunny came hurrying up to stop her. "You're not leaving already?" she said, meaning it. She glanced up at Adam. "Not when the guest of honor just got here."

"'Fraid so," she said again. "I really have to be going."

The two women exchanged a quick, warm hug. "Drive carefully," Sunny admonished.

"I will." She raised her eyes to Adam's one last time. "Happy birthday," she said and hurried out.

DAPHNE WAS wide-awake when the first pale fingers of sunlight started to pry their way into her hotel room. She lay on her back on the double bed and stared up at the ceiling, eyes dry now, thinking about the night before.

She was *glad*, she told herself fiercely, that Adam had come to Sunny's party with another woman. It had kept her from making a complete fool of herself.

Elaine had suggested that she be up-front. "Just say 'Listen,

Adam, I enjoyed the other night, let's do it again soon.' He'll take it from there.''

But Daphne couldn't have said anything like that in a million years. What she'd had in mind was more subtle. Invite him out for a birthday drink, maybe, and then let nature take its course. Yet, both alternatives sounded so calculating and Daphne was a woman who had always expressed her emotions more spontaneously. Well, it was a moot point now. Blinking back tears she sat up and reached for the telephone. She would leave San Francisco on the first available flight. Elaine could fly out and handle her accounts.

The phone rang just as Daphne put her hand on it.

"Hello?" she said, after three rings.

"Daffy? It's Adam. Did I wake you?"

"No. No, you didn't wake me," she said, startled to hear from him after spending all night thinking about the man. It was almost as if she had conjured him up.

"Well, I thought...we didn't get much of a chance to visit last night. And I thought you might have time for breakfast before your business meeting."

"Meeting?" Daphne said, forgetting that had been her excuse to leave the party. Comprehension dawned. "Oh, the meeting at I. Magnin. Yes, well, it's not for several hours yet." Actually, it wasn't until Monday. "But I—"

"Then you're free for breakfast," Adam said eagerly. "You stay where you are. I'll be right up."

"Up?" she squeaked. "You mean you're in the hotel?"

"At a house phone in the lobby."

"Fine, then you stay—" she began, intending to say that she'd come down. But he had hung up on the word "fine."

Oh, my God, she thought. She wasn't dressed, hadn't combed her hair, and her eyes were all red from crying half the night.

She snatched her velour robe off the floor by the bed and stepped into it, then hurried toward the bathroom. *Lord, what a mess,* she thought, peering at herself in the mirror. She brushed her teeth first and then scooped handfuls of cold water over her face.

Better, she decided, *but not good enough.*

There was a sharp rap on the door.

Daphne started, smearing lip gloss all across one cheek. "Just a minute," she called, and yanked a tissue from the dispenser.

There was another rap on the door.

"Damn." She threw the lip brush down in exasperation, seeing how little improvement it made. Waving a dismissive hand at her image, she left the bathroom.

Another rap, louder and more impatient.

"I'm coming!" *Impatient as ever,* she thought, as she opened the door.

"Adam," she began brightly and then stopped.

He was dressed the way she had always liked best, casually, in faded jeans, a dark periwinkle-blue turtleneck that intensified the color of his eyes and enhanced the golden glow of his skin, and a Sam Spade trench coat with the collar turned up. Standing there with a paper sack in one hand, he quite literally took her breath away.

Oh, Adam!

"May I come in?"

"Please do." Daphne inclined her head and stepped back to allow him entrance.

He set the paper sack down on the small round table at the window and opened it, releasing the fragrant aroma of coffee. "Do you still like raspberry Danish?"

"You've got raspberry Danish in there, too?"

"Sure." He held a cup of coffee toward her. "Coffee's no good without something to dunk in it." He pried the lid off a second cup. "Here. A raspberry Danish for you." He handed it to her. "A cinnamon roll for me and—" he pulled out two more plastic cups "—orange juice for both of us. Well, come on, sit down."

Adam shrugged out of his trench coat, draping it across the

back of the chair, and sat down, too, pretending interest in his cinnamon roll. "About the other night," he said.

"Last night?" She frowned.

"No. The night of Sunny's charity thing."

"Oh. *That* other night." Daphne forced herself to hold his eyes. "What about it?"

"I wanted to apologize."

Daphne sipped her coffee. "For what?" she asked.

"For leaving so abruptly like that. I didn't...I mean, it wasn't—polite," he said finally.

Not polite, she thought, wondering if that's all that was bothering him; a breach in the etiquette of brief sexual encounters. "Well, don't worry about it," she said lightly. "You had an emergency, so you're excused." She gave him a false, brittle smile. "Feel better now?"

"No." The words were intense. "I didn't want to leave you that night." He put his hand on her arm. "I wanted to stay and make love to you again. Slowly, all night long. In every way possible." Daphne began to feel faint. "I still want to," he said quietly.

Daphne eased her arm out from under his hand. "You didn't call," she accused, surprising herself. It was the last thing she had intended to say.

Adam let her pull away. "I wanted to." He ran his hand through his hair. "But I thought it would be better—for both of us—if I didn't. We've got separate lives now," he went on, half to himself. "*Successful* lives," he emphasized, "on separate coasts. And it's been eleven years." He looked up, his eyes faintly accusing. "I actually thought I was over wanting you," he amended. "But you're like a..." He shook his head. "Like a drug to me, Daphne. All I have to do is see you again and I ache like a sixteen-year-old boy who hasn't had his first woman." He took a deep breath. "Why the *hell* did you have to come back here?"

"Because I ache for you, too," she said simply.

She knew that it was probably unwise to admit how she

felt. But it must have been hard for him to lay his feelings out in the open and so, she could be no less open about hers.

"You, too?" Adam's hand tentatively touched hers.

"Me, too." She lifted her hand, palm toward him, and let him lace his fingers with hers. "After that night I couldn't get you out of my mind. Couldn't forget how good it had been." His fingers tightened. She squeezed back. "I told myself it would be best if we didn't see each other again. But then Sunny called and invited me to your birthday party and I thought 'Why not?' We're both adults now. We could be friends. Lots of exes are. Right?"

Adam nodded slowly, his expression wary.

Oh, hell! Who am I trying to kid, she thought.

She straightened and pulled her hand from his. "No, that's not true." She laced her fingers together on the table. "The truth is," she said, "that I decided to come to Sunny's party to start an affair with you."

"What?" Adam's blue eyes opened wide.

She met his eyes straight on. "I thought that would be the way to get you out of my system. I mean, this intense…*thing* we seem to have for each other would have to fizzle out sooner or later and—"

"It hasn't fizzled in eleven years."

"No, but I think that's because of the way it ended. We parted still wanting each other physically, even though the emotions were gone." *On your part, anyway,* she added silently. "And I thought, if we had an affair it might, uh, might—"

"Get me out of your system for good," he finished for her. His tone was tinged with hurt but Daphne didn't notice.

She nodded, forgetting that she had spent most of last night deciding that *nothing* would get Adam out of her system for good. "Yes." She smiled ruefully. "Do I sound crazy?"

"Maybe. But if you're crazy, then so am I."

"Huh?" Daphne lifted her brows inquiringly.

"I think we should have an affair," he elaborated.

"Oh."

They both fell silent, picking at their respective pastries.

Daphne spoke up after a minute. "Well," she said a bit breathlessly. "Should we start now?"

"What about your appointment at I. Magnin?" Adam asked.

She paused, considering. "There isn't one," she said. "Well, there *is,* but not until Monday."

"You mean you lied?"

"I didn't *lie.*" Daphne said. "I just rearranged the facts a little."

"Why did you feel it necessary?"

"Because you came to Sunny's party with that—friend of yours."

"Ginny? What's Ginny got to do with it?"

"Because, when I realized that you and Ginny were a couple my little plan for…an affair suddenly didn't seem to be too smart. The 'other woman' is *not* a role I'm interested in playing. Even for you." *Oh, no! Had she really said that?* "Satisfied?"

"No." Adam took her chin in his hand. "Ginny and I are not a couple," he said, eyes blazing into hers. "If we were I wouldn't be here. Is that clear?"

"Yes, Adam," she replied meekly, something inside her flaming into sudden joy. *Ginny and I are not a couple!* Had he ever said seven more beautiful words to her?

"Good." His hand caressed her throat. "Now, if that's settled, can we get back to what we were doing?"

A slow grin spread over Daphne's face. "Breakfast?"

Adam shook his head, his lips set in an answering grin. "There's the little matter of our affair. I thought we'd start with, say, a little heavy necking." He led her over to the bed. "A bit of serious petting, then—"

Daphne's stomach growled loudly. "Just ignore it," she advised, reaching up to pull his head down to hers.

Their lips touched.

Daphne's stomach growled again.

Adam sighed. "Come on, get up." He stood, pulling her to her feet. "I refuse to make love to a woman whose stomach is growling at me."

"But, Adam," Daphne began.

He stopped her words with a quick, hard kiss. "The next time I make love to you, Daffy," he said, "it's going to take a good long time. Not ten minutes like the other night. Hours," he promised gruffly. "I intend to savour every luscious inch of you and I don't want you fainting from hunger right in the middle of it. So…" He released her with a last quick kiss on the end of her nose. "You go get dressed and I'll take you out for a real breakfast. Okay?"

"Okay," she said reluctantly.

She showered quickly, then washed and styled her short hair in less than twenty minutes. Her makeup took almost no time. A dab of sheer ivory foundation, a dusting of peachy blusher, was all her complexion needed to make it glow.

She had never looked better in her life, she thought. That's what love did for a woman. It made her sparkle as if she were lit from inside by a thousand candles.

She had loved Adam since she was seventeen years old. And had continued loving him, in absentia so to speak, since she was twenty. What if he set her adrift again before she was ready? And he would, she told herself, staring wide-eyed at the woman in the mirror. That had to be faced up front. Because Adam would eventually get her "out of his system" and she would be left alone again, still loving him.

"So what else is new?" she murmured. She had survived it then—and even gone on to make a success of her life—she would survive it when it happened again. As it surely would. But until then…she would enjoy every minute of every day with him and not think about the future. They were going to have a glorious affair. Simply glorious!

*

"UH-HUH. Yes, got it." Daphne sat in one of Adam's velveteen, padded dining room chairs, her bare feet propped on another one, rapidly making notes as she listened to the voice on the phone.

Adam's invitation to stay with him during her next trip to San Francisco had turned into almost six weeks of conducting her business on a transcontinental basis. She was getting very good at it.

"Yes, the sketches arrived in perfect condition. No problems. Umm-hmm. Well, maybe you'd better double-check that."

She pushed a huge marmalade cat off her notepad and then relented, idly scratching him behind the ears.

"And the shelter people were pleased with the fundraiser?" she said. "That's great, Elaine. You did a fine job," she congratulated her assistant warmly.

She paused for a moment, listening. "This coming Monday," she answered. "Flight 487…no, I'll take a taxi…plenty of time," she said airily. "Mr. Chan isn't due until Wednesday. You can hold the fort for three more days, can't you?" She smiled to herself. "Yes, I thought so. Oh, and tell Hiram—" Hiram was her lawyer "—that I'm sending him a copy of a partnership agreement I'd like him to look over."

"A partnership agreement?" Elaine said carefully.

"Uh-huh." Daphne smiled at the gray Persian who sat on the opposite end of the table cleaning herself. "It's about time I gave you a piece of the action, don't you think?"

Elaine's voice rose. "You mean you're making me a partner?"

"Not a *full* partner," Daphne warned. "Just twenty percent to start and—"

"Twenty percent! Of Night Lights?"

Daphne chuckled. "What else have I got twenty percent of to give away? Anyway, you've earned it."

"Oh, Daphne, I don't know what to say. I—"

"Well, don't say anything," Daphne advised. "I haven't got time to listen to you. Sunny'll be here any minute and I've got to get some of this mess straightened up before I leave or Adam's housekeeper will have a fit." She hung up before Elaine could say another word.

"Go on, Queenie," she said, shooing the gray cat off the table. "You're in my way."

Quickly, she straightened the sketches and notepads spread out across Adam's dining room table, sorting them into haphazard piles according to size. She picked up a coffee mug and a plate, leaving the dishes in the sink for Mrs. Drecker to do when she came in, then Daphne hurried back down the hall to the bedroom.

No longer excessively tidy and impersonal—except after Mrs. Drecker had just left—the bedroom definitely looked lived in, especially with three cats sprawled across the middle of the unmade king-size bed.

Daphne claimed long-term kinship with two of them; Queenie, the aloof gray Persian, and Mack, the fat orange marmalade so named because of his resemblance to a truck, were strays that had taken up residence in her New York apartment years ago. She had brought them with her on her last bi-coastal trip at Adam's urging. It had taken them less than a week to settle into his house, and now they treated it as their own.

The third drowsing feline was a half-grown kitten, christened Tiger, who had wandered up the front walk one foggy night recently, begging for food. He had been fed and offered shelter for the night and had decided to stay.

"Don't bother to get up, guys," Daphne said, rummaging around in the closet among the "few clothes" that were taking up more and more of Adam's rack space. She was trying to find something that would be appropriate for both office hunting and a protest march. Nothing seemed quite right.

She finally settled on a pair of pleated-front, straight-legged camel slacks, a loose ivory silk shirt and a camel Shaker sweater in case the May weather turned breezy. She was just stepping into a pair of low-heeled pumps when the doorbell rang.

"Ah, Mrs. Drecker. Finally," she muttered, as she hurried toward the front door.

It wasn't Mrs. Drecker. "Oh, Sunny, come on in. I was hoping it was the cleaning lady. She's late." She held out her arms to the toddler who was clutching the neckline of Sunny's T-shirt. "Hello, Mollie, me darlin'. How's my favorite red-head?"

The child changed hands willingly. "Mack," she said.

"Right this way." Daphne nuzzled Mollie's neck. "Come on to the bedroom. I haven't quite finished dressing."

"Isn't that a little, um, elegant for a protest?" Sunny said.

"That's just what I was wondering." Daphne set Mollie down on the bed. "It's been years since I've been to one so I wasn't sure what the current mode of dress is," she said, taking in Sunny's olive-green corduroy pants, camouflage T-shirt and Nike running shoes. A tomato-red cashmere sweater was tied around her waist and a diamond the size of a small ice cube graced her left hand. Her inch-long nails matched the sweater.

"Is that what every well-dressed radical is wearing these days? Camouflage and cashmere?"

"What? This old thing?" Sunny picked up a sleeve of her sweater. "Strictly utilitarian."

Daphne snorted and turned toward the mirror to fasten a pair of thin gold chains around her neck. "I guess I'll stick with what I've got on," she said, slipping small gold hoops into her pierced ears. "Besides—I've got to look at some of-fice space this afternoon."

Sunny pounced on that. "Office space? Are you finally moving Night Lights here?"

"No," she replied, but that's *exactly* what she was thinking of doing—if things worked out the way she hoped.

She and Adam had been getting along very well these past

six weeks; their relationship was calmer than it had been eleven years ago. More adult. Adam had mellowed nicely and she had become much less volatile. They had both grown up. They were careful of each other's feelings. Solicitous of each other's opinions. Why, they hadn't had one argument.

Was that normal? she wondered.

"So why are you looking for an office?" Sunny prompted.

"Because I've been spending more and more time in San Francisco—" she paused "—*over the last year or so.*" She emphasized the last few words but if anything, Sunny's know-it-all grin got wider.

"All right, you can just wipe that smug, silly look off your face, Elizabeth McCorkle," Daphne said sternly. "I've been thinking about opening a branch office out here for the last six months at least."

"Uh-huh," Sunny snorted.

"Well, I have! I have as many customers here as I do in New York, if not more. In fact, my line sells better in California than it does anywhere else. And it's much closer to Hong Kong," she said. "So it will save me time and money in the long run. On freight and…so forth."

"Uh-huh."

"Well, dammit, I can't just keep spreading my stuff all over Adam's house," Daphne said. "Mrs. Drecker is threatening to quit."

"Whatever." Sunny waved a manicured hand dismissively and sat down on the edge of the unmade bed. "Is it really so hard to admit that you're still crazy in love with Adam and you'd give your eyeteeth to be married to him again?"

Daphne sank down on the bed beside her friend. "If only it were that simple!"

"Why isn't it that simple? You love Adam. Adam loves you. Ergo, wedding bells."

"Ergo, nothing. Yes, I love Adam. I've always loved Adam. And he loves me…but that's not the point."

"So what is?"

"The point is, when Adam and I got married it was because I talked him into it. Remember? I wouldn't listen to any of his arguments against it. We were too young, too different. We'd be poor. But I thought nothing mattered except that we loved each other. I'm ashamed to admit it but I even tried using sex to get my way."

Sunny's brown eyes brightened. "Is that what finally did the trick?"

"In a way." Daphne laughed softly, remembering. "Adam always thought that he shouldn't have been sleeping with me in the first place. I was only seventeen when we met, remember? And still pure as the driven snow. I think he felt guilty about leading me down the path to wickedness." Her eyes sparkled gleefully. "Completely forgetting that the first time I practically had to push him into bed." She gave a little shrug. "Anyway, when I threatened to cut him off until he married me, he said he thought abstinence was a good idea." She giggled. "And then I spent the next three days convincing him it wasn't."

"Sounds like fun."

"Mack gone," Mollie said mournfully, standing up on the bed to lean against her mother's shoulder.

"How did that get you married?" Sunny asked.

"When Adam realized that we couldn't keep our hands off each other, we decided to elope. You know the rest." She shook her head slightly, as if to clear it. "Anyway, this new relationship is sort of a...a trial," she said, putting it into words for the first time.

"What?" Sunny's start of surprise sent Mollie tumbling back against the bed. "You mean like a trial marriage? And Adam agreed? Old conservative Adam?"

"We're doing it, aren't we?" Daphne responded. "We both agree that there's something, uh, special between us," she said then, trying to explain it to herself as well. "So we're taking this time to find out what it is—"

"It's called love," Sunny interrupted dryly.

"And if it will last," Daphne went on. "We're getting to know each other again, finding out if we can be friends as well as lovers. If we can live together. Which is exactly why I have to find some office space," she concluded.

She stood up and hauled Sunny to her feet. "Come on. Pick up that child and let's go to this protest of yours before I get smart and change my mind."

THERE WERE already twenty or so people milling around in front of the research center when Sunny pulled her yellow Mercedes station wagon up to the curb.

"Now what?" Daphne said as Sunny set the parking brake.

"Now, we pass out the signs." She gestured over her shoulder. "There's a card table back there, too, for the petition. Jason will set that up." She waved at a young man. "Why don't you get Mollie out of her car seat while I get the signs?"

"Fine," Daphne agreed. "Looks like it's you and me, kid," she said, lifting the child into her arms as she got out of the car. They watched Sunny organize her troops.

In less than five minutes she had everyone wearing black armbands—for the deceased animals, Daphne decided—and marching in front of the medical research center. Most carried one of Sunny's hand-lettered signs. Stop Slaughtering Our Pets and Vivisection Is Killing Puppies seemed to be the favorites. A few carried placards with rather gruesome representations of small animals that had apparently been the unfortunate victims of medical research.

It was an emotional, heart-wrenching scene—as Sunny had fully intended it should be—because no one, no matter what side of the question they stood on, wanted to think of their own beloved pet ending up as an experiment.

And that was why, despite some reservations, Daphne had agreed to come today.

"Here, let me tie this on," Sunny said, wrapping a strip of black cloth around Daphne's biceps. "You, too, sweetheart." She tied another one around Mollie's plump little arm, and for the first time Daphne noticed that her sweatshirt sported a grinning dog face and the legend, I Love my Dachshund. Mollie didn't have a dachshund.

"Have you no shame?" Daphne chided mildly. "Using your own child as propaganda?"

"Mollie'd love her dachshund if she had one," Sunny said, taking the child from Daphne's arms. "Hold on tight to Jason," she urged as he lifted Mollie to his shoulders.

Mollie clutched the young man's hair with both hands. "Gid'up," she ordered gleefully.

Jason galloped to his place in the picket line.

Sunny thrust a sign into Daphne's hands and hoisted her own. "Come on, the TV crews should be here any minute."

The police arrived before the TV crew but apparently only as a precaution. Aside from warning the protesters not to block the sidewalk or physically harass anyone going in or out of the building, they merely watched. And waited.

Daphne waited, too, shielding her face behind her picket sign, and hoped Sunny had been wrong. She wasn't. The TV crew arrived ten minutes later.

At a signal from Sunny, the protesters began to chant louder, thrusting their signs into the air as the Minicam zoomed in.

"Excuse me, ma'am," a reporter said, thrusting a microphone under Daphne's nose. "Could you tell us what you hope to gain by this demonstration?"

Daphne ducked behind her sign, pointing at Sunny. "Ask her," she mumbled.

"Excuse me, ma'am…" The reporter repeated her question to Sunny.

"We hope to arouse public concern for what's going on in that—" she gestured "—that torture chamber there."

"Torture chamber? Don't you think that's a bit strong?" the reporter said. "You make it sound like a concentration camp for animals when, in fact—"

"Isn't that what it is?" Sunny interrupted. "Tell me what

else you would call it when perfectly healthy cats and dogs—
children's pets—are being purchased from city pounds to be
used in painful, crippling and unnecessary experiments.''

"Poor puppy,'' Mollie said, her high childish voice clearly
audible over the noise of the crowd. The reporter—and the
Minicam—turned their attention to the adorable three-year-old
on Jason's shoulders.

"Do you have a pet, honey?'' the reporter said gently, taking her cue from the front of Mollie's sweatshirt.

"Poor puppy,'' Mollie repeated, her bottom lip out. "Poor,
poor puppy.'' She was shaking her head sadly.

"Shame on you!'' Daphne hissed in Sunny's ear. "Teaching that child to tell lies.''

"What lies?'' Sunny hissed back, brown eyes wide and innocent. "All she said was 'poor puppy.' ''

"...this is Karen Zachary, reporting live from the Hillman
Medical Research Center.'' The Minicam was lowered, the
reporter and her crew hurried back to their van.

Sunny handed her placard to one of the other protesters and
opened her arms, lifting Mollie from Jason's shoulders.
"Mommy's brilliant little girl,'' she said delightedly. "Say
goodbye to Jason.''

"Does this mean we're leaving now?'' Daphne asked.
"That's it? Five minutes in front of the cameras is all the
protesting you're going to do? Elizabeth McCorkle, I'm surprised at you!''

"Why?'' Sunny was strapping Mollie into her car seat.
"I've done my part here today. Jason and some of the others
will stay for most of the afternoon and try to get some more
signatures on that petition.''

"And just what was your part?'' asked Daphne.

"Focusing media attention on an issue of vital importance,''
Sunny said promptly. "By giving that reporter something
more interesting to film than a bunch of people carrying signs.
I've practically assured our cause a spot on the nightly news.
And maybe we can stop what's going on in there.'' She waved

at Jason and slid behind the wheel. Daphne scrambled in. "Now," Sunny said, "where shall I drop you?"

ADAM'S forest-green BMW was in the driveway when Daphne's taxi pulled up at his Russian Hill address.

Damn, she thought, paying the driver. *One of the few days Adam gets home from the hospital before six and I'm not here to greet him.* The perfect opportunity to show him what suitable doctor's wife material she had turned into was down the drain because of a rental agent's faulty transmission. Well, if she was lucky, she thought, he had only just come in himself.

She hurried up the brick path, mentally reviewing the contents of the refrigerator, and unlocked the front door. Holding her breath, she pushed it open. The living room was clean and tidy. Mrs. Drecker hadn't quit yet.

She continued down the hall toward the low hum of voices coming from the bedroom.

Fresh from the shower, Adam was stretched out on top of the striped bedspread, propped up on a pile of pillows at the teak headboard. His long hairy legs were crossed at the ankle. A wedge of his equally hairy chest was exposed between the open edges of a white terry bathrobe. He was surrounded by cats: Mack, sprawled across his stomach; Queenie, perched on the headboard; and Tiger on the bedside table with his paw in a ceramic bowl, fishing for an M&M.

"Hi," Adam said, looking up as she entered the room. "You're just in time. Sunny called a few minutes ago and said to be sure to tell you to watch the evening news." He popped an M&M in his mouth. "I was going to tape it for you but this is much better." His smile was warm and welcoming. "Come watch with me," he invited. "There's plenty of M&Ms for everybody."

Daphne stepped out of her shoes. "Best offer I've had all day," she quipped, crawling across the bed to cuddle up in the warm curve of his arm. It closed around her, drawing her in. "Umm." She snuggled against his side. "Heaven."

"Don't I get a kiss hello?"

Daphne looked up at him. "Depends. Do I get an M&M?"

He held one up in front of her. "Trade?"

Daphne tilted her head back, eyes closed, and opened her mouth.

The kiss was deep and satisfying and quickly threatened to develop into something more. Adam's big body shifted toward hers, but Mack dug his claws in, protesting the move.

Adam fell back. "Damn cat's trying to emasculate me," he said, and dropped the M&M into Daphne's mouth.

Daphne chewed and swallowed before answering. "Get tough," she suggested. "Tell him to move."

"Move," Adam ordered, and Mack opened one yellow eye. Disgruntled, he rose, stretched languidly, and stalked off to the more settled regions at the foot of the bed.

"You're so forceful," Daphne sighed, "and I'm a sucker for forceful men." Her hand was plucking deliberately at the fine hairs around Adam's navel.

Adam's stomach muscles contracted. He growled playfully and turned toward her, one hand pushing hers even farther down his stomach. "I'll show you forceful."

Daphne giggled, her eyes golden with desire. "Promise?"

His mouth came down on hers just as her fingers closed around him. Daphne felt him jerk, his muscles tightened in reaction to her touch, and then his tongue invaded her mouth, filling her with the taste of him. It was a long sweet moment before either of them moved except to press closer.

"I missed you today," he murmured. "All day I thought about you. About this." He moved his hips against her hand. "It played hell with my concentration."

A part of Daphne thrilled to his words, but another part of her stood back, hoping for more. He missed her, he wanted her, but did he love her? She *thought* he did, hoped he did, but in the past six weeks he had never said the words.

"I missed you, too," she said softly, then she pulled his

head back down to hers, afraid that if her lips were free, she might say the words he wasn't ready to hear.

"Helpless animals are being systemically tortured..." Sunny's voice broke through their building passion.

"The TV," Daphne murmured, shifting a little.

"Hmm?" Adam turned to squint at the television. "Oh, God, Sunny's on the warpath again!" Adam chuckled and levered himself from Daphne's supine form. He lifted her a little more upright so she could see the television, too. "I wonder if poor Brian knew what screwball thing she was up to today."

Daphne cringed at his words, and hoped that the camera hadn't caught her face, too.

"Poor puppy," Mollie piped up right on cue.

Adam hooted. "She's got Mollie in the act, too! Brian will be fit to be tied."

"Do you really think he'll be angry?" Daphne began hesitantly. "I mean it *is* a good cause...isn't it?"

Adam shook his head, his eyes on the TV screen. "Animal research is absolutely vital to the advancement of medical science. And if Sunny would stop letting her emotions rule her head for a minute, she'd realize it."

The camera angle changed again, slowly panning back to bring the reporter—and the protesters—into full view.

Daphne's body stiffened, anticipating the explosion.

"Good God, that's you!" Adam shot upright on the bed.

For just a moment, Daphne considered denying it. But, "Yes, I guess it is," she admitted reluctantly, struggling to sit up as the screen faded into a close-up of the anchorman back at the studio.

Adam turned to look at her. "I didn't know you were going to be involved in that today," he said calmly.

"I didn't, either," Daphne hurried to explain. "That is, I knew I was going, but not about the reporter and—"

"Hey." Adam halted her. "You don't owe me any explanations. You can get involved in as many, er, causes," he said

judiciously, "as you want to. It has nothing to do with me."
He swung his feet to the floor. "So, what do you say we go
get something to eat?" he said.

The subject, she realized, was closed. Instead of yelling at
her as he would have eleven years ago, instead of telling her
what an idiot she was making of herself, he'd very calmly said
that it had nothing to do with him. Didn't he care what she
did?

Daphne sat upright, Indian fashion. "I thought we might eat
in tonight," she said, her voice as calm as his.

"Sure, if you like. What did you have in mind?"

"Oh, I don't know. Whatever's in the kitchen."

Adam looked doubtful. "I don't think there's much of a
choice. But I'll see what I have."

Daphne was up off the bed. "Oh, no. I didn't mean for you
to make it, Adam. I just feel like doing something domestic
tonight, that's all."

"Domestic? You?"

She scowled at him. "I get these impulses once in a while.
Even I can get tired of eating out all the time."

"We could order something in," he suggested.

"I get tired of that, too," Daphne said, wondering why he
still seemed so intent on treating her like a guest.

"Why don't you just relax. Here on the bed," she invited.
"Let *me* see what's in the kitchen. Come on." She propelled
him back to the bed. "Relax. Let Dan Rather tell you what's
going on in the world." She plucked the bowl off the bedside
table. "Have some more M&Ms," she advised. "I'll get you
a nice glass of white wine."

"With M&Ms?"

"So, I'll get you a glass of rosé," she said airily. "It goes
with everything."

The refrigerator was better stocked than the first time she
had looked into it, but not by much. A quart of cream, several
half-full foil-covered cans of Seafood Supper, Creamed Kid-
ney Bits and Chicken Nibbles, a carton of eggs, a closed plas-

tic container with a selection of cheeses, three different kinds of deli meat, a loaf of sourdough bread, jars of pickles and olives, a six-pack of imported beer, several bottles of wine; all the ingredients for tomorrow's picnic but not the makings of a great meal.

"Noodles," she said to herself, remembering a package in one of the cupboards. She could make a halfway decent fettuccine Alfredo with those noodles and what was on hand in the refrigerator.

She filled a large pan with water and set it on the stove. Opening a bottle of the promised rosé, she carried it back into the bedroom with two long-stemmed glasses.

"Dan Rather's on vacation," Adam said sheepishly, explaining why the TV was now tuned to reruns of "The Love Boat."

Daphne flashed him a knowing look. "You have the most juvenile taste in TV shows," she said, pouring a glass of wine. "Well, enjoy." She handed it to him with a flourish. "I'm going to go take a quick shower."

Adam leered up at her. "Need some help?"

"I said a *quick* shower."

But her shower wasn't as quick as she'd planned. She couldn't find the shower cap so her hair got wet and she ended up washing it. Which meant drying it, too. Finally, she slipped a silky peach-colored caftan over her head. It had a wide V-neck, fluttery split sleeves and a hem that brushed against her ankles. It was also very nearly transparent.

Deftly, she touched up her makeup and fluffed up her hair. *The very picture of wifely devotion,* she decided.

Despite a slight delay, she had finally managed to put her plan into action. Adam had his glass of wine, she had slipped into something slinky, dinner was well on its way to being done.

The only problem was that Adam was sound asleep. The wineglass, empty now, tilted precariously from his right hand.

Mack had crawled back up on his stomach and lay sprawled in feline abandon.

Daphne stood silently for a few moments, disappointment building inside her. Then she sighed in resignation and moved across the carpet on bare feet. They would have all day tomorrow together, she reminded herself.

*

"WAKE UP, sleeping beauty." Daphne leaned over the figure on the bed, waving a cup of freshly brewed coffee back and forth near Adam's nose.

His nostrils twitched, but he didn't wake.

My sleeping Greek god, she thought tenderly, feeling the urge to brush the hair back from his forehead.

Instead, she blew gently across the top of the cup. "I've got coffee," she singsonged. "Wake up."

Adam's nostrils twitched again, narrowing as he inhaled deeply. "Coffee?" he said groggily, and rolled to his side. He pulled on her caftan then, tugging until she was forced to sit down on the bed.

"Careful, Adam," she warned. "You'll make me spill it."

"Put it down," he suggested, rolling over onto his back again. His eyes were fully open now, and Daphne recognized his expression.

"Oh, no, you don't," she said, laughing. "You promised we'd go to the park today. Have a picnic, remember?"

Silently, still smiling that sexy sleepy little smile of his, Adam took the coffee cup from her and placed it on the bedside table.

"You mentioned roller-skating, too," she reminded him. "And then maybe some shopping."

His left arm curled around her back, drawing her down. Daphne pretended to resist. The loose open neckline of her caftan slid halfway down her arm, completely baring her left shoulder and breast. Daphne ignored it.

"Then there was dinner at that new Chinese place and dancing at—"

"Hmm," Adam said. "We will." His lips touched her bare shoulder. "Later."

"Uh-huh," Daphne scoffed. "How much later?"

Adam grinned lazily. "About thirty minutes later?" he suggested, touching his lips to the upper slope of her bared breast.

Daphne sighed, melting against him. "Only thirty minutes?"

Adam laughed softly, deep in his chest, and rolled over, carrying Daphne with him so that she ended up on her back beneath him, her legs trapped by the sheet that had been covering his golden body. His left arm was still wrapped around her back, making her spine arch, thrusting her breasts forward like an offering.

"We'll take as long as you want," he promised, his voice no longer teasing as his eyes made a slow, thorough survey of her lush breasts. The right one was only lightly veiled, but her left breast was totally bared to his heated gaze.

He moved his right hand, cupping her exposed breast in his palm, and lowered his head. He took the puckered nipple into the warmth of his mouth, laving it with quick little flicks of his tongue. It hardened instantly, drawing up, tightening, aching for a firmer pressure. Instinctively, Adam began to suckle more strongly, his cheeks flexing as he took as much of her breast into his mouth as he could.

Daphne arched even farther off the mattress, lifting up to him, feeling the sensual, primal pull of his mouth all the way to her womb. She moaned softly, seeking a way to touch him.

Adam lifted his head. "What?" he murmured.

"I can't move," she breathed. "Can't touch you."

Adam shifted, turning and lifting her body until she lay on top of him. "Better?"

"Hmm, yes. Much." She sat up in one fluid motion, her knees sliding open to straddle his hips. With a sensuous little roll of her shoulder, she dropped the right side of her caftan and slipped both arms out of the sleeves.

She looked both elegant and sensual sitting there astride him, her long smooth torso rising up out of the peach silk draped around her hips.

Adam lay passive for a moment, drinking her in with his eyes, and then he raised his hands to her waist, sliding them down under the peach silk to curve around the swell of her hips. His thumbs touched the soft, curling hair that hid the secrets of her body.

Daphne's eyes lifted, meeting his, and her palms continued smoothing the hair-roughened sinews of his forearms until they came to rest on the backs of his hands, stopping them. For a moment she hovered there, her hands covering his, devouring him with a heated gaze of her own.

Then Adam's hands tightened under hers, demanding, and Daphne surged forward. She pressed her soft full breasts to Adam's chest, her belly to his belly, her lips to his lips.

As if in slow motion, Adam rolled over again, pressing her down into the mattress. His mouth took hers in a gently savage kiss and his hands palmed her breasts, kneading their fullness with gentle skill. Urgently, maddeningly, his hips ground into the cradle of her open thighs, tempting her with that part of him that was still separated from her by the thin layers of peach silk and crisp brown sheets.

Daphne whimpered slightly, wanting more, and Adam lifted himself off her, turning to one side to help her rid them of this last impediment to their lovemaking. Then he was on her again, entering her slowly, moving slowly, driving her mad.

Daphne ran her hands down his sleek back, her nails scraping lightly along the indentation of his spine, reveling in the feel of the muscles that rolled beneath her fingers with each slow thrust of his hips. She smoothed her palms down the slight inward slope at the small of his back and over the hard curve of his buttocks. There her fingers tightened, pressing, urging him to a more frantic pace. But Adam refused to be hurried.

Even as he moved within her, even as he whispered soft, sexy words into the damp curve of her neck, she could feel him holding back some essential part of himself. But she was too far gone to figure out what it was. Her hips bucked beneath him, urging, hungry, out of control.

"That's it," he murmured into her mouth. "Let it go. Let it come," he urged, retaining his control, his awareness of self and place, to the end, holding back until she had cried out in mindless pleasure...once, twice. And then, deliberately, he let go, thrusting forward into her welcoming body with a fierce cry of his own.

It was wonderful. It was satisfying. It left her sated and replete. But it wasn't the same as if he, too, had gone beyond control, had lost himself in loving her.

They lay tangled together for a moment more, letting the world right itself around them, and then Adam levered himself up and off her and rolled over onto his back.

"I bet my coffee's gotten cold," he said, grinning at her out of the corner of his eye.

For just a moment, Daphne contemplated grabbing the cup and pouring its contents over his head. That he could lie there looking so natural and so...*relaxed, dammit,* while she was still trembling inside from the strength of her response, made her want to scream. *How can you be so blasé,* she wanted to shout. *Don't you care?*

Instead, she calmly leaned over his supine body and stuck the tip of her index finger in the coffee cup. "Still warm," she said, drawing back with the cup in her hand. "Here." She gave him a look over her shoulder, and disappeared into the bathroom.

THE TELEPHONE rang as Daphne was trying to fit a second bottle of wine into the picnic basket.

She let it ring, sensing that it was the hospital. Adam, she knew, would answer it from the bedroom extension. Five minutes later he came bustling out to the kitchen, a worried look on his handsome face.

Daphne was already unloading the picnic basket.

"That was the hospital," he said unnecessarily, shrugging into a tan suede sport coat as he spoke. "Tiffany Jenkins has developed an infection." The little girl had had her third skin graft operation less than a week ago. "I've got to go. I—I'm sorry, Daffy, but this is important."

"You've got to go to the hospital. I know."

Adam stood there speechless, not knowing what to say.

"Hey, it's all right," she said, forcing a bright little smile past the lump in her throat. "I understand."

Adam looked skeptical.

"Really, I do." She came over to him.

Adam put his hands on her shoulders, knees slightly bent as he tried to look into her face. "You sure you don't mind?"

"Of course I *mind*," Daphne said. "But I understand."

"And you're not mad?" Adam's voice was still doubtful.

"No, I'm not mad," she denied. *For God's sake, Daphne, try to act like a reasonable adult! A canceled picnic isn't the end of the world.* "I'm disappointed, that's all. I was looking forward to spending the whole day with you."

"I know." Adam squeezed her shoulders. "I was, too."

"Maybe you won't be all day?" Daphne asked hopefully.

"It's hard to say. Maybe. It depends on exactly what the problem is." She could tell he was anxious to be off.

"You'd better get going," she said in a flat little voice.

He looked for a moment as if he wanted to say something more, something...important. Instead, he reached out, curling his hand around the back of her head, and lifted her into his kiss. It wasn't quick. It wasn't distracted. It was long and thorough and turned Daphne's knees to jelly. "I'll be home as soon as I can," he whispered. "Wait for me."

She finished dealing with the contents of the picnic basket, merely transferring everything, still neatly wrapped, to a shelf in the refrigerator. She was skeptical that Adam would be back in time for a picnic that afternoon—but maybe tomorrow.

She went back into the bedroom then, intending to do a little light housekeeping. Mrs. Drecker wouldn't be in again until Monday, and a whole weekend of not picking up after herself would make Adam's lovely house look like a tornado had hit it.

"You guys can have it back in a minute," she told the cats, shooing them off so she could make the bed. When she'd finished, they clambered back up, settling in for their midmorning nap.

The phone rang for the second time that morning, surprising her with yesterday's clothes bundled up in her arms. She dropped them on a convenient chair.

"Hello?" She sat down on the bed. "Oh, hi, Sunny. What's up?"

"We've arranged another little demo at the research center. I thought you might like to come with me."

"Two days in a row? Don't you ever give it a rest?"

"Nope. Do you want to come?"

"Well, I don't know," Daphne hedged. "Adam didn't seem too thrilled to see me on the news last night and—"

"You mean to tell me you're going to let Adam, a man you're not even married to, dictate your conscience? Daphne Granger, I'm surprised at you."

"He's not dictating my conscience," Daphne defended him.

"So, are you just going to sit home and do nothing?"

"Well, I…"

"Hundreds of people's pets, cats just like Mack, are being slaughtered."

"Yes, but…" Oh, what the hell, Daphne thought. *I haven't got anything better to do today.* "Okay, sure, pick me up."

"Good," Sunny said approvingly. "I knew I could count on you."

"Now I know why you're so good at fund-raising," Daphne said, as they drove to the research center. "Nobody would dare say no to you."

Sunny grinned. "Persistence has its uses."

"Intimidation, you mean."

"Who, *moi?*" Sunny said.

"Yes, you!" Daphne replied as they pulled up across from the research center.

Daphne followed her friend across the street to the group marching in a tight circle in front of the center.

She recognized a few faces from the day before, but the mood was different today. More unsettled and...rebellious.

Someone handed Daphne a sign and she took it automatically, as Sunny tied on a black armband.

The protesters were chanting loudly, thrusting their placards into the air with youthful zeal. As she began marching, Daphne noticed a squad car parked halfway down the street. There were two uniformed policemen sitting inside, silently watching again.

"Stop vivisection now!" the protesters chanted. "Vivisection is murdering our pets!"

Suddenly, someone hurled a brick through the front window of the research center. Glass went flying in every direction. Several people fell to the ground, protecting their heads with crossed arms. A woman screamed. Protest signs clattered to the sidewalk. A police siren blared.

Daphne's first instinct was to run. But she couldn't move. She just stood there, frozen, as another brick sailed through the half-shattered window, breaking the spell that held her captive. She started to turn away, looking for Sunny, when someone grabbed her wrist. She jerked away, startled, and dropped her sign.

"Come on now, lady. You don't want to add resisting arrest to the rest of it, do you?"

Cold steel clamped around her delicate wrist and Daphne looked up into the eyes of a uniformed policeman.

"But I didn't...I wasn't... "

He gave her a little shove, urging her toward the police paddy wagon that had appeared on the scene. Another policeman stood by the open rear door, helping handcuffed protesters into the back.

Someone jostled her and she glanced up as Sunny, her hands cuffed behind her back, stumbled into the seat across from her.

"This is all your fault," Daphne hissed.

"My fault?" Somehow, Sunny managed to look indignant. "I didn't throw that brick." She grinned. "But I'd sure like to thank whoever did."

"What!"

"Just think of all the publicity," Sunny said gleefully.

"This is going to make the papers, isn't it? And the evening news?"

"I sure hope so."

"Adam is going to bust a gut," Daphne said.

THE HANDCUFFS were removed as soon as they got to the police station. Daphne rubbed her wrists, surprised there were no bruises, and looked around her with wide eyes.

She had only been in a police station once before, that time when she had tried to hit the TV cameraman over the head with her protest sign. She hadn't liked it then. She didn't like it now.

"How long do you think we'll be here?" Daphne asked.

"I don't know. Hours probably," Sunny replied.

And it was hours. One by one, they were booked, searched, fingerprinted and photographed like common criminals. The charges were disorderly conduct and criminal mischief, both misdemeanors. Then, finally, a judge arraigned them, setting bail at two hundred dollars apiece, payable in cash. Neither Daphne nor Sunny had that much on them.

"Now what happens?" Daphne asked hesitantly.

"You can call someone to come down with the money,"

an officer told her. "A family member or friend. Or a bail bondsman. In the meantime you wait in the tank."

The "tank" was segregated by sex, one for men, one for women. It was the worst place Daphne had ever been. But finally, the two women were allowed their phone call.

"I got hold of Brian," Sunny said.

"Was he mad?"

"Are you kidding? I could feel the steam coming right through the telephone wire."

"But he's coming to get us?" Daphne asked hopefully.

"He said he ought to let us stew for a while but, yes, he's coming to get us." She patted Daphne's hand. "Are you sure you don't want to call Adam?"

Daphne shook her head. "I don't want to bother him at the hospital. If he's home now, I left a note telling him I'd gone out with you for a little while."

"Oh, that'll put his mind at ease."

Brian arrived forty minutes later. He wasn't nearly so angry as Sunny had indicated. In fact, he now seemed to see the funny side of things. Adam, however, apparently didn't see anything funny in the situation at all.

"I didn't tell Brian to call him," Sunny whispered. "Honest!"

"Well, well, if it isn't the two little jailbirds," Brian said teasingly. But he hugged Sunny hard. "Are you all right?" he said against her hair.

"Fine, now that you're here," she replied.

Daphne wished she were being held, too. But Adam just stood there, a somewhat wary expression on his face as he waited for her to claim her valuables. He was, she thought, absolutely furious with her. She didn't blame him. She was furious with herself.

"Are you all right?" he asked when she came away from the desk. His voice was low, his words clipped.

"Yes, Adam," she said, head down. "Fine."

He reached out and lifted her chin with his forefinger, forcing her to look at him. "You're sure you're all right? We heard that there was broken glass."

"No," she said softly. "I wasn't near the glass. I'm fine."

"Good." His hand dropped. "Then, shall we go?" he said.

They exited the police station to the glow of the late afternoon sunlight slanting across the pavement—and the flash of a newsman's camera exploding in their faces.

"What the hell—" Adam began, shielding his face. He drew Daphne closer, as if to shield her, too.

"Dr. McCorkle, how do you feel about your wife being involved in the anti-vivisection protest?"

"No comment," Brian muttered, heading his wife toward the yellow Mercedes. Adam and Daphne crossed to the forest-green BMW parked right behind it.

"Dr. Forrest, how does having your wife involved in a criminal protest against a medical research center affect your new position at Children's Hospital?"

Daphne's eyes widened at that. She hadn't given a thought to how this might affect Adam. At least, not careerwise. After all, she wasn't his wife anymore. Even if she were, it should have no bearing. She opened her mouth to say, "I'm not Mrs.—" but a hand clamped down on her arm, silencing her.

"We have no comment," Adam snapped, assisting Daphne into the passenger seat of his BMW. He stalked around to the driver's side, inserted the key into the ignition and gunned the engine to life. And then careful, controlled, always-in-charge Adam left rubber on the road as he peeled away from the curb.

Daphne sat silently, unable to think of anything to say to defuse his anger. "If I had known what Sunny was up to," she offered at last, "I wouldn't have gotten involved."

Adam didn't even glare at her. "A bit late for regrets, isn't it?" he said, downshifting as the car crested one of San Francisco's famous hills.

"I didn't say I *regretted* getting involved," Daphne snapped back. "But, I'm sorry you had to get involved."

"I suppose you'd rather I just left you sitting in jail?"

"Brian would have bailed me out," she said, shrugging.

"Brian would not!" Adam exploded. "You're my responsibility!"

Daphne's head came up, all her senses ready—eager—to do battle. "I am not your responsibility," she said firmly, as Adam turned onto their street.

He swung the car into the driveway, bringing it to an abrupt halt only inches from the garage door. Daphne reached for the door handle, then stopped when she realized that Adam hadn't turned off the engine. "Do you intend to finish this—discussion out here? In front of all your neighbors?"

"I don't want to finish it at all. I have to go back to the hospital." He revved the engine as if to emphasize his impatience.

"Oh, that's right!" Daphne said. "Hide behind your white coat. Well, I've got news for you, doctor. Your problems will still be waiting for you when you get back," she informed him icily, shoving the car door open.

He turned. "Will they?" he said, very softly.

For just a moment Daphne hesitated, caught by the look on his face. It was hopeful and worried at the same time. She almost said something soothing, but then she realized the car was still running.

"Count on it!" she shouted, springing out of the car before he could say another word. Tires squealed as Adam roared off down the street. "Damn the man!" she cursed aloud, wishing she had something to throw. "He hasn't changed a bit!"

Oh, he was older, smoother, more expert with words of love. No, not love, she thought. *Seduction.* He knew all the right words to say when he had her in his arms. But when it came to emotion, he was as closemouthed as ever. Be it love or hate or anger, he couldn't say the words. Couldn't tell her what was in his heart.

Well, that was coming to an end! And soon. Very soon. She would wait until he cooled off, and then she would confront him with her feelings, all of them, and demand that he expose his own. There would be no more pussyfooting around the edges of this relationship. If it was love, the real, committed, ending-in-marriage, forever kind of love, she wanted to know. And if it was just a sexual fling…well, she wanted to know that, too.

Somewhat calmer now that she had made a decision, she walked through the deserted house to the bedroom, shrugging out of her jumpsuit as she went. She dropped it on top of the wicker clothes hamper and reached into the shower to turn on the taps. Her jumpsuit wasn't all that felt dirty after her little run-in with the law.

The phone was ringing as she stepped out of the shower. For a moment, she considered not answering it. Then she reached for the receiver.

"Hello?"

"Thank goodness I finally got you." Elaine sounded breathless. "I've been calling all afternoon. Where have you been?"

Daphne hitched her towel a little more securely around her damp body. "Believe me. You don't want to know." She sighed. "So—what's the problem?"

"Mr. Chan is here *now* and he's leaving tomorrow night. And he wants to see you. I told him you'd—"

"What happened to our Wednesday meeting?" Daphne said.

"His oldest grandson is having surgery on Tuesday—or is it Wednesday? Anyway, he wants to be back and that means he's here now, two days ahead of schedule."

"Can't you handle it?" Daphne inquired. "You're a partner."

"I told him that, Daphne. But he insists on seeing you. You know how he is about dealing with the 'head man.' "

"Yes, I know." Mr. Chan had the worst timing in the world! She needed to be *here* right now, dealing with Adam. But business was business. And Mr. Chan was there about the fabrics for her new lingerie line. She had to see him now, too, if the line was going to launch on schedule. Damn!

"Daphne, you there?"

"Yes." Her voice was resigned. "Have someone meet the next San Francisco plane at La Guardia. Unless you hear otherwise, I'll be on it. And send a basket of fruit to Mr. Chan's suite with my—*our*—compliments. And make reservations at someplace fancy for dinner tomorrow night for three. You, me and Mr. Chan. It's high time he got used to dealing with someone other than me. Yes. Bye."

Daphne pressed down on the telephone button, breaking the connection with New York, and dialed the airlines. Then, she called a taxi and finished putting herself together.

In less than twenty minutes she was dressed in trim ankle-length slacks and a matching unlined jacket in a nubby beige fabric with a russet-colored string knit sweater beneath it. Large copper discs adorned her ears. She stuffed a few essentials into a large carryall and headed for Adam's den to write a note.

While dressing, she had debated whether or not to call him, but just thinking of his thundercloud of a face put her right off that idea. A note, she decided, was the safest bet.

As she was writing it, she heard the front door open. Apparently the decision had been taken out of her hands. "I'm in here, Adam," she called.

There was no answer.

Daphne came out of the den. "I was just writing you a note," she explained. "I know it's terrible timing but I have to fly to New…" Her voice trailed off as she saw who it was. "Oh, hello, Marcia," she said coolly to the younger woman. They had silently agreed to a truce of sorts; at least there were no outright hostilities. "I'm afraid Adam had an emergency at the hospital."

"Yes, I know exactly what kind of emergency Adam had. It's all over the hospital that he had to go down to the police station and bail out his ex-wife!"

"Oh, dear," Daphne said, sincerely sorry and sincerely distressed. Above almost anything else in life, Adam valued his professional image. Quite rightly, too, she thought, since he had worked so hard to attain it.

"Is that all you can say? 'Oh, dear'?" Adam's sister scoffed. "Not that I expected anything better of you after what Adam's told me." She advanced on Daphne like a lioness all set to defend her cub. If looks could kill...

"I told him you'd be nothing but trouble! I told him that you still had the same crazy, radical friends and believed in the same stupid causes. That you were no better doctor's wife material now than the first time around. And you've proved it." A particularly nasty smile curved her pink lips. "*Now* maybe he'll listen to me."

"Maybe," Daphne agreed softly, her voice as level and calm as she could make it as she digested the rather disturbing fact that Adam had obviously discussed their relationship with his viper of a sister.

"Maybe?" Marcia's voice rose to a near shriek. With a visible effort, she controlled it. "Oh, he'll listen all right. He can't help but listen with the evidence right in front of him."

"Maybe," Daphne said again. She brushed past Marcia and went into the kitchen to tape her note to the refrigerator door, crumpling her earlier one. "That's something we'll have to discuss when I get back." She gave Marcia a deliberately arch look. "Adam and I, that is." She paused consideringly. "Although, if what you say is true, I'm sure Adam will let you know what we decide."

A horn sounded outside, three sharp blasts, and Daphne silently blessed the efficiency of San Francisco taxi companies. "That will be my cab," she said, heading for the front door. "Feel free to make yourself at home until Adam gets back. I'm sure he won't be long. And I'm sure you'll have plenty to say to him," she said sweetly, and left.

"MRS. GRANGER." Elaine's assistant hurried into the workroom, her manner flustered. "There's a man in the lobby. He insists on seeing you and he...he's *drunk!*"

"I am not drunk," corrected Adam, coming in behind her. "I have been drinking," he said. "Two brandies, to be precise. The second of which the flight attendant spilled all over my jacket."

Daphne just stared. Never, ever had she seen Adam in this condition. Maybe he wasn't drunk, she thought, but he certainly looked it.

"Adam, what are you doing here?" She rose to her feet, truly alarmed. Adam all undone was a frightening sight. "What's wrong?"

"You're what's wrong," he said, coming toward her with purposeful strides.

Daphne shrank back from the murderous look in his eyes. "Me?" she squeaked.

"Yes, you!" He grabbed her by the upper arms, completely oblivious to the four grinning women and one puzzled Chinese man who stood gaping at them. "You've run out on me for the last time. Is that clear, Daffy?"

"No, Adam, I don't. I—"

"The last time, Daffy," he repeated. "I won't let you leave me again."

"I haven't left you, Adam. I had a meeting with Mr. Chan that couldn't be put off. I was coming right back."

"You *left* me," he went on angrily. "*Again.* Without a goodbye. Without even a note to tell me where you'd gone."

"But I left you a note. I—"

"Without a note!" he roared. "I had to find out from Marcia that you'd gone back to New York. You were too much of a coward to tell me yourself."

"Marcia?" Daphne said, stunned. And then it hit her. Obviously Marcia had destroyed her note. "That bitch!"

"You leave my sister out of this, do you hear me?" He shook her. "This is between you and me."

Daphne wrenched herself out of his hands, furious now. Neither of them spared a thought for their fascinated audience.

"Don't you yell at me!" she shouted. "Yell at that interfering sister of yours!"

"Marcia, hell! It's *you* who ran off at the first sign of trouble, *you* who couldn't face up to what you had done."

"It was for a good cause!" Daphne defended herself.

"That's beside the point."

"And just what is the point, Dr. Forrest?" she asked.

"The point is you." He jabbed a forefinger into her chest for emphasis. "Why the hell can't you act like a reasonable adult instead of some flaky, irresponsible hippie?"

"I was never a hippie! You just thought so because you were always such a pompous stuffed shirt. And I did not run away!" she added furiously. "You divorced *me*, remember?" she reminded him angrily. "And you haven't changed one bit."

"I haven't changed? You're the one who hasn't changed," Adam roared.

"Even love," Daphne continued as if Adam hadn't spoken. "Oh, I should have known it wouldn't work," she cried. "I don't know what made me think it would. I guess I just wanted it so much that I didn't think it through."

Adam clamped her shoulders tighter. "I want it, too!" he shouted.

"Want what?" Daphne shouted back.

"You! I want you to come back to me."

Daphne went very, very still. "Why?" she demanded.

"Because you're my wife!"

Daphne shook her head stubbornly. "Not anymore."

"Then because I love you, dammit!" he bellowed.

Daphne's mouth fell open. It wasn't the way she had envisioned him saying he loved her. But he had said it. And it was the sweetest, most wonderful thing she had ever heard. "Oh, Adam," she whispered. "Adam." It was the only word she seemed able to say. It was enough.

Adam slid his hands from her shoulders to her back, enfolding her in a tentative embrace. "And because you love me, too,'' he said softly. He hesitated a moment before kissing her, his eyes hopeful. "Don't you?"

"Oh, Adam.'' Daphne threw her arms around his neck. "Oh, Adam, you fool. Yes!'' she said, punctuating her words with quick little kisses. "Yes, yes, yes.''

His mouth came down on hers then, abruptly stopping the joyous flow of words. He pulled her more firmly to his body, his arms hard around her, his eyes glistening with unshed tears of happiness. Their lips touched...and parted...and touched again.

"I love you,'' he whispered into her mouth, his hands firm and warm against her back.

"I love you,'' she echoed, as she tangled her fingers in his tousled hair. She pulled his head closer, demanding more.

"Way 'ta go, Gorgeous!'' Elaine's voice, brimming with laughter, urged them on.

Adam raised his head a fraction and looked around. Four beaming female faces, and one very puzzled male one, were watching them with avid interest. Adam blushed, as spontaneously, the women burst into applause. Mr. Chan, not wanting to do the incorrect thing, joined them.

Daphne grinned happily and executed a sketchy little bow. "Elaine, you're in charge,'' Adam said, dragging Daphne toward the door.

"But Mr. Chan...'' Daphne sputtered.

"I'll take care of him.'' Elaine slipped her arm through Mr. Chan's. "We'll get along just fine, won't we?'' she said.

Mr. Chan smiled tentatively and bowed.

"AND YOU'D really thought I'd left you for good?''

"Really.'' Adam finished lathering up his hands and reached beneath the water for her foot. Holding her heel in one hand, he began to massage the floral-scented soap over her arch and between her toes. "What else was I supposed to think?'' he asked. "I come home to an empty house. Three hungry cats, begging to be fed. No Daphne. No note.''

"I already explained to you about that."

"Yes," he said. He put her left foot down and picked up the other one. "I intend to have a little heart-to-heart with my baby sister when we get back."

"Don't be too hard on her, Adam," Daphne advised. "She was only trying to save you from yourself." She grinned wickedly. "And me."

Adam grinned back. That slow, sleepy, utterly sexy grin that turned her bones to mush. If she wasn't already half lying down she would have melted.

"I don't want to be saved from you, Daffy," he said softly. "I never did."

"Never? Not even the first time around?"

"Not even then."

"Then why— Oh, that feels wonderful." She sighed and fell silent a moment, enjoying the feel of his strong, gentle hands caressing her foot. "Why did you file for divorce?" she finally asked. It was an old issue, an old hurt.

Adam stopped caressing her foot, placing the sole against his bare, hairy chest. "I don't know exactly," he said. "I was angry. And—hurt, I guess."

"Hurt? What had I done to hurt you?"

"You left me," he stated simply. "To follow your career."

Daphne pulled herself upright and her foot slid down his stomach into the water. "But it was only going to be for a couple of months! I was coming back. You knew that!"

"I know but..." He shrugged, looking like a small boy admitting to something that embarrassed him beyond words. "I couldn't have left you, Daffy. Not for any reason. And it hurt like hell to think that you could leave me."

"Oh, Adam." Daphne leaned forward, causing little ripples of water and bubbles to lap against his chest. "Why didn't you say something? Why did you get all macho and *order* me not to go? We could have worked something out."

He shrugged again. "Pride, I guess. If you didn't want to stay, I wasn't going to beg you to."

"But if you felt the way you say, why—" her hand slithered up his wet arm and she touched his cheek "—why did you file for divorce if you loved me?" she said.

"I had some half-baked idea that filing for divorce would bring you back to me. That if you really loved me, you'd come back and fight it." His eyes lifted to hers briefly and then dropped. "When you didn't, I thought, well...that you'd decided you didn't love me after all. That your career was more important."

"Oh, no, Adam! How could you think that? I loved you then like I love you now." She moved forward until she was kneeling between his thighs and took his face in her hands, forcing him to look at her. "I loved you passionately. When you filed for divorce I thought you didn't love *me!* What else was I supposed to think? You didn't want to marry me in the first place and—"

"You were so young," Adam said. "I didn't want to push you into something you'd regret."

"Push me!" Daphne sank back on her heels, incredulity written all over her face. Her breasts swayed with the movement, drops of water glistening on their tips. "I practically had to blackmail you into marriage. How could you think you were pushing me?"

"Because I wanted it..." He licked his lips, his eyes suddenly caught by her swaying breasts. "Wanted you so much that I *didn't* think. I just felt. And what I was feeling was driving me crazy." He looked up and grinned. "Just like it's driving me crazy now."

"But that doesn't make any sense," she said indignantly. "You didn't want to marry me because you loved me. You divorced me because you loved me. You...*Adam!*"

Adam had reached out, cupping his warm wet hands under her breasts. He slid his palms to her sides, his thumbs resting under the lower curve of her breasts, his fingers curling toward her back.

"Adam, I'm trying to talk to you," she said, putting her hands on his shoulders.

He shook his head. "No more talking."

"But we're not finished discussing this."

"Yes, we are. It's yesterday's news. Over. And what matters now is *now*—and the rest of our lives."

"But I need to ask you one more question."

"All right." His thumbs flickered across her nipples. "Ask. I'm listening."

"You are not. You're—" She gasped as his thumbs brushed her nipples again. "I can't talk when you do that. I can't even think when you do that."

His hands tightened, pulling her to him as he slid down into the water. "Good," he murmured.

Daphne let herself be pulled forward until she was lying on top of Adam, her breasts resting high on his chest, her bare bottom poking out of the bubbles like twin moons. But she wouldn't let him kiss her. Not yet.

"I still have one question," she insisted.

"Now?" He ran his hand along the curve of her spine, smoothing it all the way down to the swell of her buttocks.

"Yes." Daphne's voice faltered only slightly. "Now."

"But—"

"No 'buts,' Adam. That's how we got into trouble the last time. We made love instead of talking things out. I'm not going to let that happen to us again."

"You're right," Adam said, resigned. "Ask your question."

Suddenly, Daphne didn't know quite where to start. "Well, I…that is…" Surprising herself, Daphne blushed. "Well, it's just that you've been so… Oh, damn! This isn't going to come out right, especially after what just went on in that bedroom in there."

What had "gone on" was loving so abandoned, so intensely emotional that Daphne wondered how she could ever have thought that Adam was holding anything back. Assured of her love, he had given everything to her. And she, freed by his lack of constraint, had given him all of her.

"Come on," Adam prompted. "What have I been?"

Daphne's blush deepened. "You've been so, well, so standoffish with me these past six weeks. So distant."

She felt, rather than heard, the rumble of his laughter beneath her breasts. "Standoffish? Are you kidding? You call *this* standoffish? When I've practically ravished you every time we got within two feet of each other?" He grinned wickedly. "Not to mention what 'just went on in that bedroom.' "

Daphne's eyebrows rose. "That isn't what I mean and you know it. What I mean is," she began again, "well, why didn't you get mad when I appeared on the evening news in Sunny's protest march? And why didn't you get upset when I left junk all over your nice clean house. And—"

Adam put a finger on her lips. "I think I get the picture," he said. "I didn't get upset for the same reason, I suspect, that you didn't get upset when I had to stay late at the hospital, or when I was called back after we'd already settled in for the night. Compromise," he stated succinctly.

"Hmm," Daphne said, digesting this. "But you were so angry when you came down to the police station to bail me out. What happened to the compromise then?"

"That wasn't anger, Daffy. Well, not all of it, anyway. It was fear. Stark terror. I thought you'd gone stomping out in a huff because I'd had to cancel our picnic."

"But I wasn't in a huff at all. I understood. Really."

"I know. I know. But that's what I thought. When Brian called to tell me that you and Sunny had been arrested that was the last straw."

"So," Daphne crowed. "You *were* mad."

"Furious," he admitted easily, his thumbs stroking the sides of her throat. "And terrified that I'd blow up and we'd end up arguing. And the last time we argued, it—" his voice got very quiet "—it was eleven years before I saw you again."

"Oh, no, Adam! It wasn't the argument that kept us apart. It was—"

"I know," he said quietly. "Intellectually, I know—knew," he corrected himself. "But I was still afraid that it would happen all over again. That, if we argued, you'd leave. When I got home last night and you were gone I thought it *had* happened again."

"But it wasn't the arguing that drove us apart all those years ago," she said. "It was the silence. If we had really argued...really discussed things, it would have been okay, don't you see?"

"Yes, I do see. And from now on..." His hands tightened on her back. "We'll talk things out. No matter what. Agreed?"

"Agreed," she echoed softly, her eyes shining golden.

"Good!" He grinned suddenly. "Because if you didn't agree, I was fully prepared for a fight...whatever it took to get you to come back to me."

"After two brandies," Daphne reminded him.

"Actually, I had those brandies on the plane, *after* I'd decided to come after you." His palms curved over her wet silky rump. "Speaking of which, do you think I'll ever get the smell out of my clothes?"

"We won't know for a while. They won't be back from the cleaners until tomorrow."

"You mean I'm without clothes until tomorrow?"

"Uh-huh. Not a stitch." She smiled seductively.

"Don't you think we ought to take advantage of that?" he suggested, curling around the backs of her thighs.

Daphne's knees bent at the urging of his hands, coming to rest on either side of his hips. He bumped his pelvis against hers, causing water to slosh against the sides of the tub. "What do you say?" he murmured, lifting his mouth toward hers.

"I say yes," she answered, lowering her head to meet him halfway.

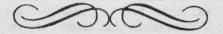

Blaze

Red-hot reads!

Save $1.00 off the purchase of any

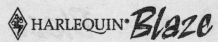

◈ HARLEQUIN® *Blaze*

series title.

$1.00 OFF!

any Harlequin Blaze series title.

RETAILER: Harlequin Enterprises Ltd. will pay the face value of this coupon plus 8¢ if submitted by customer for this product only. Any other use constitutes fraud. Coupon is nonassignable. Void if taxed, prohibited or restricted by law. Consumer must pay any government taxes. For reimbursement submit coupons and proof of sales to: Harlequin Enterprises Ltd., P.O. Box 880478, El Paso, TX 88588-0478, U.S.A. Cash value 1/100¢. Valid in the U.S. only.

Coupon valid until December 31, 2001.
Valid at retail outlets in the U.S. only.
Limit one coupon per purchase.

107401

5 65373 00076 2   (8100) 0 10740

Visit us at www.tryblaze.com
T5V2CHBUSR
© 2001 Harlequin Enterprises Ltd.

◈ HARLEQUIN®
Makes any time special ®

Blaze

Red-hot reads!

Save $1.00 off the purchase of any

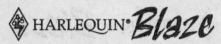

HARLEQUIN® *Blaze*

series title.

$1.00 OFF!
any Harlequin Blaze series title.

Coupon valid until December 31, 2001.
Valid at retail outlets in Canada only.
Limit one coupon per purchase.

52603307

HARLEQUIN®
Makes any time special ®

~Presents~

Seduction and Passion Guaranteed!

Save $2.00 off the purchase of any 3

series titles.

$2.00 OFF!

any three Harlequin Presents series titles.

RETAILER: Harlequin Enterprises Ltd. will pay the face value of this coupon plus 8¢ if submitted by customer for this product only. Any other use constitutes fraud. Coupon is nonassignable. Void if taxed, prohibited or restricted by law. Consumer must pay any government taxes. For reimbursement submit coupons and proof of sales to: Harlequin Enterprises Ltd., P.O. Box 880478, El Paso, TX 88588-0478, U.S.A. Cash value 1/100¢. Valid in the U.S. only.

Coupon valid until December 31, 2001.
Valid at retail outlets in the U.S. only.
Limit one coupon per purchase.

107419

5 65373 00051 9   (8100) 0 10741

HARLEQUIN®
Makes any time special®

~Presents~

Seduction and
Passion Guaranteed!

Save $2.00 off the purchase of any 3

series titles.

Visit us at www.eHarlequin.com
T5V2CHPCAN
© 2001 Harlequin Enterprises Ltd.

HARLEQUIN®
Makes any time special ®